REA

9-7-94

P9-EDO-006

✓

WHEN A MONKEY SPEAKS

WHEN A MONKEY SPEAKS

*and Other Stories
from Australia*

Damian Sharp

HarperCollins*West*
A Division of HarperCollins*Publishers*

HarperCollins West and the author, in association with the Rainforest Action
Network, will facilitate the planting of two trees for every one tree used to
manufacture this book.

Part of this book was written on a grant from the Literature Board of the
Australian Council for the Arts.

"Ena Waiting" was first published in *The Chicago Review.*
"The Defeat of Big Flo" first appeared in *The Denver Quarterly.*

Text design by George Brown
Set in Janson Text

FIRST EDITION

Sharp, Damian.
When a monkey speaks : and other stories from
Australia / Damian Sharp. — 1st ed.
p. cm.
ISBN 0–06–258500–2 (alk. paper)
1. Country life—Australia—Fiction. I. Title.
PR9619.3.S465W44   1944
823–dc20   92–54817
                                  CIP

94 95 96 97 98 ❖ HAD 10 9 8 7 6 5 4 3 2 1

CONTENTS

Ena Waiting

HE DROVE OFF with his arm waving out the window of the car, a sunburnt hand carelessly hung in the dust: limp, almost as if it were severed from the elbow, but it was a gesture, no matter how dead, a faceless farewell from which he never returned. The hand that waved didn't care. Its owner was looking away now, and moving away across the flat land both he and the automobile were swallowed by the intractable dust, the trees, the void of the continent into which countless men had disappeared as though they had entered a time warp, and were lost to the rest of us forever.

"Good riddance," said Ena, watching him go. She turned around and headed back to the kitchen. "I care about as much as 'e does," she said, throwing a pot into the already cluttered sink. "He can go to the other side of the sky for all it matters."

She stood solidly in the kitchen as if barring someone from entering, her big hands lodged firmly on her hips in that attitude of defiance with which she had watched him leave and which she had held all morning as though it were evidence of a personal, internal glory that he might have never known about, or even considered.

Ena was approximately one-eighth Chinese, and the rest of her was Irish-Australian. She was, in spite of the size of her hands and feet, quite a beauty, although her features had hardened over the years. Her hair was black and wiry, and if not pulled back behind her neck fell in wild dark locks about her shoulders and gave her a look of untamable innocence. Her shoulders were square, her lips full. Her mouth and eyes were Oriental. Her legs were long with strong and sinewy muscles.

She was tired now and sat down at the table and brushed her hair that was like long dark moss out of her face. Outside magpies were warbling in the trees, the chickens growled and whined in the brown yard like leaking sacks of air, and a yellow dog, sprawled on the back door step, snapped at flies. Things had started to return to their natural state.

She had not lived long on the farm, nor did she care to. It was a place for her to mark time, away from the world. When she moved from the hotel to live there with her two children, everyone thought that Ena must've been doing quite well, but she was poorer than she had ever been, and the house had been abandoned for quite some time. The floors were covered in a fine layer of red dust, the curtains dirty and torn, the wire screening rusted and broken. Possum excrement stained the ceilings of the big, once grandiose house. Its walls had been painted in bright and gaudy colors, all faded now in the damp and crumbling plaster, so that in places there was only the suggestion of a color, of a green or a red or a blue or a yellow. In the stale pungent indoor gloom the rooms had the feeling of an uncovered Mediterranean mausoleum. There was one room, all in faded purple, that Ena entered only at night, in the raw yellow light of the single naked electric light bulb, to make love to forgotten strangers, sometimes real, and sometimes phantoms spun from her nighttime brain. The farmhouse was entirely hers to fill with her fancies, and whatever she had left behind in her entire life seemed to be able to find her there at a moment's notice.

She did not care about the mess, or the starkness of the place. She had brought no furniture with her; there was only what was in the house: a kitchen table, some chairs, two single beds, one with a tattered and hard black and white striped mattress, and a large double bed with wrought iron and brass bedsteads. That was her bed. The two boys, Tom and Indigo (so named because he was born blue), slept together in a room off the veranda. They avoided the purple room and in fact never ventured into that area of the house for fear of what lurked there. Although they were only six and four years old, they had already seriously considered burning the entire place down. The younger of the two, Indigo, listened to his brother's haunting talk of how ghosts are destroyed by fire, and in the night, lying in bed on the veranda, suspended in a place without shape, he would hear the muffled sighs and the thumping and knocking of the ghosts trying to get out of the walls in which they were trapped.

The boys had left the house early in the morning when Ena shut herself in her bedroom and said that she was not coming out again until she died. Things had passed.

She buried her face in her hands and closed her eyes and breathed deeply through her nostrils. When she opened her eyes, looking through her fingers that were red in the sunlight, she saw a man she had never seen before standing in the door to the passageway. In the dark yawn of the doorway, in a bushman's hat and pale shirt, he seemed only half in reality, a molecular configuration not yet complete. She could not see his face. The figure, both squat, square, yet somehow ethereal, faded before her very eyes as he stepped into her room of reality.

"My God," she said to herself. "I didn't think those buggers ever left the other end of the house. I wonder how 'e got out."

LATER ENA saw him across the yard, and when she went out to water the chickens he was in the chicken coop, almost obscured by the sunlight as though made of dust. She decided to ignore him. She watched the chickens' throats throbbing in the heat, and the thick and warm scent of the eucalyptus was almost suffocating to her. The afternoon buzzed in her ears. When she turned to go back to the house he was standing at the door to the coop, and she could see his face in the light, and was sure she had never seen him before.

"I don't know you," she announced. "Now fuck off." And he left her in an instant; but as they came up the drive in the mid-afternoon heat, the two boys saw him standing in the drooping, scented shadows of the eucalyptus trees by the house. They did not know how long he had been there, and as they approached they saw that he did not seem to care about them at all but remained indifferent, as though totally preoccupied with his thoughts. They found Ena in the kitchen washing dishes and told her about the stranger, who was now sitting under the trees. "Jesus!" she yelled. "There's been more than enough madness."

THAT NIGHT Ena locked herself in the purple room with a flagon bottle of red wine and drank and smoked until she passed out. The two boys played outside in the yard in the warm night air until they decided to go to bed, and then they walked around to the front to the screened-in veranda rather than walk through the all but empty house. A sliver of moon hung above the shaggy outlines of the trees and in the loud breathless aromatic stillness of the summer night the deep black current of the nearby river filled Ena's sleeping ears with the faint, almost indiscernible murmur of its passing.

The next morning she awoke inspired by a virulent anger and told the boys that if they saw the stranger again they were to throw stones at him and drive him away. Her hair was wild, as though blown by the wind, and she had the look and stink of a woman who had been ravished. All of a sudden, it seemed, Ena had been bitten by a lustful rancor against the world, and it formed such a crust around her that for the first time in their lives the boys faced a personality in their mother that they had never met before. They quickly left the house and headed for the river. When Ena went out to the chicken coop to fetch eggs, the stranger was sitting in the middle of the enclosure as though he had become one of the chickens, the birds scratching around him obliviously. He moved into a corner and eyed Ena as she collected the eggs, squatting down on his haunches like a native, his bare feet dark and calloused. He started to chant, almost a whisper:

Dad a da da
Dad a da da
Dad a da da
Da kata kai

"Shut up," snapped Ena, closing the door to the coop behind her as she left.

All day long he sat in the coop and chanted. His voice would sometimes swell, other times it would grow small. Soon it came to her like the wind. When the boys returned they went out to the coop with sticks and threw stones and garbage at him through the wire, and he did not move. The stones hit him and cut him so that he bled, and the slop they showered on him made him look pathetic and ridiculous, and still he squatted, stopping his chant and eyeing them as if from behind a mask, and then turning his head away from them as he was seized by a gargling coughing fit that was the most violent the boys had seen. They left in disgust when he turned toward them and started spitting at them and laughing coarsely.

"This is out of hand," cried Ena. "He's taken over the chicken coop and spitting at anyone who comes near. Who in the fuck does he think he is?" And she went out to the chicken coop with a stick to beat him, but he had gone away.

ENA, DRESSED in a red and white checkered summer dress with short frilled sleeves, was startled by the radiant figure of bucolic wholesomeness and feminine innocence that looked back at her from the mirror. She was a woman able to startle primitive desires in almost any man, and the image in the mirror told her that she was ripe, if not inspired, to do so. Her large bare feet rested flatly on the cracked floor. It was unfortunate that the fate of such a woman should have led her onto the paths of stupid men. Watching herself in the mirror she hardly moved at all, and the dress slowly slipped away from her shoulders and fell around her feet. The mellow light of dusk, a deep apricot, filled the room. Going to the large closet, she picked her way through rows of old Victorian dresses, selected one of white silk and lace with a high frilled neck, and put it on, buttoning and clasping its various devices with a mindless and methodical patience. She then gathered up her hair onto the top of her head and pinned it with a comb of white mother-of-pearl.

The dry rustle of her skirt seemed loud in the dusk stillness as she crossed the room to the French windows and opened them to the dank afternoon smelling veranda, which was encrusted in the shade of the poplar trees and the morning glories that had overgrown it and the sharp, sweet liniment smell of the gum trees. Crying, the white cockatoos flew over the house. They sat in the trees away from the house and saw Ena standing in the long open window looking out at them.

Dusk spread out across the sky, silhouetting the trees. The new moon hung in the diaphanous sky and it seemed to Ena, sitting at the open window, that she could hear the growing of the wild grape vines around the house. She looked at her wrists. In the long elegant sleeves of the dress they were delicate and feminine, as were her sunburnt hands. Coming out of the white dress like two flowers those big hands were almost beautiful, almost capable of a mysterious softness that came from a hard sinuous but brittle strength, as though the strength of flesh and fiber was contradicted by the delicate framework of bone that gave it its shape.

She had not worn this dress in months. It seemed that she had been surrounded by old things from places beyond her own time ever since she was a little girl. She had owned a shop that sold old things, clothes, and she had accumulated the best of it for herself, a wardrobe of theatrical costumes, of memories that remained hidden to her and forgotten by their owners.

Somewhere in the bush a moepoke sounded. She listened to the reverberation of the crickets and cicadas while she sat at the window and smoked the last of her silver vial of hashish. The taste of it coated her lips and tongue. She stood up abruptly, as if some invisible external force had pulled her up, and stepped out into the long abandoned garden, the shrubs, the trees, all wild and bursting forth with impervious and uncontrollable profusion. She stood under the almond tree in the middle of the garden, herself a ghostly figure under the branches and the murmuring dark outline of leaves.

Now, in the warm night air, the sounds of the boys playing, joking, arguing, searching, came to her from inside the house like the dim light that bloomed from one or two of its windows and from the boys' room on the veranda. The night air was filled with moths and giant scarab beetles, clumsy armored creatures that fell on their backs as if dazzled by the light they sought, and the moths came to her even in the dark and left their dust in her hair. Mosquitoes needled the air. She remembered then that for a short time she had felt the dread power of wifehood, felt it with her firstborn and his father, an eyeless eternity in which he owed her his potency and fidelity and she owed him her womanhood, and neither, it seemed, ever received their due. He left her one night and disappeared into the erotic anonymity of the city in summer; he left her all alone with her one-year-old child and a wild concupiscence with which she blared her blasphemies against love, and out of which a second child, a half-brother to the first, was born as testimony to and evidence of her independence and self-sufficiency.

Standing under the almond tree, Ena seemed to lose all comprehension of time; for suddenly she was in the house again, and although the kitchen light was burning, the house was still and sleeping. She had spent the evening remembering and now was thinking about the night ahead of her. It was a shame there was no one around to see her in her dress. The boys had seen it before and it appeared to mean very little to them, but a grown man would be different. There was, indeed, a national shortage of men, and that simple and meaningless statistic seemed to be affecting her directly. She remembered the wild grape vines floating in the billabong when she had visited there two days before, and the pink and gray galahs that watched her from the tree branches as she walked along. She sat at the kitchen table, the picture of colonial serenity and old world allure, and smoked a cigarette. Her hair was starting to slide in heavy locks from the top of her head. The frilled, white, delicate lace embraced her long throat. Ena did not know what she was waiting for. She thought about the man who had left her two days ago. She did not expect him to return. She never expected any of them to return. Only Marriot Burke returned. He gave her money. He was an older man, perhaps fifty. He was a rich man, too, inheritor of a squatocracy, and everyone knew that he visited Ena. Sometimes he came to the farmhouse and sat around like an old man, grabbing Ena whenever she was near and interrupting her, causing her to snap at him irritably. But she was always available to him, and she would hitch up her dress and bend over on the spot to give him satisfaction while she chided him for his childish dependencies. But his presence was too much of a dull irritant to her, and one day when he asked her to make him a cup of tea and come and sit beside him she told him that he had become nothing but a nuisance, and that the time had come for him to leave and not return, like everybody else. He had cried. The next week he came back and cried again, and then sat inert on the veranda for hours.

"Fuck twenty-four flamin' pigs in a barn!" Ena shouted at him through her teeth. "Get outta here and leave me be. I want to be alone." Marriot Burke did not move. Ena's eyes were wild like a frightened animal's, and her lips were full and red. He turned toward her, his lips trembling.

"How many men have been in that purple room?" His throat was dry. He watched Indigo's pet tortoise try to climb up the wall and topple onto her back, swimming with her short legs in the air, the dust of the corner sticking to her long snake-like neck and head. Ena rushed to her and flipped her back onto her stomach.

"The poor cumbersome thing," she said remorsefully.

"Well," said Marriot. "How many?"

"I don't know. Why don't you go away? Go back to your wife and your sheep."

"I feel weak," said Marriot. "I have never felt weak like this before."

"Jesus," she said. "I'm not up for any old man acts. I'll make yer a cuppa tea. Then I want ya t' go."

He followed her into the kitchen, wanting to touch her, feeling older, fainter, by the minute, as though his very image was fading in the light. Marriot was a handsome man for his age, in a country-bred way. He was proud of his white sideburns and brown face, and the clear healthy blue of his eyes. When he was drunk, and when Ena first knew him, he would laugh out loud and slap his thigh and yell, "Look at that! The powerful buttocks of a kangaroo," and Ena would laugh, admiring the bawdiness of this man of the land where she now found herself. Some said that Marriot gave Ena the money for the farm, or at least some of it. It was never really known for sure. What was known was that she very quickly got tired of him. Even at the hotel she was known to complain about his groping ways and heavier-by-the-day dependency. He seemed to forget any notion of a facade very quickly, not because he wanted to make a defiant statement to his wife or anyone else, he would never have wanted to do that; but because he seemed to abandon himself to her, and was therefore abandoning his generation, which in the end was something he could never do without giving up completely.

She plugged in the electric kettle to boil some water. Marriot pressed against her from behind and reached around and took hold of her breasts with his hands. He was trembling and holding her gently. From far away, from a nearby orchard, came the long cry of a peacock.

"Come on, now," he said feebly. "You can't just shake me off like that." She shrugged him off and slipped around him back to the center of the room. "Just this once, Marriot, and then I have no more time for you."

"Just this once," he repeated tearfully.

THERE WERE wild grape vines floating in the billabong, their branches, joint by joint, spreading over the water and moving to and fro with the motion caused by the wind. The tortoises were swimming in the billabong, raising their heads with the morning. In her sleep Ena asked, *What is that crying?* The parakeets, nestling in the trees about the house, let out long cries as they flew over the roof in darting flashes of red and green and saw the warm rays of the sun rising in the east. In the bush the kangaroo moved his buttocks. Ena sat up in bed, hearing the last cries of the parakeets. Sunlight quickly filled the room, although it seemed to Ena that she had at first awakened to darkness. She had awakened with a start, with the sudden realization that she was, indeed, awake and cognizant of the world around her.

The morning settled windless and arid, but full of vigor. Ena threw back the covers and drew her big feet out of the nighttime depths into the bleaching morning light, and walked out onto the veranda in her white cotton night dress and rubbed her eyes. She looked out at the drive, the long road swallowed in the shade of the trees and the tree ferns that lined it on either side all the way up to the house and beyond, following the channel, as if she expected to see someone or something, but the drive was empty. The morning heat had not yet reached the house, and she listened to the boys waking further down the veranda, and saw their dark, tiny forms through the heavy wire screening, there to protect them from the mosquitoes.

When she turned around and went back through the French doors into her bedroom, she spied the stranger sitting in the living room, half immersed in the dank lime-smelling faded green and maroon gloom, half in the dusty morning light that fell in through the glass double doors that were open to the veranda. She heard the possums scraping inside the roof while she dressed quickly. Whoever the stranger was, spun out of whatever the spell was that had formed in Ena's heart, he was certainly becoming a nuisance. There was no one Ena could go to to help her exorcise herself of his unpredictable presence. She seized the broom from the corner of the room, and thus armed stormed into the living room like an avenging banshee, only to find the room empty and a hollow clock-clock sound coming from inside one of the walls.

"Good," she said. "At least he doesn't want to face me now. He can stay inside the walls, trapped there by his own cowardice." She was momentarily filled with triumph. All morning, off and on, she heard the tapping and thumping from inside the living room walls, and each time she heard it she smiled, and felt a warm, tingling sensation of liberation, and thought, *There now, he's in his place, there'll be no more trouble from him.*

AT MIDDAY, on the precise point of the clock, almost at the exact position of the sun, the cockatoos, perched high in the trees, saw Marriot Burke drive along the sandy road in his green Land Rover. One of them flew over him screeching as he turned onto Ena's road. He was a little nervous today. As he drove up toward the farmhouse, the sound of his engine stirred the ibis that were fishing in the brown water of the channel, and the swirling pillar of dust that hung on behind him, and which had already caught Ena's attention before she heard the noise, was more than enough to make him feel self-conscious and foolish, as though the dust was some embarrassing significator that clung to his coattails in public, pointed him out as he tried to move anonymously across the impervious land. A kookaburra laughed. Marriot Burke felt that he was the Fool of the Bush, Nature's idiot seduced by a Lilith. When he stopped the car at the corner of the house, in the dank shade of the trees and the vines, the childhood sensation of being in a place where he was not supposed to be almost suffocated him. He put his feet on the ground with a hesitant timidity. He stood up on them, moving away from the car, feeling the movement first of all in his toes, then in the back of his legs, and then in his back. He opened the frail screen door of the kitchen, and stepped inside, letting it swing shut behind him with the flat hollow and brittle clap of old wood on old wood. Ena was in the living room, the room of faded green and red like dry blood, the biggest room in the house.

He listened to her singing as she worked, and stood fumbling with his hands, not knowing which way to turn. He sat down at the kitchen table. When Ena came into the room and saw him sitting there, she stopped in the doorway and put her hands on her hips and laughed at him almost raucously, only it was a contemptuous, tempting female laugh, shrill like a bird.

"I thought as much," she said. "It's like trying to chase away a stray dog after you've fed it once or twice."

He did not know what to say. He tried to look at her, and found it easier to fix his eyes on her belly. She was indeed beautiful. He allowed his eyes to roam, and trembled inwardly at the idea of her being a woman beyond possession. Something frightened him beyond the condemnation to uncertainty and irretrievable desire that she meant to him and he did not know what it was. Perhaps it was the fear of death. Ena filled him with wild and confusing sensations, making him feel younger and older, stronger and weaker. Around her he spent his time contradicting himself.

"Do you wanna cup of tea?" She began moving around the kitchen in a busy and hurried manner, letting him know that her time was precious.

"Yes," he said, "I'd like that."

"Yer know, Marriot, you're a real education."

"Why?"

"Yer a persistent bugger, too."

He looked at his hands.

"I thought I told you I didn't want you back."

"You need me here."

"Ha!"

She opened the door and threw the cold contents of the teapot into the yard, and then returned to the sink to wash it out.

"You need me here because you have two small boys and I care about them as though they were my own."

"You mean you don't care about me?"

"Of course I care about you," he said flatly, "but the kids are important to me. They've become important to me, even though they're not my own."

She left the room and came back again as the kettle started to boil. She made the tea and poured him a cup and handed it to him.

"I have to go to town today to get some things," she said.

"I'll take you."

"No you won't. It's not good for you to be seen with me. I'll drive in myself."

"You'll need some money."

"I have some money."

He took out his wallet and laid fifty dollars on the table.

"That should do you for this week," he said.

"This week!" she exclaimed. "You're so fuckin' extravagant. That'll do for a couple of weeks."

"If you need more . . ."

"I don't need any more."

He sipped his tea quietly and smoked a cigarette while he listened to Ena moving about the house, in and out of its various colored rooms. He could stay there for most of the day, even while she went to town, and rest and be comfortable while he waited for her to return. He took a long draw on his cigarette and listened with a warm mindlessness to the almost indiscernible tapping that came from inside the walls of the house.

A Native Son

FOR YEARS, as a boy, he ranged the bush that bordered his father's orange groves on three sides and which spread for miles, how far he did not know, on either side of the river. Beyond the eucalyptus forest were miles of savanna-like grassland and beyond that was desert. In another direction there were mountains, where the river started. He wandered the bush paths often with his dog, accompanied by the white cockatoos that screeched overhead or flew from branch to branch, tree to tree, following and watching. An uncanny sensation, to be held in the eye of the cockatoo. And for years that bush, that land crushed under the cruel glare of the Australian sun, was neither beautiful nor real to him, but alien. He neither saw it nor listened to it. In his mind were Celtic songs and in his eye he saw only gentle, green Northern forests. His gods were Northern gods hewn from fog and oak. So for years the bush seemed ugly, hostile, and barren. Yet he roamed it, came to know it, found in himself the desire to accept it as his own. The cockatoos never ceased their screeching indignation and mockery. It occurred to him, after a while, that they were trying to tell him something.

Occasionally his father shot the cockatoos. They were pests. They were pests. They raided the fruit trees. So the parrots stopped flying over the farmhouse, but would loop around it and settle in the tall gum trees just beyond the gate, waiting and watching. When the boy appeared they would fly up, screeching with what seemed more like excitement than alarm, and fly ahead of him as he crossed the red sand road and climbed through the fence into wild and uncultivated country.

Aborigines were seen only on occasion, more often around the town pub. But sometimes, wandering along the river, he came upon camps, humpies made of corrugated tin, ragged tents and lean-tos made of sticks, and sometimes there were people, but more often not, only the evidence of people who had moved on. The river had been the scene of many bloody battles in the old days in which the black people had been massacred. There were not many local people left, only half-castes with little to no tribal memory.

"The Abos are hopeless," his father told him. "The bastards won't help themselves. They won't work. You give 'em work and still they won't work. Hopeless."

"Have you ever tried?" his mother interjected. "Have you ever had one work for you?"

"You don't know what you're talking about, dear."

"I know you've never hired an Abo, not as long as I've known you."

"Well, that's as much as you know."

His mother was a tall, handsome woman with long brown hair and a youthful complexion. She had married young and given birth young and was still very much in her prime. His father was fifteen years older than his mother, with a sunburned and wrinkled country man's face, hard, handsome, green predatory eyes, his body tall and lean, well muscled like a strong, slender rope.

"It's well and good to theorize, to think there are simple solutions, but unfortunately reality is just a little bit more complicated than that."

This was at the breakfast table, and apart from their conversation the morning was very silent. The heat had not yet begun, was still a white haze in the distance, but it was rushing toward them and soon they would be engulfed by it.

"Well, your business is your business," said his mother, rising from the table. "I sometimes find you too severe, Harry. Way too severe. Anyway, it's hot and I'm going for a swim."

"It's just that I don't think I can solve the world's problems. I have enough trouble just living with 'em," said his father, watching her back as she walked away down the long veranda.

It was that very same morning that a half-caste Aborigine named Jackie Swan appeared in the packing shed and asked his father for employment.

"Got any work for a black fellah, boss? A fellah like me needs work an' works hard, boss."

His father eyed the man curiously, glancing his thoughts off of him, and Jackie stood there smiling through his short white whiskers and wiped the sweat from his bald crown. And then his father said: "Alright. You're hired. I need fence posts sunk." At the table, over lunch, his father grinned like a satisfied cat and said to his mother: "Well, dear, I hired an Abo this morning."

"That was very nice of you, Harry. I hope the bugger's a good worker. I don't want you coming in here a week from now complaining about blacks and telling me you told me so."

"Well, we'll see, won't we? What are you doing this afternoon?"

"I'm taking a book and going back to the river."

"Don't get too much sun. You're getting awfully dark."

She looked at her arms and her brown eyes glowed with delight.

"I am, aren't I. Look like a true native daughter."

"You'll be old and wrinkled before your time if you're not careful."

She was a defiant, sensual, and haughty woman, and all through the long summers she held his father's attention and kept him occupied and happy.

"Maybe I'll take the shotgun and see if I can bag some rabbits for dinner," she said, brushing back a thick strand of hair, wet with perspiration, that had stuck to her forehead.

Jackie Swan was a short, thickset man in his late forties with skin the color of chocolate but tinted with red, like the undercoat on a Titian canvas. He had a round, protruding belly, which trembled when he laughed, and he laughed a lot, loud and raucous. Everything, which included the company of the boy, delighted him. He called the boy by his name, David, but he could not pronounce the V, and so when he addressed him it was as "Daybid," barking at him playfully in his ludicrously loud voice. He addressed the boy's father as "Boss" with that same voice, nodding his head up and down and saying "Yes boss" and "Gotchya, boss" and "Will do, boss" and "Okeydoke," as his father gave him instructions—his mannerisms, the contortions of his face, exaggerated and comical. His father liked Jackie even though he was not a "good worker"; was, in fact, "a bit of a ratbag," talked "a mile a minute," and got "sweet Fanny Adams" accomplished, but he kept him on just the same. He was a "funny bugger" and knew a lot of good fishing spots. There were nights when Jackie Swan and his father and the boy were out on the river until dawn, setting pots for giant crayfish and lines for cod, and always they hauled in big fish. Sometimes they pulled the boat up onto a beach, especially if there was a moon, and built a fire and sat around and talked and the men would drink. This became a ritual of intimacy between them, this sharing of the night and the fire, an intimacy that did not exist so much between them on the farm during day.

The boy started to roam further from the farm on his days off, his awareness of the bush, of the deities that dwelled there, increased with each new step into what for him was still unexplored territory. One day he crossed a dry swamp bed, working his way along a path through coarse blue and yellow needle grass that rose several feet above his head. The afternoon was bright and hot, and beyond the swamp the land rose and fell in low embankments, the grass long and dry and bright between the trees, quivering in the heat waves, the light rushing into his eyes from the gleaming blue sky and the radiant land. As he came out of the swamp and started up the gentle slope of the first embankment, he stopped short. There was a sound, a new sound, beyond the twanging of the cicadas—a dry rustling of grass, as of a man running, light of foot. He looked all around. There were no cattle or kangaroos, only the white cockatoos perched high in the tree branches, watching and strangely silent. And there was no wind. The bush was still. Large red ants scurried around his feet. A few stood looking up at him with small, glittering eyes.

He listened, puzzled, all of his nerves alert. The bush, drowned in sunlight, was empty and silent. He continued to the top of the rise, his legs tired and heavy. He had started out with his dog just after dawn, expecting to be back for breakfast, carrying a gun and a water bottle—the gun in the hope of seeing some ducks or quail, the bottle as a quirk, for he had told himself he would not be out long. But now it was the middle of the afternoon. The world was at rest, unconscious in the glare and heat. He had walked for hours without stopping. The dog had left him about an hour ago, following a scent, and he knew he would find him soon enough.

As he started to walk he startled himself by almost stepping on a large red-bellied black snake. It was coiled, sleeping, in a pothole, and he saw it just as his foot was about to come down. He stepped over it and then turned and looked back. The snake had raised its head slightly, narcotic in the sun, its black skin glistening like water. It was then that he heard the sound again, and something, a short, lean, dark shape darting between the trees, flickered across the corner of his eye.

He advanced toward the trees where he had detected the movement. His eyes narrowed. In the middle of a step he stopped. There was the sound again, and then his face showed puzzlement and then bewilderment. A black figure, small, lean, and epicene, was running away from him on two legs. For a moment he doubted his own sight. It was a man, and then before his very eyes it turned into a lizard.

The snake who walked as a man, he thought, and he felt the hair on the back of his neck prickle. The sight was both awesome and ghastly, triggering in him an ancient memory and an ancient fear. It was a figure from a dream, and for an instant he was seized by something like terror. The image had entered into the farthest corners of his brain, had been seized by his imagination, and it would never leave him.

Yes, he thought. *I have seen the ancient demon of the land. The snake who walked as a man. God has not yet sent his angel here and cursed him.*

The lizard dropped down into the grass and disappeared. The boy stood perfectly still, waiting and listening, and slowly a chill feeling grew up the small of his back and into his shoulders. He shuddered involuntarily. At the roots of his hair, a tingling sensation began which spread down over his face and arms, leaving him goosefleshed as though cold. He had a sudden, new fear of isolation. He turned and looked uneasily over his shoulder, wishing the dog would appear. He was amazed by this sensation. In all the years that he had roamed through the bush, he had never had the slightest feeling of uneasiness. He walked on, turning around constantly in search of the shapeless menace that now stalked him. The forest began to thin. He came upon the skeletons of several dead cattle and then abruptly, as though nature had drawn a line across a map, the bush ended and red sand dunes rose before him and he was on the edge of an undulating desert that stretched to the horizon.

He thought: *One day I will cross that desert. But not today. This is the boundary of my territory. The forest is my Eden and I will go into the desert when I'm finally expelled.*

He got back to the house well after dark. His parents were sitting out on the veranda under the electric light, screened in against the mosquitoes. He saw the light and heard their voices, the high, lyrical sound of his mother's tipsy laughter, his father's deep mumbling, as he came up the driveway. The dog was with him by then, its head down and its tongue dragging. Ahead of him, through the trees, just in front of the woodshed, a small campfire glowed. It was Jackie Swan's fire. The boy was hot and tired and hungry, but he headed straight for the fire, and as he drew near he heard Jackie's voice, low, guttural and coarse, as he sang drunkenly to himself. He sat before the fire on crossed legs, a half-empty bottle of port between his feet, bent forward and swaying from side to side. He stopped singing and looked up as the boy entered the circle of light.

"Gedday there, young fellah."

He went to rise but seemed too drunk to stand up. The boy nodded a greeting and sat down beside him. The day of wandering in the bush had cast an aura of animal silence over the boy. He was content to sit and simply enjoy the company of the older man. He was not yet ready to go into the house and face that other world. And Jackie was delighted to have the company. As soon as the boy sat down, Jackie started leaning sideways toward him until their shoulders were touching, and he was talking the whole time, telling the boy how much he liked to work for his father, how much he liked the farm and the fishing on the river. It was the drunken, free associative ramble of a man who needed or wanted desperately to talk. Suddenly he pulled his head into his shoulders and looked around furtively and started to speak in a rapid whisper.

"When I was your age. No. A little younger. But anyway, when I was that age, you know, they took me out and put me through the rites. They did all that to me. They cut me. Hang on. Can't speak now."

He waved his hand and then raised his elbow, as though trying to protect his face from an imaginary assailant. He turned away to avoid looking at something he did not want to see, something that had interrupted him, in the presence of which he could not speak, reveal to the boy the secrets of manhood as he now so very much wanted to do. The thing was a woman, the boy's mother, and for him to speak of such matters within range of her hearing was the worst and most final form of taboo.

"Can't talk now. Can't." Jackie mumbled into his chest. He turned his head, bird-like, and looked at the boy, his eyes glistening, filled with a curious mix of fear and something wild, burning, fierce.

"If I break the law I'm in trouble."

There was a fatalism in his voice, as though there was a perverse and powerful side to him that would speak, that would find the compulsion irresistible.

The boy looked up into his mother's smiling, glittering eyes. Her smooth, suntanned face was covered in small pearl-like beads of perspiration. Her hair was a little messed up on top of her head and fell in dark, tawny locks around her shoulders. It was obvious to the boy, looking up into her smiling, glowing face, feeling her eyes riveted on him devouringly, that she, too, was a little drunk. His father, still back in the house, was probably drunk as well.

"So here you are, David. I was getting quite worried about you, but I suppose I ought to know better by now."

She took in a deep breath through her nostrils, tasting the eucalyptus in the air.

"It's such a beautiful night. How are you this evening, Jackie?"

Jackie shuffled his feet uneasily and stooped forward, mumbling: "Okay thanks, missus." He kept his eyes on his hands. The boy's mother sat down across from them, apparently unaware of Jackie's discomfort, and smiled at the two of them, viewing her son with delight, and then settled into studying the fire. She too now desired to share in their bush communion, in that unspoken intimacy of the fire. She seemed to gaze deeply into the flames, her handsome profile ablaze, and then glanced quickly at the boy and the man, hungry-eyed and pleased with herself.

Jackie looked up from his hands and then quickly down again and then at the boy, licking his lips, the movement of his head quick, nervous, again resembling an eccentric bird. He wanted to speak badly. It was building up inside him, making his face twitch and his body jerk in little spasms. He leaned in toward the boy, so that his lips brushed his cheek as he spoke, whispering so low, and his speech now so drunkenly slurred, that the boy found it hard to understand him.

"They took me out into the bush. The men. I wasn't supposed to be part a no tribe, but they came and got me. I tried to run away and hide. I didn't want to be part of any tribe. But they came and took me away and then they cut me." He covered his face with his hands and then looked through spread fingers at the woman, who sat gazing at him serenely.

"Can't talk now." He waved her away with a loose gesture of his hand and then stared long and hard at the boy.

"Mum. I think you ought to go back to the house." The boy's tone was gentle, reflecting his embarrassment, and he was trying to appeal to her by inflecting his expression with a hidden undercurrent of meaning, but it seemed to wash over her head.

"What?" She sounded suddenly irritated.

"It'd be better. I don't think Jackie is used to women in his camp."

"Oh rubbish, David. Ask Jackie how he feels. He's just a little drunk, that's all. I want to stay, just for a little while. I'll ask Jackie if I can stay. If he minds my being here, then I'll leave. Really, you men can be so incredibly boring."

She looked across at Jackie, seizing him with her moist, dark appealing eyes.

"Do you really want me to leave, Jackie?"

Jackie kept his head lowered, his eyes on his hands.

"That's okay, missus." The words, barely audible, had the flat tone of defeat.

The boy felt now that there was nothing more that he could do. There were natural and conditioned limitations to his own behavior. At fifteen he did not yet feel truly like a man, had not yet earned the right to instruct this haughty and youthful woman, his mother, in the ways of men. They sat in silence for several minutes. From somewhere near at hand a bittern roared. An owl hooted. Mosquitoes needled the darkness, and large brown moths with iridescent blue circles on their wings flew around the fire.

Jackie took a long drink from the bottle. Then he reached over, offering a drink to his mother, his way of making peace. She smiled and took the bottle in both hands and put it to her lips and drank. She handed the bottle back, coughing as she did so, and wiped her mouth with the back of her free hand.

"That's pretty raw stuff, Jackie," she said.

"Good company in the night, miss. Ah, er, missus."

"I'm sure it is. My name's Rachel."

"What's that miss. Ah, missus?

"Rachel. My name."

"Yes, miss."

"My name's Rachel."

She reached into her shirt pocket, a white shirt of his father's, and withdrew a wrinkled packet of Drum cigarette tobacco. She held the paper on her wet lower lip while she rubbed some tobacco between the palms of her hands, then quickly and dexterously rolled a cigarette and lit it with a burning stick from the fire. Jackie sat perfectly still, looking at her while he pretended not to be looking at her. She made him jump when she threw the packet of tobacco into his lap.

"Have some tobacco if you want," she said jovially.

Instantly Jackie seemed to relax. She had made the right gesture, had pushed a button, had even made him forget, for a moment, that she was a woman. His silence, as he concentrated on making a cigarette, was comfortable and self-possessed.

He smoked and drank the rest of the port. He was very drunk now, swaying again, staring hard at the boy. He seemed to have forgotten completely about the woman.

"They took me out." His voice that rapid, rasping, wet whisper. "An' they did those things like I was tellin' yer. They cut me all over. On my chest, and into my parts, to make me a man. You know. I was yellin' and screamin'. This wasn't the life I wanted. Not even then. But I got marked and initiated."

He became suddenly rigid, paralyzed, his face contorted in a silent scream. He turned his head slowly, like a mechanical doll, and looked at the boy's mother. She had stood up, and was gazing down at him with knotted eyebrows, her expression one of blank, alcoholic confusion and instinctive, almost subliminal horror. She knew. The boy knew that she knew. But it was too late. Jackie stared up at her, wide-eyed with fear. She turned, her head reeling, and stumbled off into the dark.

Then, abruptly, Jackie sprang up onto his feet. He looked down once at the boy, and then ran, stooped and ape-like, down the driveway.

When the boy came into the house he found his mother sitting alone on the veranda. She had been weeping, and was quite sober.

The next morning his father found Jackie hanging by a rope from a tree in the bush, just across the road from the farm.

When a Monkey Speaks

IT WAS NOW the middle of the afternoon and she sat by the window with the louvered shutter up, looking out at the high sand dunes alongside the tracks. The dunes shone brightly and were as deep and as high as a canyon, shutting out the view of the desert plain and the immensity of blue sky.

"You don't have to be that way," she said. "There are other things you could do that would make me happy." She watched the shadow of the train sliding across the wind-rippled, yellow surface of the dunes.

"Like what?" he said feebly.

"It doesn't take much. A bit of imagination. A new approach. You're smart enough. The same thing all the time gets boring. All you have to do is please me and then things'll be fine. We can have a good time, even out here."

They were alone in the compartment and the blinds on the door and the corridor windows were drawn. The man sat facing the woman. His pants were still undone and his shirt was out and he was perspiring uncomfortably in the heat.

"Why does it go so slow?" she asked, turning her face from the window and looking at him.

"It's the heat. It buckles the rails during the day. You notice how we roar along at night, to make up for time?"

She didn't reply but turned back to the window and he looked at her with hot eyes, his face red and hot and wet and his lips dry.

"You know," he said musingly. "I've thought about you a lot lately. You're a very curious person. I don't think I understand you."

Alongside the tracks now, half buried in the sand, were three derailed freight cars lying on their sides in a haphazard line. She looked down at them and the shadow of the train as they moved slowly by.

"Malcolm, please stop trying to be interesting." She sighed and leaned back and ran her fingers through her hair.

"No. I mean it. I think you're fascinating. Difficult but fascinating."

The sand dunes started to level out and now she could see the plain and the sky and the bright shimmer of the heat on the flat horizon. They were in a second-class passenger carriage on the end of a long freight train, directly in front of the caboose, traveling from Adelaide to Alice Springs across the Simpson Desert, in the dry center of Australia.

"Why don't you give your mind a rest and look at the desert," she said impatiently.

"I've already seen the desert."

She stood up and opened the blinds on the door and the interior windows. Through the glass, across the corridor and through the outside windows, she could see the great, flat, glaring white expanse of a salt lake.

"That must be Lake Eyre," she said, sitting down.

"Yes, I believe it is," he said flatly and his bored tone immediately irritated her.

"It was your idea to get on this wretched train instead of the regular express," she said shrilly. "So why don't you be creative and take something in instead of drooling over me. Climb up on the roof. Leap between the carriages like in a Western, the way you were going to. Remember? You said that was the one thing you've always wanted to do. Well, now's your chance, and we're only doing ten miles an hour."

He stood up and did up his pants.

"You know, Vivian, you're an inspiration. That's exactly what I'm going to do."

He stepped out into the corridor and slammed the sliding door shut behind him. He would climb onto the roof and get himself burned black and then, probably, he'd be able to sleep. He hadn't slept properly in three days, not since they got on the train, and it was all because of her. She was difficult to be with at times, lonely; as though nothing much mattered to her except herself. And although he knew she'd be miserable for a time if he left her, she could accept being alone better than he could. She didn't seem to need affection or be reliant on him the way he thought he would like her to be. A lot of men had come and gone in her life, and when she talked about them it was always as though that was what she had expected. It was all she had ever really wanted. It was different with him, of course. But he too could go like the others and she let him know it wouldn't mean the end of the world. She had always been self-sufficient, and that had nothing to do with the fact that she was born rich and American, although she admitted it made her different— being rich. She could be cruel, he thought, capable of a subtle and cold terrorism if she didn't get her way. He was in love with her and he didn't quite know how to handle her. Yes, he thought, opening the carriage door and looking out at the glaring salt flats. She could be cruel and hard. She called it honesty. He saw it as evidence that she didn't really need anybody be-cause her life had always been well provided for and that she had suffered for it. Yes, suffered. In a private, lonely way.

She was not what most people considered beautiful. She was striking. Very tall and long legged, with a powerful, sexual body and a handsome face with clearly defined, patrician features.

She had dark, thickly handsome eyebrows and long, slanted, be-witching green eyes. The eyes were beautiful. They had a mysterious look that spoke to him of some ancient race in her blood. Like the eyes of Medea, he thought. Jason had looked into those eyes and drowned. She was striking and handsome in the street or in a restaurant with her dark, leonine mane, but in bed she was beautiful. Most men could sense that; and those who couldn't, he quickly concluded, were simply not very intelligent. All men knew she was difficult, though. A real handful. So did the women, especially the older ones. Since he had been with her he had been told on several occasions by women much older and wiser than himself that she was "very interesting" and "a special kind of challenge." She was unique but no devastating beauty in the traditional sense, although she was certainly beautiful out here in the desert.

He climbed out between the cars and a hot wind blew against him and immediately he felt the sun burning his skin. As he started to climb the ladder on the caboose the train came to a lurching, skidding and screeching stop and he heard men shouting further down the tracks.

Inside the compartment Vivian sat by the window just out of the sun. She had been looking across the low dunes to the plain where dust devils whirled and danced, at a mob of red kangaroos, when the train started to skid on the tracks and then there was the crashing boom of couplings hitting and she was thrown forward as the train jolted and then stopped. For a moment she thought they had been derailed and she remembered Malcolm on the roof and sat perfectly still, listless in the heat, and waited solemnly to see what had happened. She thought about getting up and going out to look, but she was tired and irritable because of their failure to pass the time in lovemaking and because of the endless, heat-soaked desolation that surrounded her, and she did not feel like moving nor care about anything.

She heard men's voices shouting and laughing from the other compartments. They were a strange lot, these outback men, she thought. Wild and crude and reckless, uneasy in the company of women and apparently drunk all the time. She had managed to shun their immediate assumption of intimate friendship toward them as a couple, and the men now left them alone and maintained a polite distance, although she still sensed them stalking, looking for the smallest opening to engage Malcolm and draw him into their back-slapping circle. Well, she thought, right now they can have him. Let them get him rotten drunk. It'd probably be good for him. Right now I'm sick of him. He's one of them, really, even if he doesn't know it himself.

The conductor came angrily out of the caboose, and as he walked by the compartment she heard him mutter: "Bloody fuckin' ants."

She stood up and went to the door and called out to him.

"Excuse me."

He stopped and turned around. He was a heavy man about five feet, ten inches tall and dressed in a battered wide-brimmed hat and a blue singlet and baggy shorts and dilapidated, knee-high Texas-style cowboy boots. His shoulders and arms were covered in black hair and he was deeply sunburned and had a round, fat, beard-stubbled face. He looked at her with expressionless, dull blue eyes.

"What's that you said, about ants?" she inquired.

"Yes, miss." He tipped his hat awkwardly. "Pardon my French, but the fuc—" He caught himself, twisting and rolling the syllables, struggling to disguise the obscene slip of the tongue. "—frolickin' ants."

"Frolicking?" Her voice sounded both amused and quizzical.

"The ants get on the tracks, miss. Millions of 'em, followin' the straight an' narrow. Then a train comes along, mushes 'em up, and skids to kingdom come. Where are you from? You're an American, ain't ya?"

"That's right," she said, giving him a big, white-toothed American smile. He looked at her, obviously puzzled as to why she was on this particular train.

"Well, out 'ere, miss, ants derail trains." He turned and continued down the corridor shaking his head. She went back and sat by the window and looked out at the desert and saw that the kangaroos were gone. The train started to move again, only in reverse, going back into the high dunes.

HE SAT on the edge of the caboose roof with his legs dangling and looked out at what they had been unable to see before and it all looked the same as what they had seen the day before and the day before that, with the exception of a mountain range they had passed north of Port Augusta and the occasional dry wash where trees grew. The air was hot, the sky and the land glinted like aluminum foil, and the sun was burning him through his shirt. Way off beyond the dunes he could see the strange, prehistoric shapes of emus, distorted and vaporous in the heat waves, running away from the train. He was starting to forget about the difficult woman sitting alone in the compartment. He was a different man now, very different from the man who had met her in the mountain temple in Bali and saved her from the monkeys. She had not liked the monkeys and the monkeys had not liked her, and they came at her screeching and showing their teeth. She left another man, an American, for him, and now it seemed she was growing tired of him and had noted the change herself. It was because of him. He had changed, was different. He noticed it yesterday, when he looked at himself in the toilet mirror. The desert was changing him, only he didn't know how.

The train stopped after about a mile and then started forward again at the same slow, monotonous, wheel-clicking pace. He stood up, looking down at the rails, blurred with motion, between the cars. The train was starting to pick up a little speed. The cars rocked from side to side. He held himself very erect, the hot wind blowing in his face and hair, and then leapt onto the passenger car, where he stumbled but managed to keep standing. The long caterpillar of freight cars stretched before him. He laughed out loud, exhilarated and confident, and ran along the roof and leapt onto the next car. Then he turned back, seeing the long empty track behind the caboose and the salt bush plain, dotted with mallee scrub and desert oak. As he leapt back onto the passenger car, the train suddenly skidded to a stop and he was thrown off, landing on his side in the deep sand of a dune. As he sat up he heard Vivian's laughter coming from the compartment window directly above him. He looked up and saw her face, animated with mirth, and smiled foolishly, more from relief at seeing her finally amused than from his own comic mishap.

A scuffle was going down at the other end of the car. There was the loud, vicious sound of men snarling like cats, then the door flew open and a very black Aborigine with long, oily hair was pushed violently from the train. He landed on his face beside the tracks. He was dressed in a soiled pink T-shirt that was practically torn in half down the back and blue jeans and his feet were bare. He pulled himself up slowly onto his knees as the conductor climbed down off the train. The Aborigine was a heavy man with a protruding belly and thick arms and an ugly, much battered face. He was bleeding from the nose and mouth and looked dazed. As he tried to stand up the conductor kicked him hard in the mouth and knocked him sprawling and unconscious onto his back. The white man turned around immediately, without looking at him, and climbed back onto the train, where he leaned out from the door and signaled with his arm for them to proceed.

"You better hurry and get on board," said Vivian flatly. "I doubt you want to be left out here with the likes of him."

He looked up and saw the cool, unperturbed expression on her face. She saw the way he was looking at her and said:

"That's the way it is out here. You ought to know that. You can't let it get to you. I'm sure that guy's used to it. Now hurry up and get on."

The train was not yet moving. The conductor was hanging out of the door looking down the tracks into the shimmering mirage of heat through which a figure moved, floated, above the black, glinting rails, looking more like a kite hovering, flapping, as it came steadily toward them. He saw the conductor looking and then he saw Vivian's head, straining out of the window, her long eyes squinting and giving her an Oriental look.

"What is it?" he said, trying to ignore the bleeding Aborigine and feeling vapid and idiotic. He knew her eyes were better than his and that she could describe things at a distance that he couldn't even see.

"It's a man." Her voice sounded distracted. "It certainly doesn't look like a giant ant."

"What?"

"Nothing," she said, laughing. "Hurry up and get on, will you."

She looked younger and fresher now that she was smiling. The surly mood seemed to have evaporated in the heat, and as he climbed on board he wondered what was in her heart.

The train moved slowly and they were lulled into a restful silence as it clicked and rocked along through the bright afternoon. They were passing through a barren, red lunar landscape of scoria desert that they had seen in the distance, noting the change from yellow to red, and now they were in it and it was an endless wasteland. There were no crows nor emus nor kangaroos, and absolutely no vegetation. Not even a snake or a scorpion could live in that, she thought. The desolation seeped into her like a narcotic, putting her into a trance-like state that was neither sleep nor wakefulness. Perhaps that is the ultimate nothingness I'm looking at right now, she thought, and closed her eyes. Bright circles of light, like rings of phosphorus, swirled in the darkness behind her eyelids.

The sound of the compartment door sliding open startled her into consciousness. She opened her eyes and saw a man, about middle height with sandy hair, reaching up and placing a knapsack and a rifle in the wire baggage rack above the seat where Malcolm lay fast asleep. He wore a wide-brimmed bushman's hat pushed back on his head and a faded khaki shirt and trousers. His face and arms and hands were very tanned. It was he she had seen coming down the tracks, and although she had not seen him clearly she recognized him now. He looked at her with bright, distance-seeing blue eyes that already seemed to be laughing at her inwardly. The eyes disturbed her. She could not help finding them beautiful.

"Don't mind me, miss," he said softly, tipping his hat in that characteristically old-fashioned display of manners toward a woman that she found so comical and awkward and charming. "All the other compartments are full. Besides, I don't much care for the company of those yahoos. Hope you don't mind."

"No. Not at all," she said, sitting up.

He sat down and smiled at her and took off his hat, and she looked away from his face at the way his brown shoulders sloped beneath the loose, well-worn and dusty shirt and the way the pale cloth contrasted strongly against his dark skin. She noticed his very dirty boots and the smell of dust and what she thought was the smell of cattle or horses that he brought in with him.

"That was you on the tracks before, wasn't it?"

"I'm afraid it was. Lost my camel two days ago." He smiled again and faint lines grooved merrily at the corners of his eyes. She saw that he was looking at her legs where her skirt had slipped up over her thighs.

"How did that happen?" She put her legs up on the seat and tucked her feet back under her buttocks without adjusting the skirt.

"I bought her from an Afghani trader and he didn't tell me she was in heat. Then she started makin' blue bubbles and I knew there was goin' to be trouble. And sure enough, it came the other mornin'. Three males attacked my camp just as I was wakin' up and took off with her. Left me high an' dry."

"Male camels?"

"That's right. Wild ones. Bastards nearly killed me."

"What were you doing out there?" He looked at her and then at Malcolm curled on his side, still asleep and breathing heavily and his dark hair wet with perspiration.

"He with you?"

"Sort of. Tell me, what were you doing?"

"You're American, huh?"

"Yes," she said and smiled at him and looked straight into his face.

"Him too?"

"No. He's an Aussie, just like you. I take it I asked the wrong question."

"No. No. I'm a prospector. Opals. Been out west for a while, got lucky, and thought I'd take a look around here."

She looked out the window and then back at his eyes.

"I'm amazed there's anything out there," she said.

"Oh, there's a lot out there." He grinned knowingly and his eyes flickered over her. He reached into his trouser pocket and drew out a small leather bag, opened it, picked out a stone, and handed it to her.

"Take a look at this," he said proudly, placing it in the palm of her hand. It was a small, black opal and it shone with a green iridescence.

"It's beautiful," she said. "Strange and beautiful."

"It's yours."

"No!" She looked up at him with bright eyes and smiled with coy and warm embarrassment. "It must be worth quite a lot."

"It is."

"I can't keep it, really."

"Yes you can. It's just a rock. This desert is full of 'em, be-lieve me."

Malcolm moaned and stirred and sat up and blinked at the stranger.

"Gedday," said the newcomer, putting out his hand. "The name's Tom Bryant."

They shook hands and Malcolm said: "Malcolm Savage." He leaned forward, his elbows rested on his knees, and buried his face in the palms of his hands.

"Jesus, I feel ill," he mumbled.

Vivian looked up from studying the opal in her hand. Her fist closed around it as she spoke.

"Malcolm, is something wrong?"

"Sick. I feel sick."

He stood up painfully and hunched forward, his arm over his stomach, he pulled the door open and staggered out into the corridor, his legs almost too weak to hold him against the rocking motion of the train. He put his head out an open window, into the hot, dry and now breathless air, and vomited.

"Must've been the water you brought on board at Marree," said Tom Bryant, looking at Malcolm sprawled, asleep, on the seat opposite him. There's dysentery and gastro in some of the wells out here. Always a good idea to boil the water. You can't be too careful. Are you alright?"

"Yes, thank you. I'm fine," said Vivian.

"A good night's sleep and he'll be okay. It's common enough. Suffer from it meself from time to time."

"You look none the worse for wear."

"I've managed to get by," he said, looking at her in the dim, yellow electric light of the compartment. A wind came in the open window and blew her hair across her face and once again she was allowing him to look at her legs and he saw the way she was looking at him. He leaned back, looking at her with hard, unflinching eyes, seeing her skirt drawn taut and stretched straight against the tensed muscularity of her parted thighs, the dark V between her legs exposed beneath the dress and the wild splash of black hair inside her upper thigh that spread from the tumescent, pubic bulge of what he thought should be her secret of secrets, revealed without modesty and without underwear right there in the clickety-clack-clack of the fast-moving train.

My God, he thought. *I feel sorry for this bastard and I want this Yankee bitch for myself. Maybe he doesn't care or give a damn, but I do. I know how these women are but I can't say I don't care about him because I do. I feel sorry for him and for feeling this way about her while he's so helpless but really it's his own fault and she's asking for it. Jesus Christ forget about him. She's a person too and it's his fault and she's asking for it.*

THE DUSK had passed and the night had settled upon them but it was still hot. It was not the same as the Moroccan desert as she had known it in the night when the great cold descended. It was summer in Australia and the desert night was hot and smelled of dust and the vast, insatiable dryness of the brown continent. During the day the spinifex plains, dotted with smooth, white rocks, had reminded her of Africa, but it was not like Africa at all. It was much older than Africa and seemed to reject man as though it was a totally alien world. It had a quality that was strangely quiet and ancient and wild, as though some intangible but palpable force pervaded its essence, a force that was invisible and fierce and older than any human memory, deeper and more arcane than the most secret recesses of the unconscious mind. She looked out the window and saw the reflected electric light from the carriage compartments and the blurred shadows of men sliding rapidly over the flinty land beside the rails. The train was traveling at breakneck speed, swaying violently as it roared along. She looked at Malcolm. He had not moved all night, not since being violently ill, and had been so still that she had almost forgotten about him. The illness had come on suddenly and he had gone inside himself to deal with it. He certainly was no whiner, she thought, and she appreciated him for it and remembered the way he had made the monkeys cower in the temple and the hot, dark, sugar-sweetened tea they had drunk together on the roadside afterward and how good it had been with him then. She did not think about the man who had taken her up to the temple on the motorbike and who had been as frightened as she was of the monkeys. She remembered him briefly, and then in her mind she heard the sound of the temple gong and realized he was best forgotten and looked at Tom Bryant, the beautiful Tom Bryant, she thought, who was sitting opposite her trying to conceal his satyric preoccupation. His eyes were so excruciatingly honest and unabashed that she was both excited and amused by them.

She thought about giving herself to him in a friendly act of shared pleasure. A man like him would certainly appreciate such an encounter, she thought, and seeing the way he looked at her but kept holding back not only aroused her but elicited her female compassion. She stood up confidently and drew down the blinds on the door and the interior windows and then turned out the light and sat back down opposite him. Light from the other compartments, streaking the desert floor, paled their profiles to a livid bronze. They sat in silence and listened to the rapid clicking of the wheels on the tracks and Malcolm's heavy, exhausted breathing.

Finally she said to him: "That's a beautiful opal you gave me. A stone like that is a rare gem. I want to let you know that I really appreciate it."

"You're welcome," he said. "Have a nice day."

She laughed, more out of surprise than amusement.

"How did you know about that?" she asked.

"About what?"

"Have-a-nice-day."

"Oh." He shrugged his shoulders but kept his eyes on her. "I've been around."

She leaned forward and slid onto her knees on the floor in front of him and placed her hands gently on either side of his face and kissed him, flicking her tongue between his lips. He kissed her back softly and she put her long arms around his neck and pressed herself against him and kissed him hard and passionately, smiling against his mouth as she felt his hands reach down and grope beneath her dress, stroking the backs of her naked thighs and then her buttocks, and then his fingers parted her flesh and probed the moist, willing opening below her rectum that wanted him sooner than she had anticipated and which she imagined, at that moment, to be a lush, refreshing oasis in an otherwise arid wilderness.

Through his sleep Malcolm felt the crazy rocking of the speeding train and recognized the sounds of Vivian's whimpering love moans but did not move nor open his eyes. The nausea and the stomach cramps that had gripped him earlier were finally subsiding and he could feel his body settling and his mind clearing. He had been dreaming about Bali and the funeral pyre he had seen on the beach and the wailing shrieks of the mourners and the flames leaping and the intense heat and the odor of burning flesh. In his dream there was also the smell of saffron and of clove cigarettes and there was gamelan music. For some reason he had attended the funeral and had been disgusted and frightened by the sight and the smell of the burning body, but in spite of this it was a happy occasion and he was surrounded by beautiful Balinese boys, the kind of boys that the wives of Australian executives came to Bali to have affairs with. The boys were all exquisite dancers and were in their dancing costumes and smiling at him. There was a clutter of resonant sounds and perfumes and it all looked just like one of those Balinese paintings and he did not want to wake up and lose the sensations of the dream. But the intensity of Vivian's muffled whines and sobs finally broke through and then shattered the tapestry of the dream and he was briefly reminded of the shrieks of the monkeys in the temple. He opened his eyes and lay perfectly still and watched her in what he thought at first was moonlight. He did not care about nor really notice the stranger. It was more than apparent, even at a glance, who had initiated the coupling. When it was over he closed his eyes and realized that he still loved her and that he had enjoyed watching her. She seemed so totally fixated on herself that he couldn't feel at all jealous. Envious, perhaps, if he had been feeling better. But he felt at this stage that he could grant her her fling and that it meant nothing and that he knew he had disappointed her. Besides, he felt too weak to protest. It was one night in the middle of nowhere and he had been with her for over five months—through Malaysia, Thailand, Sumatra, and Java, after Bali. He had strayed a few times in Thailand but it didn't amount to anything and this didn't amount to anything, otherwise she wouldn't have done it the way she did. He would let it go and say nothing.

The two were separated now and she lay down beside Malcolm and put her arm around him and he felt her lips on the back of his neck and her eyelids fluttering against his skin. She hadn't been there long when the train suddenly came to a screeching, grinding halt and they were thrown onto the floor. Voices were yelling at the other end of the car and he recognized the conductor shouting angrily above the general din. Malcolm got to his feet and opened the door to the lighted corridor just as an iron rod, wielded by someone outside the train, shattered the glass in the compartment windows, spraying the fragments all over the floor and seats.

"Jesus fuckin' Christ," said Tom Bryant, still sitting and looking out the window, where a tall, very thin man with long greasy brown hair and thick, dark-rimmed spectacles, was running down the tracks smashing every window on that side of the car.

Malcolm walked down the corridor to the door, where four men, all of them with large, protruding bellies and dressed in dirty white singlets and baggy short pants, stood huddled together and drinking from large cans of beer as they watched the riot outside. The tall man was yelling threats and obscenities and flailing the air with the iron rod in an attempt to keep three would-be subduers, among them the conductor, at bay. A fourth man lay at his feet, his head bleeding profusely.

"What's going on?" Malcolm asked the man nearest the door. The man looked up at Malcolm with bloodshot, frightened-looking blue eyes.

"It's our mate Ralph. Can't hold his booze. He always goes off like this after we've given him a few."

"For Christ's sake," said Malcolm disgustedly. "Why do you give it to him then?"

The man looked at him incredulously, almost as though he thought he was mad, as the conductor and another man both lunged at Ralph and dragged him writhing and cursing to the ground.

"You can't be fuckin' serious, mate!" said the man, his tone and expression full of exaggerated indignation. "A bloke's gotta 'ave his beer, no matter how tropo he is."

SHE HAD liked it. She had loved it. Tom Bryant could see it in her eyes in the morning even though, after they had finished, she had lain down next to Malcolm and much later on, when the whole train was asleep, he had heard her sighing the way she sighed with him and he opened his eyes and watched Malcolm make love to her in the dark with her long legs up wrapped around him, rocking with the motion of the train. *I got her all fired up for him,* he thought. *But I'm not complaining. Pretty amazing to see a woman who can go like that from one man to another with the same verve and passion and then wake up in the morning with the same two blokes there together, one a virtual stranger, and smile at them both and kiss one of them and act like nothing happened. I suppose he just has to take it if he wants to keep her. I know I wouldn't. A woman like that means trouble but my God she tasted good. He must've seen. We must've waked him. He looks as fit as a fiddle today and maybe he's just a good sport and maybe she always does exactly what she wants and to hell with everyone else. But she did go back to him after she'd finished with me. Suddenly it was over and she went straight back to him and couldn't take her hands off of him.*

She was just a windfall, he thought. He received them from time to time and had learned not to take them too seriously.

It was approaching midday and the train moved at its slow daytime pace across a spinifex plain and there were the low, rounded shapes of ancient red hills on the horizon. Vivian looked out at them from the open window, cleared of broken glass, where she also watched the moving dust cloud of a herd of wild horses. Her face was fresh and serene and showed no hint of any anxiety or remorse. If anything, she looked better than she did the day before and appeared unbothered by the heat or the slowness of the train. The handsome prospector had shown her kindness and generosity and she had reciprocated and given him what he desired most and it was very pleasant and she was pleased that she had that to give. Life, and men in particular, had shown her that she had the powerful qualities of a woman who could give or withhold great favors.

She did not know if Malcolm had seen what had happened or not. She hoped that he hadn't. She was free to do as she pleased and insisted on it, but men and sex and freedom were complicated matters. All she really knew was that she did not equate sex with love, and that she had wanted Tom Bryant, and in having him her desire for Malcolm and her sense of intimacy with him had been reactivated. She felt comfortable and rejuvenated by the whole episode and believed now that things would be fine for the rest of the trip. They were headed for Darwin and from there would return to Bali, and she knew that things would be fine and animated from this point on because she felt good inside. *As long as Tom Bryant doesn't complicate things,* she thought. *As long as he understands.*

She looked down at the earth passing below her, at the dry, pale, sun-bleached clumps of spinifex grass with their pointed leaves and bristly seed heads, and at the blur of thousands of small, sharp, white stones.

It takes energy to invest life with meaning, she thought. She was feeling bright and energetic. Today, for the first time, the desert actually looked awesome and beautiful. In such a state the value and meaning of things hardly seemed to matter. The world was full of illusions, anyway.

They were all hungry for lunch and their food had run out when the train pulled into the settlement. There was a general store here, they were told, where they could purchase supplies for the rest of the trip. It was the only such place between here and Alice Springs. A few ghost gums with smooth white trunks grew alongside the tracks. Apart from the store, the settlement was composed of just a few derelict-looking buildings made out of buckled sheets of rusted corrugated iron with the doors and windows boarded up. Beyond these buildings was the pub, a slightly more respectable-looking structure made out of the same material, with a Swan Lager sign displayed above the entrance. At the other end of the "town" was the store, square and box-like and made of bricks and mortar with a wide corrugated iron veranda overhang in front that sagged like the back of an old mule. About fifty yards from the store was a small Aborigine encampment made up of scattered lean-tos constructed from the ubiquitous metal sheets and kangaroo skins and burlap bags. Around these sat listless groups of blacks and more than a dozen brown and yellow dogs.

They climbed down off the train and walked toward the store as the other travelers made a raucous dash for the pub. Vivian was between the two men. Tom Bryant had been sullen and withdrawn all morning but Malcolm, feeling a renewed vigor after his illness, appeared to be in good spirits.

"Well," said Tom Bryant, addressing them both. "This is where I get off." He looked at Vivian, searching for the faintest glimmer of recognition now that he was offering them his farewell. Everything about her denied that anything had happened.

He put down his pack and rifle and shook hands with the two of them.

"My camel man should be through here in a day or two, or else I'll get a ride out to his station," he said. "Then I can start afresh."

"Just make sure you don't get stuck with another bitch in heat," said Vivian, laughing.

"Oh, I'll make sure of that alright. Ain't nothin' but trouble."

Her brashness caught him off guard, and he tried to sound light and merry but wasn't sure that he had succeeded. They wished him luck and went into the store. She had changed into jeans and a shirt and he watched her back and the way her hips moved, noting the concupiscent, female quality she had even though her walk was almost mannish. She was taller than both he and Malcolm and he had to admit he had never met anything quite like her. They disappeared through the door beneath the deep shadow of the veranda and then he looked up at the bright and incredibly blue sky and thought about his luck and the fact that he was glad it was all over.

The inside of the store was bare looking and smelled of dust and tobacco and the rank, close odor of human sweat. A large, bald man with a freckled face and scalp stood behind the counter and next to him was a pretty girl with very blond hair and wide, soft, blue eyes. She was of medium height and powerfully built, with broad shoulders and large, pendulous breasts that looked full and ripe in the brassiere beneath her yellow T-shirt. She gazed longingly at Malcolm as he placed their order, and Vivian noticed the gaze and shot her a quick, green, predatory glare that made the girl's peach-colored face flush red, although her eyes continued their doleful and inviting appeal.

"So you two are on the goods train, eh?" The man spoke with a German accent. "The train people tend to be a rough crowd. Not often we see a couple like yourselves."

"We thought it would be a good way to see something of the desert," said Malcolm.

"Oh, ya, it is that," said the man.

"Cheap, too," said Vivian.

"Oh, ya. It's cheap."

"A couple of weeks back the train brought in a real wild bunch," said the girl, smiling. "They wrecked the pub. Went crazy. Reto closed the store and stood outside with a rifle until they'd gone."

"It's like that sometimes," said the man. "The heat gets to people, and they go tropo. I've been out here for twenty years and it's crazy but I love it."

"Reto's a little crazy himself," the girl told Malcolm. "He's been out here too long."

"Oh, ya, I'm crazy alright," said Reto, addressing Vivian. "Are you two married?"

"No. We're just traveling together."

"That's the modern way," he continued, his voice loud and jovial and his expression hungry, eager to converse with the newcomers.

"Oh, look," said the girl nonchalantly. "The train's leavin'." She was slowly packing their goods into a cardboard box.

"What!" Malcolm turned and saw the caboose pass across the frame of the open door.

"Not to worry," said Reto. "There'll be another in a few days."

"Jesus Christ!" said Malcolm. He threw down a twenty-dollar bill and snatched up the box and headed for the door, Vivian following close behind.

"Your bill is only sixteen seventy-five," yelled the man, laughing, as they ran out. It always amused him to see people in such a hurry. After twenty years in the desert he could never understand why they were that way, and he felt superior because he never was that way himself.

They ran out onto the tracks, the box falling apart in his arms, as the train cleared the settlement and picked up speed. Neither of them spoke. They stood there, panting and out of breath, and watched the rear of the caboose grow steadily smaller, eventually disappearing into the vanishing point where the straight, black lines of the rails converged on the flat horizon.

He turned and looked at her to see if she was upset. She looked back at him, her face red and moist. She drew in her breath very slowly and deliberately, and then slowly exhaled, as though the breath was meant to both measure and release her exasperation.

"Well," she said, looking up at the huge blue sky where she saw tiny black dots that were crows circling as they surveyed the plain and the town in the afternoon sunlight. "I guess that's that. All we can do is wait."

"I suppose you reckon it's my fault."

"Don't be silly. It's no one's fault. There'll be another train in a few days. All we can do is wait."

"I'm glad you're feeling so philosophical."

"There seems to be no other choice."

The girl came out of the store. She smiled and waved at them to come back.

"It'll be okay," she yelled. "Reto said you can stay here. We'll look after you. Come inside and have a cup of tea."

"All our things are on that train," said Vivian as they started to walk. "What rotten fucking luck. Wouldn't you know it? What damn rotten fucking luck in all the damned wretched spots on earth."

"I thought you were being philosophical about it," said Malcolm.

"I am. But I'm allowed to be pissed off. I wish we'd taken the regular express, or even an airplane."

"So far it seems you've managed to actually have quite a good time." He laughed, and the laugh sounded bitter and sarcastic.

"Oh shut up, Malcolm. Just shut up and leave me alone."

That evening, after they had showered, they ate dinner with Reto and his niece, whose name was Luscha. They ate steak that came from a cross-breeding of cattle and water buffalo, a speciality, they were told, of the Northern Territory, and which was surprisingly good and tender. Reto bored them both with long, sordid, rambling anecdotes of life in the desert. It was a crude, harsh, violent life, full of bizarre happenings and brutal encounters and devoid of any semblance of refinement or what Vivian considered common decency. The men were drinking heavily and their drunkenness irritated her. As soon as the meal was over she abruptly excused herself and retreated to the shack behind the store that had a bed and a washbasin where Reto had only been too pleased to house his guests. He had not met such an interesting and handsome couple in a long time and kept telling them this, which also got on her nerves. She took a kerosene lantern with her and placed it on the concrete floor of the shack and lay down on the bed and looked out of the window at the new moon. The air was filled with a strong odor of dust and the sour, ashen smell that came from the Aborigine camp. She could hear dogs barking and the faint din of drunken male voices from the pub and she wondered why this had happened to her, that she should be stuck out here in this flat, endless and inhuman desolation, surrounded by male drunkenness, with nowhere to go. She had never seen country so empty and flat. The salt bush plains seemed to go on forever, and what had been beautiful to her that morning was now a landscape dwarfing and oppressive in its vast monotony. She tried to understand why her moods shifted so dramatically, why everything could suddenly change for her without warning. She was unhappy now, she thought, because she felt stuck, trapped, and powerless for the first time in her life. She was in the middle of nowhere and her own will and desire meant nothing and there was no escape.

He was drunk now and he did not want to be, nor had he believed he was getting drunk sitting there listening to the old German and aware of the girl looking at him. But now, outside and alone in the night air, he knew he was drunk, although not terribly or deliriously so. But he did not want to go into the shack and face Vivian this way. He knew how much she despised any form of drunkenness and he was afraid of what he might say to her. He was hurt and angry at her now and he did not want to be. It was there and he couldn't control it, but he could control his feet. They led him away from the store, toward the campfires and the native smell he knew from his boyhood, out beyond the perimeters of the white settlement.

He felt invisible in the darkness beneath the stars. The new moon was high in the sky and gave only a faint light, and he could hear the hushed, low, rapid mutterings of the native tongue as he moved closer to the camp, feeling a mindless and irresistible pull toward the fires and smelling the cooking odors of wild meat and burning eucalyptus. The lights of the store and the pub were behind him now and he crossed the tracks, seeing the dark figures squatting around the fires and the buckled skeletons of the humpies outlined darkly against the indigo sky.

A large woman in a sackcloth dress stood beside the nearest fire cooking something in the coals, which she turned with a stick. As he drew near he saw it was a giant lizard, a large Perente about five feet long, its body arched and stiffened by the heat. He hovered on the edge of the firelight, strangely captivated by the sight of the lizard in the flames, and did not see the woman frowning at him dangerously nor the low stars that cluttered the sky beyond her where the Milky Way poured down into the horizon, but only the lizard on the fire and the dark space between the stars.

The woman picked up the club she had used to smash the lizard's head with and waved it threateningly at the drunken, mad-looking intruder. White men around the camp came for only one thing, and she had seen a lot of rape and even murder in her time and Aborigine women so hopeless and desperate that they smeared cattle dung on their genitals in order to repel the loathsome violators. She was an angry old woman and ready for a fight, and she had long ago ceased to distinguish good from bad and harmless from harmful in her dealings with white men.

He was still transfixed and convinced of his own invisibility when she struck. He heard a woman scream somewhere behind him and as he looked up and turned around the club caught him across the side of the head and a hot, white light filled his skull, blinding him from behind the eyes, and immediately he felt the blood flowing warm over his forehead and trickling down his neck. He heard voices yelling and dogs barking and he was on the ground, looking up at the large old black woman with her silver hair and furious face as she swung the club high and hit him again and he heard the loud, shattering *car-wong* of a rifle and saw her brow explode and her heavy torso thrown back. He tried to raise himself up and then fell back into darkness.

When he opened his eyes he was alone in the bed in the shack and he could tell by the light that it was near midday. The side of his head was heavily bandaged and throbbed painfully. He looked into the long, still, heavily lined brown face of an outback policeman who gazed at him with tired and friendly eyes from beneath the wide brim of his bush hat.

"Now take it easy, son," said the policeman. His voice was slow and flat. "Everything's alright. Do you remember what happened?"

"I think so."

"Good. I'm gonna read this statement to ya, that I prepared with Luscha and Reto here, and if you agree with it, I want yer to sign it and that'll be the end of the matter."

"The matter?"

He moved to sit up and the policeman put his hand on his chest and gently pushed him down.

"Now just relax, son, and listen . . . 'The Aborigine woman, known as Maria Ado in English, supposedly a member of the Pitjantjajara, attacked Malcolm Savage on the night of February fourteen around eleven P.M., as he was walking on the outskirts of Oodnadatta. The attack was unprovoked, and executed with a club with which the said Maria Ado apparently intended to kill the victim, clubbing his head and bringing him to the ground, from whence she proceeded with the assault. This was observed by Luscha Rieman, who called on her uncle, Reto Rieman, for help. Reto, unable to stop Maria Ado, and in order to save the life of Malcolm Savage, was obliged to use the only recourse available at the time, and shot Maria Ado through the head with a thirty-thirty caliber rifle, killing her instantly.'"

He held the typed document on a clipboard in front of Malcolm's face and put the pen in his hand.

"Now sign this next to the other signatures and that'll be that."

He signed without thinking as Luscha came into the shack. She looked down at him and smiled.

"Where's Vivian?" he asked.

"Oh, she left this mornin' with Tom Bryant. I told her you'd be alright here with us while you recovered. She said she wanted to see the desert, and that you'd understand. She said to tell you she hoped to meet up with you in Alice, but if she wasn't there when you arrived not to wait around for her. Here then, let me get yer a nice cuppa tea."

The following night he made love to Luscha in the bed in the shack. Two days later the train came, and he sat drinking with a group of stockmen in a crowded compartment all the way to Alice Springs, believing that if he got drunk and stayed drunk the pain in his head would go away and that he would forget about the monkeys in the temple he had visited high in the mountains of Bali.

The Defeat of Big Flo

ALAN BEDFORD was witness for his father.

In the shanty town.

He stood in the hut, in its dog smell, where the oldest woman in the world was dying. She lay on a pile of hessian bags against the far wall, her shape massive and indistinct in the interior darkness. She was so old she had practically outgrown her human form. Apart from the obvious manifestations of her womanhood, the inherent nature of her sexuality seemed to have been all but forgotten in a shapeless abundance of outraged flesh. Pin shafts of dusty sunlight pierced the dark through holes in the buckled zinc roof.

The old woman was dying at the slow pace characteristic of her dry existence, surrounded by people who no longer understood her ancient nostalgia for the sea or the dream image she clung to of the giant green cod who had formed the river. Outside the cicadas were loud in the trees. When she started to sound like a sack losing air, and the shanty became overwhelmed by the liberation of her boiling innards, Alan Bedford, standing behind the women and the old men, thought, *To each his own,* remembering the very first time he ever laid eyes on the gigantic matriarch, when he was still a small boy. He was alone in the woods. He saw her knock three Aborigine men down in succession. He remembered her thick parrot's tongue, the dry croak of her animal voice, that powerful backhand swing, executed with the militant ease of a monstrous ballerina. She danced in the clearing. He saw her through the trees, lifting her dress made of burlap and revealing her awesome brown buttocks like formations of the land itself.

He remembered.

It was a bad day for a death, any death, but especially this death. His father had asked him to go, without explaining why. Already, at six in the morning, the heat was swimming in the garden, the orange trees were dusty. The old man came into his room and woke him, told him brusquely to get up.

"I can't go meself. Look at me. But I want you t' go." There was, at that hour, no love between them, and he did not want to go. He did not want to go down to the shanties, and the garbage dump they were part of, and the flies in the heat of the day.

"What's all a this shit about?" said Alan. "It's an ol' Abo woman dyin'. What's it t' you?"

The old man couldn't explain. He spluttered, and put his hands on his head.

"I—I—I—I— . . . look, Alan—" shaking his head, and pleading now "—just do this one thing for me. I'll be dead meself soon. This one thing." His voice was shaking, and full of self-righteousness. "This means everything to me. Ya gotta go. It's because of the man, the Flyin' Roo, that's all I can tell ya now."

Serial stood waiting on the veranda. "He's goin' too," said Jack. "He has 'is own reasons fer goin'."

Serial was an old man who worked on the orchard for Jack Bedford.

He had a story and a reason of his own.

"What do you want me to do, then?" asked Alan.

"Just go. Just be there when she passes, that's all."

He felt that his father was weak and hypocritical. He felt that always the old man had got his son to do what he should have done himself. Now it was this, that had nothing whatsoever to do with him, personally, as he felt that his father had nothing whatsoever to do with him. He had wanted to say, "I don't want to do your shit. Attend your own funerals. Take care of your own business." But he didn't. He rose and dressed without a word.

"Thanks," said his father. "Thank you, boy. Thank you." Hanging his head and turning away, not looking at Alan anymore and shuffling out of the room shaking his head and mumbling "thanks" over and over, and not once did Alan feel that the words were being said to him.

He stood in the sweating dark of the shanty, wondering if it was cruelty that was the measure of his courage.

The white cockatoos had gathered in the tree branches on the opposite bank of the river. The warm air of the forest was thick with the smell of eucalyptus. Above the tree tops the eternal blue sky displayed absolute unconcern, an infinite disregard for the panting and lugubrious tedium of the old woman's death on the ground below, beside the river.

Alan took a handkerchief and wiped the sweat from the back of his neck. He realized, because his head was hot and perspiring, that he had failed to remove his hat upon stepping inside the shanty, and he took it off, out of respect for the dying. He wiped his eyes. The women and the men began to chant and clap their hands. The chant broke into a high wail, melodious but not quite music, as the singing of their voices was overtaken by the growing frenzy of their lamentation. The old woman heaved asthmatically. There was the sound of the final release of her bowels, and as the androgynous spirit of that immense and ancient female rose like a pale sheet through the roof of the shanty, that death song, although potent like liquid on the spine, came also like a long moaning breath, a simple expiration of air.

Hers was definitely not the inglorious fate of a wallflower. Hers had, in fact, been a story of triumph and defeat. No, it was not defeat. Defeat was only one side of it, and it was not the whole thing. No one word was the whole thing. No one word was the summary of any given moment of her incredibly long life.

ALAN BEDFORD knew this: That Big Mumma Flo (that was what they called her; her own name, her singing name, was never revealed to the gubbah) was the only woman, ever, permitted in the saloon bar of the Wallangirrii Hotel. She would appear there, in the night, and take on the entire crowd of men, knocking them away from her as creatures trivial and anonymous with that infamous backhand. She had performed that rite for over a hundred years. For as long as any white man could remember. There were accounts of her from the very first days of settlement along the river, although in this place many things went unrecorded.

As he stepped out of the shanty and saw the wide river stretched before him through the trees, Alan recalled the obscure tale of the Flyin' Kangaroo, the only man, in recorded history, who challenged Big Flo and defeated her. That was in the days when riverboats still plowed the Murray, and Wallangirrii was little more than a hotel, two or three stores, and a railway station. There was a lumber mill and a few houses with zinc roofs and newly planted hedges. There was one street that went all the way down to the river. It was lined with squat bristling date palms that provided shade from the sun. The train provided ice, which was brought from hundreds of miles away wrapped in hessian. The train also took the fruit and grain away, and finally it brought an end to the river traffic.

The train also brought the Flyin' Kangaroo to Wallangirrii, not the river, as some would like to imagine.

He walked along the path through the trees toward the road. Serial was behind him, and Alan could still smell the smoky odors of the shanties on his shirt. On the other side of the road, on the slope of the red sand ridge, orange trees squatted in rows like a legion of giant green fowl, their feathers ruffled in the breeze that he could not feel, but only see from time to time in the gentle agitation of leaves. The sand ridges and the plain had been gradually turned into a huge orange tree by the waters of the river. There were the shiny leathery leaves, the sticky scented blossoms, the coolness and shade; it bore magnificent fruit.

The hot sun on his back, and his aching fatigue from the morning, filled Alan now with that sense of an old irritation. Images of his father standing over his bed, or drunk in the afternoons, came to him as he walked along, and already he was demanding some explanation as to why he had attended Big Flo's death. His father said it had something to do with the Flyin' Kangaroo. What a stupid name for a man, especially in these parts, where to be a hero is nothing but to remain obscure. He knew nothing, really, of this man. There were vague memories, and scattered talk. Like trees on the savanna. His father had said, once, that one day, over the orchards, he would come flying. Over the river. He was a man capable of inhuman leaps. That was his legend. Alan saw him in his mind, a socialist, a startling advocator of miscegenation on the riverbanks, and a wild debauchee who scandalized the town. His table became well known throughout the region, for he shared it with workers, wanderers, Aborigines, and even respectable citizens of Wallangirrii. He would sit at one end of it eating in silence, an eccentric patriarch, a thick shock of chestnut hair falling across his brow, his eyes holding that wild gleam of an outcast. Behind him, on the wall, a huge indigo flag with the white stars of the Southern Cross blazing on it like the canopy of the Antarctic sky, uncluttered by the imposition of the Union Jack in its top righthand corner. He was, above everything else, a true Southerner, with a deep feeling for the island continent. The republicanism he professed, and lived out, set him apart from many of his countrymen.

Alan would hear his story now. And his father's story. He pondered his legs as he walked along. This was a day, he felt, never meant for him. He was aware of nothingness, as though nothing-ness were a great beast that stalked him. He was now part of a tale, or he had witnessed its conclusion, and none of it, it seemed, moved him in his heart, and yet he saw it all, perfect in memory. He was an implacable witness, doomed to be aware that nothing existed. There was a rage in this day, in the pith of the sun.

Serial hobbled along the road behind him, a brown goanna of a man with small round pale blue eyes. A cripple, with one leg slightly shorter than the other. Alan stopped and waited for him. The old man's face, beneath his hat, had the painful look of plowed earth, and he was weeping still as he walked along. I should've taken the truck, thought Alan, squinting in the mid-day glare. Serial's father had worked in the old lumber mill (closed now), and when Serial was a boy his father often kept him tied to a tree. One day his father caught him down on the riverbank, where he was playing with an Aborigine girl. The old man grabbed the boy and took him home and tied him to the tree again. He put a heavy burlap bag over his head and shoul-ders, and then he flogged him with a stock whip, and left him tied to the tree for a couple of days, and for a long time after that Serial forgot how to speak, and when he remembered it was with a violent stutter and even then he had to relearn the names of many things.

As he walked down the road Alan heard the voices of Italian workers in the orange groves, distant, light, full of chatter and vigor as they worked through the day among the trees. He liked to work with those men. He liked their peasant ability to be happy while they worked in the heat, their languid perseverance. He walked slowly alongside the old man, occasionally studying the flies on his stooped back, which did not move, seemingly inert in the heat, riding Serial as though he were a camel. Even-tually Alan brushed them off. They scattered, briefly, and re-settled.

Years of sunlight, and the sickness of his old age, made Jack Bedford look as yellow as a sunflower. The lean old man was himself approaching death, and with his drawn and slanted green eyes he had the look of an old Asian. He sat in a cane butterfly chair on the veranda and watched his son coming up the drive, in the shade of the tall poplars. As Alan drew near the house, walking now across the garden, the old man stood up, his large and skeletal hands trembling.

"Has she gone?" he called in a voice that was already a roar of grief.

"Yeah," said Alan, flatly. "She's gone." He stood in the garden and looked up at the dark and blurred outline of his father in the shade behind the rusted wire screening. He could not see his face, and the garden was dry and full of sunlight and the buzzing of cicadas and locusts. The old man sat down again, blending into the shape of the chair. Behind him the rest of the house was closed up against the heat.

"Where's that ol' bastard Serial?"

"I dunno. He left me at the gate."

"He was with yer?" His voice, behind the screening, was somehow frail, dry, a voice that was more a long breath on which the words floated like particles of dust. Alan did not answer. The question, although asked, did not seem to have been asked at all. He heard the creak and whining sounds of the fibers of the cane chair as his father shifted his weight, or a leg. There was a long pause. Then Jack said: "Leave me for a while, will you?"

AND ALAN BEDFORD thought: To think that his old man now wept for that same monstrous female who had been his nemesis on at least three occasions; because of her Jack Bedford had suffered the indignity of being brought home unconscious in the back of a pickup, had suffered the ridicule of his wife, and, once struck by that powerful hand, had been marked like all the rest with that anonymous stigma of humiliation in the eyes of the town. Not so, contested Jack. The blow delivered by Big Mumma Flo contained a shock that could change a man's life completely. "Whenever I caught it from the ol' girl," he had said on several occasions, repeating himself as though his statement had become a prayer, "it was exactly what I needed. She brought me back to reality." And then he would laugh out loud, slapping the table, coughing, weeping, thrusting his square jaw out. "The only problem is ya can't keep goin' back fer more. The great bitch would kill ya." He would be reduced to tears by the excessive nature of his own humor, that laughter, as he grew older, taking on a sentimental tone, a tearful alcoholic animation. The old man had, in this late period of his life, become a fugitive from the catastrophes of the external world, and Mumma Flo had been his solace, his strength, even. In her, memory dwelled. She was its guardian.

Alan waited in the shade of a gum tree for the afternoon to pass, for the heat that had settled over the orchard with the afternoon to lift, and for the medicinal breath of the dusk and the blooming of stars in the vast turquoise twilight. He waited patiently, with a marijuana cigarette, amidst the odors of leaves and stripped bark, waiting for all that he had seen to become clear in his mind, not a heat-soaked blur, but images full of their own weight. He recalled the road in the morning, walking along it with Serial after word had been brought to his father that the old woman was dying. He would relive that morning instant for instant, over and over again, without fully understanding why it captured and scattered his brain so. Were Flo and Jack lovers? Was that why the old man had asked him to go, because he was too weak himself? He had walked along the road in silence, the sand drifts, in the shade of the trees, still cool from the night, listening to the impatient animal grunts of the old cripple beside him and knowing there was no hurry or urgency, that it would take hours of effort for her soul to extract itself from that thick mountain of unyielding flesh, that even death, for her, was filled with the burden and labor of existence. The shrimp mud smell of the riverbanks rose with the morning heat. Serial made the sign of the cross repeatedly, mumbling to himself, feeling the cross heavy on him every time he made the gesture, and saying, "If it has to be . . . if it h-has t' be . . . a-a-a h-holy d-d-d-eath . . . ," speaking with only a small undertone of hysteria, and Alan, now, remembering it all, as though catching up with himself, remembered other times on the road, for that road would haunt him all of his life, that never-ending road home . . .

He walked along the road in the lilac afterglow. That summer evening was a part of every evening. He went around in a state of painful arousal, awkwardly stiff in his trousers, anxious for pornography. He could see the shanties through the trees and the simple lean-tos and the dogs that ran about and the dark figures around the campfire in the increasing twilight and there was the massive form of Big Flo, bursting out of the ground in the dark like a gigantic mushroom. He could hear the parrot shriek of her laughter above the medley as a group of men, in the throes of a drunken folly, took turns at trying to lift her. He watched them straining on their skinny legs, becoming one with her in silhouette and forming some unknown demonic creature of odd shape, with a massive torso and the long and ludicrously thin legs of a grasshopper. Then the creature would separate into parts, the legs would fold at the knees, and the slender figure of a man would stumble back and collapse into a ragged form. One man actually moved her, or the creature moved, a strained shuffling of feet, a slight shudder, and she swayed imperceptibly, only to topple backward arse first in the arms of the man who held her. She sat there on top of him, her feet straight out in front of her, slapping her enormous black thighs with delight while round about dark figures lay drunkenly or openly copulating. Men fought playfully for women, like kangaroos boxing, fighting each other at arm's length with their hands. There were the shrieks and whoop type sounds of women laughing and screaming and whimpering. Their voices rippled out like water in the darkness, lapping in rings against the hard trunks of the gum trees.

He crossed into the bush, making his way through the leaf-drooping dark. Something stirred, darted away. A fox, another intruder. He leaned against a tree, hiding, pressing himself against it, peering through the forked trunk. He heard the panting, smelled the dust and the smell of the camp, that Aborigine odor. A man squirmed like a lizard between the thighs of a woman where she lay in the grass. Another woman, only feet away, her ragged dress up over her waist, her naked buttocks arched skyward and her elbows supporting her on the ground, was fucked heavily from behind by a man who wore only a shirt, a pale blur mounting a dark form, surrounded by leaves, abandoned cars, heaps of corrugated tin, broken bottles, the ashen debris of the river town.

"NOTHIN' has changed."

The old man's voice caught in his throat and he had a coughing fit. He rose from his chair on the veranda and walked to the screen door and opened it and spat into the yard. It was just before dusk. Long shadows fell across the house and there was the strong sweet smell of wet dust that rose from the orchard round about as the tall sprinklers watered the trees with a slur and clicking sound like insects. He returned to his chair and sat studying an unlit cigarette between his trembling nicotine stained fingers.

"Nothin'," he repeated, almost petulantly.

It was now the old man's weary dream simply to die in the geometric oblivion of his orchard, in a sea of oranges. The wild explorer's spirit of his youth, of which he boasted often, had, it seemed to his son, long ago been drowned in heat and alcohol. Alan sat in an old rocking chair, rocking slowly, slowly drinking from a can of beer, listening to the click and rush of the sprinklers turning, watching his father and the shadows that grew.

Alan had known his father, in the past, as a man to whom childhood meant nothing more than a period of mental insufficiency, especially where his sons were concerned. Alan had left home a boy and he returned a man, to face his father, and to settle their mutual debt with geography. The beard on his face, which at first offended the old man, was still soft and youthful, unhardened by the razor.

"There's nothin' left anymore, nothin'."

The old man sat hunched forward in his chair, one elbow rested on his knee. He was angry. His yellow skin was drawn tightly across his face and his eyes blazed with a dog-like fury.

"Get me a beer, will you?"

"I don't think you should. Look at yaself!"

"Shut up, pup! If you won't get me a beer, I'll get it meself."

He coughed again. Alan fetched him a beer, thrusting it into his face, rudely interrupting his contemplation of his stained and trembling hands and the unlit cigarette in his fingers.

"Here you are, ya stupid ol' bastard."

The old man indicated with his eyes for Alan to place it between his feet. Alan put the can down gently, but several feet out from Jack's reach, so that he had to stoop and stretch his arm out, which he did with considerable strain and without saying a word.

"Maybe what you need is another smack in the face from ol' Flo," said Alan. There was contested anger between them now, and their eyes held one another as in a duel.

"Ol' Flo's dead. Or isn't she?"

"She's dead."

"There'll be a lot of talkin' now among the Abos. She'd been around fer centuries. You oughta find out whatever ya can, but be careful. And be careful with the rest of the bastards, too. We're outcasts in this country, whether you know it or not, even if no one around you seems to know it, it's still the same."

"Why's that?"

"Simply because we have a view of a nation. Of a place t' call a place."

Darkness was upon them. The old man had not left the veranda all day. He urinated from the doorstep and moved around from time to time, looking out at the drive as if expecting to see someone, or else he sat in the butterfly chair, mumbling constantly to himself, sometimes swearing and threatening unseen persons in a loud voice.

"An' you didn't go an' fight, unlike ya older brother, an' now 'e's dead. An' what for?"

"I dunno. I didn't go. I only know why I didn't."

"There are," said Jack flatly, "one or two things you ought to know. A few things about ya mother an' me, an' why I asked ya to be at Flo's t'day, why it was important that you be there, 'cos I couldn't be there meself. It's a long story."

"I'd like to know that, even if it's a long story. I'd still like t' hear it. I'd like t' know about Big Flo and that fellah you called th' Flyin' Roo. The rest, the stuff about you an' the old lady, doesn't interest me anymore. That's between you an' her, and it doesn't interest me anymore."

"I want t' tell you everythin' an' I want ya t' listen. I'm dyin', or can't ya tell?"

"I can tell. And I'll listen."

"I never could talk to ya brother. An' then 'e went t' Vietnam an' never came back, an' now the bastards are still in power. The nation, what there is of it, has been ripped apart, has lost what soul it might 'ave had."

The old man sat back in his chair and breathed deeply.

"There are even those European carp in the river, eatin' everything."

"There's still hope. There's always hope," said Alan.

"Not if there's a third world war. Not if they keep chewin' up the forests and diggin' great holes in the ground."

"They say that where the uranium is, is the dreamin' of the giant green ant. That it sleeps there, and when disturbed will awaken and bring about the destruction of the world."

"I'm not surprised. That doesn't surprise me one bit."

"Things always seem to reach plague proportions here," Alan mused. "If it's not rabbits or insects or frogs, it's fish, foreign fish."

"That don't mean shit. Nearly everythin' 'ere is foreign. That in and of itself doesn't make something bad. Everything is foreign to everything else at some point in time."

"But the fish."

"The fish are different. The orange trees are foreign, and they're different than the fish, an' that doesn't require any argument to see the difference, and how it is on the land. That difference, I mean."

There was a pause. The old man drank silently.

"You've got to understand," he said. "That in this country we Bedfords are an exceptional race. I know you don't understand that yet, in spite of all ya learnin'."

"You are tired and bitter. I refuse to become bitter. It's an indulgence."

"Here's drinkin' to ya." Jack toasted him with his beer can. "To my perpetually sweet son. May you never become bittah like ya ol' man." He looked at Alan with his intense eyes of a Chinese temple dog. His eyes, because of his yellow condition, appeared to have a phosphorescent glow in the dark.

"You know that stuff is gonna kill ya," said Alan. "But I suppose that's your option." He stood up and went into the kitchen. He was trembling, now, with a deep unconscious rage. He thought: *He's simply dismantling himself, that's all, and then demanding sympathy.* He took another beer from the refrigerator. He did not want to go back out onto the veranda. His father would demand another beer to soak his perishing organs, and he would not get it for him. The old man was insisting on his participation, insisting, somehow, that Alan be responsible for his own self-destruction.

Once back on the veranda, seeing his father's eyes in the dark, he sat down, rigid at first, waiting for the old man's request that didn't come. The old man sat back in the deep lotus of the chair, his bony knees sticking out.

"All right," he said. "Ya said you'd listen. Are ya ready, fer once in ya life, to listen?"

"Yeah," said Alan. "I said I'd listen."

Alan felt comfortable in the darkness. It was cool, and it rested his eyes, and what heat there was came from his own body, absorbed from the day. There was a long pause. The night, the forest, grew loud, its buzz filling the house with a presence almost palpable, a sound like the whirring wings of some giant but unseen insect.

IN HIS HEART and in his mind the old man had returned to that first day he ever laid eyes on the stranger, a man dressed like a tramp, but not like a tramp at all, who leapt from the back of a boxcar into the dust beside the tracks, which were raised on a high levee. Wheat and corn fields stretched out on either side. To the west they were rimmed by a thick gum tree forest, and to the east and south the flat river plain simmered in the mid-afternoon heat, swallowed by gradual and scattered trees. Jack watched the man from his truck while he waited for the train to pass, looking down the curving track and studying the awesome length of the caterpillar of red and black cars. The truck's motor, idling, stopped. Jack swore and climbed out to crank it over. He tried once, twice. The train crawled by, whining and hissing and filling the air with its smell of oil and soot, the white and gray column of smoke and steam hanging above it like a long tongue in the wind, only there was no wind.

It was nineteen twenty-one.

Jack leaned on the rounded edge of the hood. The metal, glinting orbs of light burned him through his shirt. He kept his elbow there nonetheless, assuming that quiet and loose-bodied attitude of a country man as he watched the stranger walking down the tracks toward him. The air was alive over the land, like a flame burning, and the man seemed to float on the liquid air, a mirage without weight. As he drew near Jack heard the crunch of his boots on the iron-speckled gravel and saw the shape take human form, clear now, and earthbound. His face was half hidden by the shadow of his wide-brimmed hat. His build was square, neither tall nor short, and he moved with a languid self-assurance, a sense of physical comfort and ease with himself.

"Goin' into town?" Jack squinted at the stranger with a supercilious look of both suspicion and curiosity, a feigned enactment of indifference.

"That's right," said the stranger, stopping several feet from the truck and dropping his swag, remaining there between the tracks. "What's the name of this place?"

"Walla," said Jack dryly. "I mean Wallangirrii."

Jack eyed the stranger silently for a moment, and then he looked down at the crank handle that stuck out of the lip of the truck like the thin black tongue of some mechanical insect. He pushed his hat to the back of his head and seized the shaft with both hands and jerked it around. Nothing happened and he swore out loud and spat in the dust that was stirred by his feet.

"Let me try it." The stranger came forward. Jack looked up at him, expecting a derisive smile, but the man's face was clear and calm. There was an animated flash in the eyes, which were green and slanted. The mouth was wide and full-lipped, the chin a little too long and the forehead a little too broad for him to be called handsome. He hadn't shaved in over a week, and he seemed to possess that distinct quality of a renegade or chicken thief.

"I'll 'ave a crack at it. You've just lost heart."

Jack straightened up and stepped back. The stranger stooped, sighed, and seized the shaft. Already it had become a kind of ritual of acceptance. His back bulged like a whale under his shirt. His shoulders swung upward, his torso moved on his hips like a swivel chair, and then his entire being moved down and around and up and the motor kicked over and coughed and rattled beneath the flimsy bonnet. The stranger stood up, the crank handle in his hand, smiling now.

"Get in," said Jack, already behind the wheel. "I'll buy ya a beer."

The Wallangirrii Hotel was white and made of brick and wood and had a handsome wide colonial veranda below a high balcony on three sides. It was the biggest and most significant building in town. It was built in nineteen hundred and one, the year of federation, and had originally been named "The Federal Hotel," before the present owner gave it the same name as the town. Men lounged about in the shade of the veranda, looking out at the sleepy afternoon street, drinking or just talking or not talking at all, just drinking.

An old Aborigine, dressed as a stockman, sat on the pub veranda with his back to the wall, and it was not known whether he was drunk or mad or both. Silently he watched everything from his sitting place. When Jack pulled up in the truck and he and the stranger got out, the Aborigine, who it was said had not moved for days, stood up. The men on the veranda, first of all noting the stranger, turned to the old native, who had abruptly sprung to life. He stood there, lean and straight-backed and silent, staring at the newcomer with his black-glinting eyes of an old goanna.

"That mad ol' bastard know you?" Jack grinned at his new companion.

"Not yet," said the stranger, and together they pushed through the long double doors that had BAR MEN ONLY written across them in swirling black letters and stepped into the cool deep wooden interior of the pub. They were greeted by a blast of odor and sound, a density of bodies, of backs hunched over the bar, and the thick and smoky quietude of muffled afternoon talk. The old Aborigine followed them in, awakened from his geological dream, and found a spot for himself in an obscure and dark corner. The publican, with his long, hard horse face and his dragging lower lip saw the old man and was about to call out when an unfamiliar voice said: "Leave 'im be," a voice that seemed to have no visible owner but floated on the cool rank odor of beer and stale tobacco and leather and the sweat of country bodies.

Jack ordered two beers. He was a man who always remained true to his rough life and the river that he loved. Together he and the stranger, without exchanging names, spent the entire afternoon getting slowly and raucously drunk.

Toward the end of the day the newcomer finally revealed something of himself. He said his name was Bill, then Wally, and later on he called himself Sebastian, which elicited a light-hearted but loose-lipped mockery from several of the men at the bar, at which point he announced to them all in a loud voice that his real name was Edna.

Night descended on the river flats of Wallangirrii. A cool breeze blew in off the plain. The dry and exulted buzz of cicadas and the chirping of crickets rose from the ground and the trees that grew out of the ground. Inside the pub, under the dim yellow carbon lights, the men drank on. Some lay drunkenly about the veranda, or crawled in alcoholic states of vertigo away from illusory precipices. In the brown yard and in the stables out back, harsh and drunken voices cut the air, lanterns hung from walls burning a low orange, Aborigine and half-breed women wheezed in their drunken states of urgent brides or sighed like mares or screamed and cursed with their unpredictable witchcraft, horses stamped the hay, and the collective sound of men's voices rose like dust above the clinking of beer glasses, the breaking of furniture and the barking of dogs.

The pandemonium continued well into the night, and Jack and his lively friend Edna continued with it.

"Do ya mind if I call ya Ted?" asked Jack. The pub was full of carousers and the crowd had them pressed up against the bar.

"I do a bit, seein' that me name's Edna, an' not Edward, like you'd like it t' be."

"All right, then, Edna, but ya better be prepared to defend yaself against some a these wild river men 'ere." Jack smiled at this newcomer who he felt he understood. Edna smiled back sardonically and ordered two more beers. Both of them, it seemed, were impressed by the other's immeasurable capacity. The publican placed the beers on the bar.

"'Ere ya go, Ted," he said smiling his hard horse smile.

Yes, thought Alan Bedford. *My old man is the man who knew the man who nobody else knew really. My father knew that man and that man knew my father. That man . . .*

"What's that telescope ya smokin' there?"

"What?"

"That thing you're puffin' away on there while I'm talkin'."

"What does it look like? I mean, are you suddenly relocating yaself via my immense cigarette 'ere?"

"I dunno, smart arse. It smells peculiar. Hand it over. Where'd you get that?"

"I grew it. I am, after all, a horticulturalist."

"Murrayanna. Hey, that's what ya smokin'."

"Your pronunciation is a little off. Not everything good in the world comes exclusively from the Murray River, ya know."

"I know, now how about sending that pungent white bomber of yours over in this direction fer ya ol' man t' sample."

"Your words amaze me, old man."

"Maybe, in this 'ere autumn of my life, I'm finally bein' inspired. Besides, I've got ears, an' I hear more than you think."

"Did you just fart?"

"Shut up. This 'ere is certainly the biggest cigarette I've ever seen."

He quietly smoked. After there had been silence for a while he raised his head and looked out through the wire screening and up into the leaves and between the leaves at the bright stars, his eyes luminous but clearer than Alan had ever seen them, grave but calm, and the lips beneath the bristling dull straw-like moustache had softened, almost feminine, but drawn too and strong. He put out his trembling hand, holding it out in the darkness, and then Alan knew what was happening and he took

the hand in his and held it, firmly and affectionately, and felt the
fingers trembling squeeze his hand, once, twice, and he pressed
the hand back and felt the warmth of love that was there flow.
The old man's eyes glowed in the dark, as if with a surge of fire
or light, and Alan looked out at the leaves, suspirant in the
warm night air, and at the slow wheeling constellations that
pulsed in the sky above.

NOW, IN THE BAR, things were being said, like the nation be-
longs to all, and the Australian worker is the backbone of the
nation, and the backbone of the worker is the Australian Workers' Union.

Jack recalled.

Someone else said that the unions were all made up of Bol-
sheviks. A fight started right there, without any further elabora-
tion. The talk went on. The union brought power to the man in
the field, the worker in the factory, the shearer and the drover
and the cane cutter; "Waltzing Matilda," it was said, was a
worker's song, and a cheer went up and everyone drank to it and
forgot about it. The place was full of shearers and men from the
sawmill, who were the most drunken and the most violent,
which appeared to be the way with the people who followed the
lumber mills from town to town. There were men there who
had copulated with sheep and eaten lizards, such was the extent
of their loneliness and insatiability.

"This place has potential," observed Edna, gazing through
the smoke at the raucous heads, the anonymous hats, listening
to the crumpled talk in the human-filled room.

"Strange place t' be, really," he said with a distant expression.
"Ya know, I've been around the world twice since the war. A
merchant seaman. A man potentially ahead of his time." He
grinned a wide grin, showing his teeth, and took off his hat and
his thick short straight hair was like the mane of a mule. That
hair would grow in time into a characteristically wild shock, like

flames leaping. But that was not yet. "In some respects," he continued, in a personal tone. "I long for a place to be. Somewhere t' settle and establish the tiny republic of my mind." That was the first mention ever of the notion of a republic that Jack had heard and it stirred him in his heart, as did the drunken melody of the stranger's words, the newness of his vision of things, and the expression of his weary solitude.

"This decade we're in," said Edna, "is a decade of wanderers and lost souls. A time for men like meself." He raised his glass to his lips and drank and then brought the glass down heavily on the bar. He seemed to be overwhelmed for an instant by a sudden anger. "This is not the time for the gloomy peddlers of everyday reality. They would have us believe things that are not true."

"That's too abstract fer me, Ed," said Jack apologetically.

"The name's Edna."

"That's too deep fer me, then, Edna."

"All right then, I won't go on. Just as well, 'cos I can feel me blood risin'."

"Are ya sure that ol' bastard over by the wall doesn't know ya?"

"Quite sure."

Big Mumma Flo appeared in the bar, or rather she just happened, a force of Nature itself materializing there in the midst of that loud red-faced smoke-filled suspension of male anonymity and drunkenness. At the sight of her Jack broke wind.

Almost every night, it seemed, Flo lived out the spectacle of her intractable fate of a disturbing woman, bringing disaster upon any man whose path crossed hers. Jack shuddered at the impression of her immense haughtiness and the éclat of her public acts. She grabbed a man standing next to her and kissed him passionately while he squirmed like a fish in her hands. She released him and he stumbled backward into the laughing crowd, and she stood there, her hands on her hips, her animal eyes darting about, searching like a huge bird of prey. A kookaburra woman. He saw her, an enormous black woman discolored by centuries of sun and rain, slowly raise her arm and point her finger. "Yew!" She stuck out her tongue and licked her dark lined lips. Jack felt the men behind him move back, and he was alone in the room, puny and shapeless as he felt his bones fill with foam. Only Edna did not move. He stood at the bar, between Jack and Flo.

"Not yew!" she snarled. "Yew!"

It was Edna she wanted.

"Yew, come 'ere." A white froth oozed from her mouth, she swayed from side to side on her naked feet and her wide nostrils opened and closed with her breath, like the gills of a fish.

Edna turned to Jack with an expression of drunken humor on his face. "I think it's time t' leave," he mumbled, almost incoherent. "The resources of my imagination are beginning to fail."

Flo squinted in the smoke-filled light, her eyes shining through the slits, and stuck out her lower lip. That great wet lip glistened in the light as she came forward.

"It would appear," continued Edna, grinning, "that I am a sought-after man." He lifted his glass to his lips. "Now that's a welcome to any town. Just time to hoist one."

"Edna, look out!" yelled Jack.

As Edna turned to face his assailant he was met by the fetid gush of her breath, her odor of a river crayfish, and the licorice whistle of her screeching voice as her presence gave him the immediate impression of a seismic tremor. The hand that caught him under the chin lifted him right off the floor and onto the smooth polished surface of the bar. He slid down it, scattering and smashing glasses as he found himself out of control on a frictionless plain, a mere projectile, his shirt soaked with spilled beer and the blood that flowed from his mouth. He crashed onto the floor, where he lay quite still under the foot railing of the bar, listening to the men as they retreated from the massive she-devil who had just set the wheels of fortune spinning in his head, who had brushed him with her bright tail of an incandescent comet and sent him on a trajectory through that Milky Way of patriots and beer glasses.

THERE WAS a pause, and Alan watched his father sitting in the chair, and felt his own place in his own chair, next to the old man, and the air stirred the leaves, and their hair. The old man had broken off his story as though the whispering of stars suddenly caught his attention, and it was a familiar silence that they sat in. There was a pleasure in their privacy.

Now the old man felt around him the great space of night, the space of darkness itself, the great peace and comfort of the house in the warm night space and this immensity, this pleasant enormity of night and house and being and space was pervaded by the vague yet clear face of the old woman, by her Aboriginal presence in the waving and still shadows of leaves.

Eucalyptus, cutting the darkness.

The bittern's thunder in the night.

The sound of water spattering the ground like a handful of pebbles.

MEN STUMBLED and fell into the street. Jack had lost sight of Edna in the panic that had issued. Within an instant of disposing of him Flo had unleashed her rage on the entire bar. She flung the publican through the white glass of one of the windows, and deposited others into the mirrors behind the bar. Glass shattered and dropped all around her, reflected a myriad broken images. Up until now Jack had never been hit. He had only witnessed the consequences of Flo's anger, and having a nature that was both generous and unreflecting, he reentered the pub against the tide of countrymen that spilled from it in order to retrieve his friend. He made it as far as the barroom doors, where in a blinding flash of white light he felt himself uplifted from the floor like an angel as a hot liquid burst over his thighs and he thanked God for being born before losing himself in the inconceivable shock delivered by the cyclonic power in Flo's fist.

The rising sun found Jack in a sweat-soaked heap on the hotel veranda. He opened his eyes but could not stand up. The street was empty except for his Ford parked in front of a horse trough. The early morning sky was mother-of-pearl, and the blue of day was spreading. He managed to sit up, which brought on the unrelievable sensation of having a toad in his belly. He stank of beer and urine. His lower lip was split and swollen and he could not move his jaw without considerable pain. There was a throbbing ache in his head that blurred his vision and the side of his face felt like it had lost all shape. He closed his eyes and lay down again, feeling the hard boards of the floor against his back.

He felt nothing in the world, for a while, except the ferocity of his thirst, but he lay there with his eyes closed, not wanting to move. When he opened his eyes he saw the publican looking down at him, his face cut in several places, his long lip hanging, looking as malicious as a mule in the morning light.

"She really did it this time," he mumbled in his slow guttural country-bred drawl. He kicked a broken chair off the veranda and picked up a heavy stick. The high tinkling sound of a glass breaking came from inside the bar, the sound somehow slow, tired, but loud in the morning stillness.

"She's still in there," he said.

Jack stood up. "What happened to that fellah Edna?" he asked. As he spoke searing pain shot up the side of his face.

"I dunno," said the publican. "Maybe 'e got smart an' got outta this dead cow of a town." He looked at Jack and grinned his ugly horse grin. "I see you copped it too," he said, sounding almost pleased.

"Yeah," said Jack. "I copped it."

There was the sound of more glass breaking. The double doors burst open and the men fell back into the street. The doors swung wildly in an otherwise empty doorway.

"Flo!" yelled the publican. "Okay, Flo, it's time t' go 'ome. Time t' close up the pub, Flo." He raised the stick, ready to strike.

"You'll only break the stick," said Jack.

"All right, dear . . . Time . . . Gentlemen . . . Flo . . . It's time . . . Last call's over!"

"Let's face it, Ernie, we're dealin' with a supernatural power beyond our mortal understandin'."

"Bullshit. Sounds like you spent too much time with that smart-mouthed stranger last night." Then he yelled: "Flo, you ol' bitch, get outta my pub you great cunt!"

The sun was full-risen now and flooded the street with hot amber light. Long shadows from the buildings and the trees fell across the ground, and although it was not yet dusty in the morning light the yellow street was streaked with horse urine and occasional piles of horse shit from the traffic that had raced the sun into town. An automobile rattled past, but more often a horse-drawn sulky or a slow plodding wagon. People gathered under the overhangs of stores across the street, the talk of what had happened went round about, and within a short while an avid group of spectators had gathered in the shade. The day dragged on into the midmorning and nothing happened. Flo did not move from the pub, and neither the publican nor the local constable would dare go in after her. The publican contented himself with attempts at luring her out with loud and vivid insults. He was asked to watch his language, as there were respectable women in town and husbands who might take offense.

It was just after noon. The town dozed in the buzzing heat of an indifferent midday. A group of blacks sat around the palm trees of the town square and flicked flies away from their eyes. Jack Bedford sat under a peppercorn tree outside the general store, unprepared, as yet, to return home. He felt, now, that he had a personal stake in the outcome of the day's events, although he had ceased to participate. The Wallangirrii Hotel basked in an impenetrable aura of silence. The only sounds above the cicadas were the distant cough of a browsing engine in the railway yard, couplings settling their long chains, and the hollow metallic boom of empty cars crashing.

Edna crossed over into the middle of the street from behind the hotel. His hair was wet and he was without a shirt. He staggered a little as he walked. The blue and swollen side of his face shone like metal in the sunlight, and his broken lip protruded idiotically from his hairy face. He stopped directly in front of the hotel, swaying there like a man delirious, his mad crocodile eyes flashing and his hands dangling loosely by his sides. His chin was thrust forward in brutal defiance of his present condition. He hoisted up his chest, running his hands up his sides and over his nipples and feeling his neck and his jaw. Nothing moved. All was absolute stillness. There wasn't even a wind.

"Ay, Flo!" he bellowed, rising up on his toes and then rocking back on his heels.

"FLO-O-O-O-O-O-O-O-O-O!"

A few people stepped outside, others awoke from beneath hats or crawled out from under carts and wagons.

"Ay, Flo. You daughter of my bitch. Come out an' fight like a man. FLO! You mother of a dead race of flies. You barefoot pox-ridden shit sack! You'll die in a tin shed, ya poor bitch! YA POOR BITCH, FLO. You'll die with the shit taste in ya mouth and dog's arses to kiss goodbye. Come on Flo, I'm waitin' for ya. COME ON!"

Somewhere someone was trying to start an automobile: *ughgh ughgh-ughgh-ughgh-ughgh-ughgh-ughgh-ughghrrrrrrrrrrrrrrrrrrr-yuhyuh-rrr;* that sound giving final weight to the heat and a voice more brutal than the cicadas to the shimmering waves of air that moved up and down like pistons.

"Ay, Flo, you mother of dogs, ya dog-hearted ol' slut. GET OUT 'ERE! Remember me, Flo? I'll bet ya don't. YA STUPID DOG-BRAINED BITCH! COME OUT AN' I'LL GIVE YA A KISS."

The bar doors shot open and Flo stood on the veranda. She was obese, and even uglier than in Jack's memory, and bigger. She stood there, squat and massive, like some huge female idol. Edna reeled back at the sight of her. He caught himself and he held his ground. He too seemed to have forgotten her awesome immensity, that female power. Now he seemed to have taken on a slender figure, a defenseless air.

Flo let out a long wail, the high and painful cry of an ancient bird. Some voices, once heard, will never stop resounding in the head. She plodded heavily across the hotel veranda and down the steps into the street, her hair in her face, an ashen Medusa. As she came closer to him, dancing on her tremendous thighs and furling her brow, Edna saw how huge she really was, how overspilling and glistening in the sun, oiled like a wooden statue with her own sweat. The yells of the crowd came faintly to his ears as he went forward to meet her. Already they were intimates, the challenger and the challenged, and already, it seemed, their roles had been reversed.

She swung at him and missed, almost losing her balance. The crowd was growing fast. People seemed to have appeared out of thin air. The publican, seeing his hotel finally abandoned, quickly crossed the street and went into the bar and locked the doors. Flo cursed and spat and lunged at Edna. She brushed his shoulder and sent him sprawling in the dust. He sprang up as she came at him again and danced around her as she swatted at him as though he was an insect, and like an insect he seemed to hover around her, avoiding her swings and then moving back to irritate her. She swung at him wildly and missed. The crowd was cheering him on. Flo stomped her feet and pulled at her hair. Edna moved in again and then moved back as she swung at him. And then again and again, in an almost exact replay of the moment before. She was tiring quickly. Her huge chest heaved beneath the sackcloth of her dress, her thick tongue protruded from her lips. The front of her dress was wet with perspiration, the coarse cloth sucked back against her belly and groin. She stooped and reached down and lifted her skirt and wiped her eyes, revealing her great dark loins. No one cheered, for they were all in simple awe of the sight. A sound of clapping sticks came from somewhere.

When she looked up Edna was behind her. He grabbed her under the arms, clasping his hands together behind her neck and pressing her head down. She swung around furiously, and he rode her around, his legs dangling. She pounded at his kidneys but her blows were ineffective. He put his knee to her spine and then pulled her shoulders back and she became quite still, limp, almost, like a rag doll. A hush fell over the street, the town. Edna released his grip and then seized her around the waist, leaning into her and pressing the side of his face into her back, as though listening for her internal workings. She appeared to squat, smiling, sensing what he was trying to do and convinced of her own immovability. His feet were wide apart, his knees bent, and his back muscles twitched like an ox. He strained, looking as though he was about to burst his sack, and Flo's smile grew even wider. She seemed to be fixed to the earth. And then she moved, and feeling herself move, began to struggle, cursing and screaming and trying to hit him, and then he lifted her up off the ground. There was a loud gasp as she rose, and she became completely docile in his arms, like a child, and for the first time in her own memory of her incredibly long life she experienced the sensation of nothingness beneath her feet.

Edna staggered for about twenty feet with his earthbound burden. Then he buckled at the knees and dropped her and collapsed on the ground, on his hands and knees, coughing into the dust. Flo landed on her feet, and feeling the earth once more beneath her, turned on him now with that unrelenting fury. He looked up, and seeing her about to come down on him, his entire being coiled up, like a bow being pulled back, or a spring loaded, and he leapt at her with the amazing virtue of some animal. It was magnificent. Wild. He drew his knees up into his chest and then brought his feet down onto her shoulders. She let out a bellowing sigh of surprise as, in that same instant and action, he leapt from her shoulders out into the street. He landed yards away from her, sprawling like some Icarus in the dust.

"THAT WAS it," said Jack. "A tool da force. If ever I've seen a tool da force, that was it."

THAT AFTERNOON was the only time in recorded history that any man managed to tame Big Mumma Flo.

She stood perfectly still in a state of passive amazement and watched him as he slowly and painfully got himself up on his feet and brushed the dust from his trousers. The crowd cheered and applauded and a group of countrymen pounded on the doors and windows of the hotel for the publican to open the bar. Edna crossed the street to the deep shade of the peppercorn tree where Jack stood watching him. Already people were praising him as an unusual man. He lay down on his back on the cool dark earth. His stomach muscles heaved uncontrollably and his lips were coated with a white froth. He smiled at Jack and then turned onto his side and vomited. He rolled onto his back, totally spent, and succumbed to the convulsions that rippled through his body.

When they had subsided, he said, panting, but with humor: "Ya didn't know I could fly, did ya, ya bastard?"

"No," said Jack.

The Garden

IT WAS THE MIDDLE of winter, but the afternoon was bright and clear, the sun a disk of polished gold in the blue sky. Sister Theresa was in her room, supposedly lost in prayer and meditation, but all she did was lie on her bed and listen to the wind. The curtains on her window were drawn, but the insistent light filtered through them, so that the room, although dark and cloistered, was nonetheless invaded by the hard rays of the sun. The wind was blowing dust in from the desert. Outside the convent wall, beyond the garden that Sister Theresa attended to every day, a half-dozen Aborigines were asleep, huddled around two of the date palms that surrounded the convent and the church and made it the coolest and perhaps the most pleasant place in the town.

The town itself was small and flat and ugly, a cruel glint of severe brick houses with corrugated iron roofs and wide dusty streets that appeared to be always empty, always devoid of life. The church and the convent, with the adjoining primary school, were on the edge of the town, and the schoolyard stretched flat and empty and barren beyond the convent wall, defined and separated from the vast monotony of the endless and open plain by a rundown wire fence, a remnant of an abandoned farm, a black, broken line marking a tenuous and abstract border between civilization and nature.

Early that morning Sister Theresa had ventured briefly out into the street. The cold wind and coarse dust ripped into her face and blew her white habit up from her shoulders. She stood for a moment just outside the gate, looking at the natives, and the sight of them wearied her. It seemed to her that they had kept their mute, apathetic vigil outside the convent wall for days. It was the shade of the thick, bristling, dust-covered palms that attracted them. They had come from nowhere with nowhere to go: planted, wordless fixtures on the landscape, like old rocks that had risen out of the earth. The morning had been bright and arid, unprecedented by the usual system of omens with which she inevitably awoke and which filled her with weary and nervous foreboding. The garden was still, green, glimmering, and immaculate. The desert always appeared at its best in the half-light of dawn or dusk; each small detail took on the importance of a major variant on the countryside's repetitious theme. The dawn promised change. It was only when the day came on fully, with its blanket of light and heat, that it seemed to her that the same day had returned once again, a day that had been lived and repeated over and over. She had felt happy until she saw the natives. The sight of a large, brown, fat woman, her ragged dress hitched up, squatting and urinating in the dust, made her turn away and hurry back into her green and fragrant sanctuary.

After that the day had not gone well. First of all, there was the incident with the kangaroo. The creature was the pet of a young man who lived on the other side of town by the river. Semidomesticated, he allowed it to roam freely, and it had become something of a pest. She was watering the roses in the middle of the morning when it came flying over the high wall and landed on the convent lawn, where it proceeded to feed on the grass. When she tried to drive it out, it grunted savagely and sat back on its tail, pulling itself up to its full height, threatening her with violence. A kangaroo of that size, she knew, was capable of disemboweling a grown man or rendering him unconscious with a single blow of its powerful tail. And the creature seemed to sense her helplessness, looking at her with hard, slanted, masculine eyes, eyes that looked at the world without kindness but without malice, indifferent to her protests. The kangaroo had no fear of man, no respect. Its owner had spoiled it beyond hope. Two other nuns had come to her assistance, but to no avail. The kangaroo, when approached, was simply ready for a fight. When he finished eating he lay down in the shade of the wall and scratched his ears and watched them while he dozed.

Eventually the mother superior had called the owner. He was an anthropologist. The week before some men had been clearing an old irrigation ditch that ran along the edge of the schoolyard when they unearthed some human bones. The discovery caused quite a stir. The anthropologist identified the bones, and some of the artifacts found with them, as Aboriginal. The school was on an ancient burial site. Sister Theresa had watched him from a distance as he worked feverishly in the heat, bent on a great discovery. He was tall and lean, very sunburned and very blond. He had not spoken to her, had not even seemed to notice her. Not even when she took a tray of tea and cupcakes out to him and his workers in the middle of the day. She was a nun, dressed all in white, pure and anonymous and sexless in his eyes. Much to her consternation, she found herself wondering what it would have been like to have known such a man. She was angry and frustrated by his indifference, by her own invisibility.

Now she was in her room, lying on her bed, watching a housefly glide silently back and forth on tired wings. *What a country!* she thought. She wondered how he could stand the sun, out there working all day; it made her ill to be in it even for five minutes. And that was the second incident that had made the day disturbing. He had come in answer to the mother superior's call, and for the first time, really, she had taken a good look at him. He was polite, somewhat formal, and obviously ill at ease in the setting. He entered the garden and went straight up to the kangaroo. The big buck rose to meet him, and he simply punched it hard on the mouth and leapt back. The creature reeled and stumbled and shook its head, then it turned and hopped nonchalantly around the garden, looked back scornfully over its shoulder, and glided effortlessly over the eight-foot-high wall.

He smiled at them foolishly. "Sorry about that, sisters. You gotta be careful with him. He's a mean one." His gazing green eyes fell on Sister Theresa, flickered over her from top to bottom and darted sideways, as if he were laughing, delighted inwardly. "Maybe he just wants some religion."

"It's the grass he wants," she replied, amazed at her own brashness. "It's the drought."

"Sorry about that. I'll see it doesn't happen again. He's gettin' a bit out of hand. Clobbered a kid in the middle of town the other day. Maybe he just needs a bullet."

His tone was serious and apologetic, but still she could sense his secret laughter, still the eyes, deeply green, shining and translucent, disturbed her.

They served him tea once again, this time in the garden. He drank three cups. The wind rattled the palm fronds beyond the wall.

"You like it out here, sister?" He was looking at her, talking to her, as though the other two nuns weren't present.

"Oh, yes," she stammered. "It's quite . . . interesting."

"You're not Australian?"

"No. I was born in Europe. I'm English, really, but I was raised in France."

"This is not like Europe."

"No. Not at all. All the things that make sense in Europe don't make any sense at all here."

"That's true. But Europe is old. Worn out. This is a new country, a new land. Vast and—"

"Empty," she interjected. "But Europe still has many things to offer. A past."

"Didn't like it. I'm too much of a bush baby. Too cluttered and redundant. A man needs room in this modern age."

"Well, there's plenty of that here," she said, her anger rising. "In fact, that's all there is. There's nothing but—" She caught herself. The other two nuns, Australians, were moving uneasily, starting to resent her. Inside the convent a bell rang. The two nuns rose and hurried away, but Sister Theresa remained, not knowing exactly how to leave, nor wanting to.

"I have to go and pray. It's midday. The Angelus, you know."

"No, I don't. I'm not a Catholic. In fact I'm not anything."

"I shouldn't be late. I could get in trouble. They don't like me much here, you know."

"Because you're English?"

"Perhaps. Thank you for coming, Mister . . . ?"

"Harrison. Sam Harrison."

"Goodbye, Mr. Harrison. Perhaps you'll come back and have tea with us again. In the garden. That is, if it's permitted. I'm never sure of the rules."

"Tell me, sister, are you about to leap over the wall?"

"I beg your pardon!"

"Are you about to leap over the wall? Break out? Leave all this behind?"

"That's a very personal question. In fact it's very rude. Goodbye, Mr. Harrison."

He stood watching her as she hurried away. Then he turned and walked out through the convent gate.

She thought about him all afternoon in her room, listening to the wind. The violent days seemed to satiate him—the hot sun, the vast, open, and raw land, the unearthing of the continent's secrets—the physical life—there seemed to be no other form of happiness or fulfillment in this country. She got what little she could of it in her garden. Yes, it was her garden. No one else seemed to bother about it, to nurture it the way she did. She loved it best in the early mornings and toward dusk, when it was cool and fragrant and the parrots came and nestled and chattered in the palm trees beyond the wall. At those times she didn't know whether she was happy or felt like crying. There were times when she felt that she would leave the convent, become a woman of the world, feel the hot sun on her exposed flesh, change her life completely. But she had known it so long, that life, without ever questioning it. She had entered the convent at an early age. You just don't give up on something you've devoted your whole life to and walk away from it, hoping for something else. Changing trades is nothing, but hers was a vocation, a calling. It was something far more than a simple apprenticeship.

In her room a faceless voice whispered to her: "The soul is the weariest part of the body."

Deep in the night she awoke with a start from a dream in which the kangaroo, larger than life, came sailing over the wall and wrought a terrible devastation on her garden. The wind had dropped, and now the night was strangely still. An almost imperceptible humming sound became audible, was lost, and became audible again. She listened: now it was gone, now it was a little stronger. It continued that way for quite a while, disappearing and then returning. At first she thought it was the wind, but then the sound became quite recognizable as that of a motor. It was a truck, and the sound of it had jolted her out of her dream into the realm of the possible. Inexplicably she wanted to see it, to go out to meet it. She rose, and dressed in her nightgown, stepped out into the cold and dark passageway.

In the dark the convent that she thought she knew became a labyrinth, a chaos of passageways and turnings. She made her way on tiptoe, her hands guiding her along the wall in the dark. It was necessary for her to get out into the garden, and then into the street, and they were both perhaps a long way off. To her amazement she realized that she did not know where she was. Between her and the street, in the darkness, she might meet the mother superior, a known insomniac. "What would I tell her?" she thought, and then she almost giggled. She was playing a ridiculous, childish game with herself. Her teeth began to chatter, and she shivered in the cold night air.

Suddenly the wall came to an end, and she stumbled on a downward step, landing on the floor a short distance below. She took a few cautious steps forward and ran straight into a wall, hitting her face and cutting her lip. She tasted her own blood, fascinated by it. She was in a narrow corridor now. As she turned a corner she saw a narrow band of light coming from beneath a door, then she heard a faint, high voice singing softly, the voice of an old woman that sounded strangely off-key, lonely and insane. She could not readily identify it. It was a secret voice, one that she had never heard, belonging to someone she supposedly knew. Beyond the door with the light, at the far end of the corridor, she knew, was the door to the veranda and the garden.

As she passed the room where the singing was, she noticed that the door was slightly ajar. She stopped short, hesitating, listening to the noise of her own breath. The singing continued, frail, plaintive, mad. Her hand reached out and pushed the door so that it opened enough for her to see in. The room was lit by a single candle, and the mother superior, dressed in her nightgown, her thin gray hair little more than a tight, scant screw on top of her head, was sitting in a chair, her arms parallel on the rests, her pale eyes wide open. Sister Theresa looked straight into those eyes and realized that they did not see her. She closed the door silently, and silently continued along the corridor. Now she saw the dark looming mass of the large door ahead, and when she advanced toward it she found that she could not budge the giant bolt that fastened it. Through the window above the door a narrow moon gave a white light.

You've got to move it, she thought, but she felt too weak as her fingers pressed against the cold metal of the bolt. She was trembling violently, her heart was beating too hard. And then, with sudden and remarkable ease, the bolt gave and she was out on the veranda, looking up at the vast star-cluttered night sky and the bristling forms of the palm branches outlined sharply in the moonlight.

The night was still, silent. The truck had gone, and she was convinced that he had been in it. It seemed to her, at that moment, that no other human being existed beyond the wall except him. She crossed the garden to the gate, and as she lifted the latch and opened it she remembered the sleeping forms beneath the palms. What if they were still there, and if they were, if they should awake and see her? She stepped away from the gate, and then she turned and started to run back along the path toward the convent. She stopped after a few short steps, turned back around, and in a few seconds she stood in the silence of the empty street.

She started to walk, not in the direction of the town, but away from it. Not a breath, not a sound, except that of her feet on the cold sand disturbed the solitude that surrounded her. Above her, in the vast reaches of the cold dry night, the slow Southern constellations wheeled. Her eyes, now, were open to the night. She ran along the road, ankle deep in the cold sand, away from the sparse, distant electric lights of the town. The air burned her lungs, but still she kept running, hoping to beat the cold. She felt the night absorbing her, the land, vast and ancient, rising up to embrace her. She ran faster. Tears were in her eyes now, and as she looked upward at the stars they seemed to pulse and drip, falling like snowflakes and melting into the desert below. Breathing deeply, running, she forgot the cold. She had stopped trembling. Then suddenly she fell. She neither tripped nor stumbled, but had the distinct impression that something grabbed her and dragged her down. She lay flat on her stomach, a ponderous weight on top of her, pressing her down into the earth as she struggled to rise toward the moving sky. Everything was spinning: the earth, the sky, the stars, had all become one gyrating mass that had sucked her up, as in a whirlpool. She was spinning into oblivion, leaving everything behind. Then she must've passed out, for when she came to the world was still again, the earth and sky had separated, and she lay inert, overwhelmed by an unbearable gentleness, hearing nothing but the beating of her heart.

As she stood up, a terrible cry came from beneath the shadows of the palm trees. It was like nothing she had ever heard. It had the indignation and outraged innocence of a small child, but it also sounded like a grown man. She started to run again, this time back toward the convent, desperate to be safe within its walls. No one appeared as she passed the trees. Soon she was back in the garden, panting and horrified by what she had just done. "I must be going mad," she thought. "Like the mother superior." She wondered what was happening beyond the wall—the source and nature of that singular cry. Then something moved in the shadow of the high wall. There was a heavy thump, and then a scraping sound. Turning, she saw the kangaroo, down on all fours, coming slowly toward her, his large, twitching ears and the hump of his bent back and his great thighs and tail in startling and demonic silhouette in the faint light of the stars and moon. She stood perfectly still, unable to move. And neither did she flinch nor offer even a whimper as the kangaroo, now crouched at her feet, reached up his hand-like paw and took hold of her wrist. He gently sniffed her palm and the tips of her fingers, and finding that she showed neither fear nor resistance, he directed her hand to the short, soft fur between his ears.

"There, there," she whispered soothingly as she scratched his scalp. "There, there, sweet being. Yes, now we are friends."

Boxing

IT SEEMED to Ernie Jimson, just eighteen, that all of his life he and his father and older brother had struggled with barren land and insects and bush fires and floods and rabbit plagues. Too often had he seen a year's hard work ruined in one black night, or a fiercely burning day. "It's all a question of luck," his father, Old Lyle, would say, blowing his nose into his hand and wiping it on his old brown dungarees. "No matter what you do out here, in the long run it's all in the hands of the fates. You learn not to whine. There's no place in country like this for whiners."

Old Lyle was a hard man with a long, dark, peculiarly Australian face, with dark animal eyes, their look slow and lingering, sometimes strangely dead, flat, as though they were seeing nothing at all. His wife had left him years before and he had raised his sons in his own hard and idiosyncratically unsympathetic masculine way. He seemed to frown on the very love he felt for his boys, as he had frowned upon, and even resented, the love he had once had for the woman who was their mother. He loved reluctantly. This emotion confused him.

From him, his sons inherited their sense of recklessness and that recklessness, that indifference, was not something Lyle had been born with, rather it was a product of the land, the great Australian mindlessness, the sun-drenched torpor, that the old land overwhelms its inhabitants with, so that men like Lyle, and for that matter his sons, seemed to live out their lives suspended in a dream. It was a bright dream filled with heat and dust, in the company of men. And animals.

No one really knew why the woman had left Lyle and the two boys. It was not for a lover, that they all knew. In the minds of most people it was not because of Lyle, but because of the place. She had hated it from the very beginning, and Lyle and the place were inseparable, were one. The old man had himself been born in a cabin down on the riverbank and had seen his father drowned in a flood. Lyle grew up a stockman and a sheep farmer and he became known generally as a hard man, temperamentally like the country around him; his oldest boy he had made mean and somewhat vicious, but the youngest was gentler, nervous, not soft, but not mean either. People observed the difference in the two boys, in the look in their eyes, one smiling, one with the mean and sullen eyes of a bad dog, a look that suggested a force that was caged inside. And they wondered what it meant, how it could come about, that two boys brought up in exactly the same circumstances, with the same mean old bastard for a father and the same anonymous and forgotten mother, could be so different from each other.

The only thing anyone knew for sure was that one day Lyle got on the train to Sydney and three weeks later he was back with his bride, a powdered and perfumed salesgirl from a big city department store. She was a small, slender, and pale woman in a fancy city hat and a fancy city dress, dark blue almost black and already covered in red dust, as were her matching high-heeled shoes. The men on the station watched her walk with Lyle to his truck, saw the roll of her hips and the little precarious steps she took on the dry rough ground and her thick yellow hair beneath the fancy blue hat. Later they laughed about her and Lyle in the pub. Can you see her out there with crazy Lyle Jimson, with nothin' but sheep, crows, and goannas? Where did he meet her? In a big city store, in the women's lingerie department. Much laughter. More drinking. Well, we'll see. We'll see.

And the women too, the farmers' wives, laughed and made jokes and gossiped and waited to see what was going to happen. To all of them it was inevitable. What surprised everyone was the fact that it took seven years and the birth of two sons and the worst drought and dust storm that anyone could ever remember. The wind and dust that hid her departure became a veil of secrecy that shrouded her entire being in an aura of mystery. Even after seven years no one could righteously say they knew anything of her. After the dust storm had passed, and everything cleared, it was as though she had never been there, was simply a figment of the imagination. The ghost did leave behind two sons as evidence of her sojourn in the real world. But that was all. Neither the boys nor the father ever mentioned her or seemed to know what became of her. Like many people she seemed to simply disappear into the great inland glow of the continent, to be swallowed by the cannibal Australian sun who devours shadows and memories.

Everyone knew that Lyle's own father had worked his mother to death, that Lyle had been raised raw and hard, and that he was bringing his own sons up the same way. Everyone could see it, and were all amazed by life, by the way things seem to go on fiercely repeating themselves generation after generation. Especially out in that heat-soaked place with its vast, mindless horizons, where men tried to make vegetables grow in a desert and time seemed to be caught, trapped, suspended in an endless and unchanging present.

THE LOW afternoon sun is a bright shimmering jellyfish above the flat red and gray land. The cloudless sky glinting blue. Shadows are deep and long. Ernie Jimson, on horseback, looks through red dust across the backs of one thousand sheep at the lean-tos of bark and corrugated iron along the riverbank. The river is low in the drought and sandbars stretch out into the water like pale, dozing crocodiles or goannas. Eucalyptus line the stream, and beyond them the plain is swallowed gradually by salt bush and mallee scrub. The white cockatoos fly up out of the dry grass, screech overhead. The sheep start to cry and leap about. The dogs run back and forth.

Jimson has been in the saddle off and on since dawn and now he's starting to hate and resent the hot smell of dust and sheep shit and lanolin. His tired eyes gaze at the humpies, a shipwreck in the dust (*or,* he thinks, *wallowing in a swamp of rust whenever it rains*). The sun stings his shoulders through his shirt. He moves languidly with the horse, rocking gently from side to side, half asleep in the saddle, listening to the creak of the leather. (*Yes,* he thinks, *creaking like an old ship drifting slowly in a calm festering sea toward those reefs of abandonment.*) A black woman walks through the trees away from a lean-to, her breasts like melons beneath the loose sacking of her dress. The lean-tos sag in the heat and dogs snap at flies. The sun refracts from the sorrel coat of Jimson's horse. He wheels his horse to the left and rides out to turn back some stragglers, whistling to his dog. Get behind, Frank! Get behind! The dog is all nerves and speed, snapping at the sheep, leaping onto their backs and onto their heads, packing them in close and keeping the herd moving. Slowly they move toward the gates, the pens and shearing sheds in the distance glint white in the sun. Jimson thinks of town. Of a cold beer. Of Brenda Ferguson unbuttoning her blouse and her big teats spilling out and her hard but pretty country girl's face. Her thick butter blonde hair. The bright sun bathes his thighs in lazy heat. An impatient pulsing in his loins. Yeah, it's been a long hot day. Now everything is reduced to cliches. His dry mouth tastes only dust and the sour bile of labor. There is still another mile to go. He is sunburned and his thighs are chafed. Yet he is surprised by the sense of satisfaction he has at the end of such a day of drudgery in the hot sun. And anger. Anger that he should even be there, stuck out in the middle of nowhere. But not quite knowing where else to go and feeling the pressure to content himself with what he is and what he's got. A flock of green parakeets flies toward the river.

In the sheds the shearers are hard at work. Their hands are soft like women's from the lanolin in the wool.

Back at the house his father sleeps on the veranda in a cane chair, his singlet soaked with sweat. Flies crawl across his belly. He looks at the old man through the broken wire-screen door. Jimson is weary and irritable. Tom, his older brother, is out the back hunting snakes in the woodpile. His favorite sport. Australia is the land of snakes and sharks. His older brother hunts snakes in the woodpile and along the channel. Red-bellied blacks and tiger snakes and copperheads. He grabs them by the tail and cracks 'em like a stock whip, quick as lightning. The snakes are all deadly poisonous. The broken snake bodies quickly bring the flies and the big red ants.

Hunting kangaroo and mustering sheep and breaking horses hardly amounts to much time at all, given the full length of a year. There are the other things. The nights in town at the pub. The drunken fights. The time spent with wild and rough women, and the slow times around the station, thinking about those women. The occasional dust storm or bush fire. The monsoons that blow up river, lifting the roofs off houses, dropping a sudden rain that floods a town in two hours and then clears, the sun inflaming the wet land. The long lonely nights looking up at the sky, marking the Southern Cross. The walks along the bush paths, seeing the humpies by the river, the green and gold flies glinting against the dark corrugations and the orange colored litter of the garbage dump. The listless and unsteady groups of blacks.

The rusting shell of an abandoned automobile in which a young half-caste male adult, wasted on cheap port, sleeps like death.

A black woman screeches outrage and indignation like a cockatoo, lifts her ragged skirt and squats beside the road and urinates in the dust. The white men, watching the stream of her honey, seeing her naked buttocks, laugh at her from the pub veranda. Dirty coon. Lousy boong. Hopeless Abo. Blood flows from her mouth. The man who hit her is big and blond. He hit her when she came at him, demanding the money he said he'd give her. Black power, he chortles. Everyday outrages. Cliches about white men in hot places well up in the mind. Nothing nobody doesn't already know. A dead child is found in a humpy. A half-caste woman is raped and bashed. An Abo is stabbed. These things simply go unnoticed. Some people feel only the heat. Go blind in the light.

There are Saturday nights on which Jimson and his brother drive fifty miles one way to a dance. They meet the same girls, the farmers' daughters who look at them with soft but hungry eyes, sad and weary like the eyes of old tigers. There's never any trouble scoring, not for a pair of robust and good-looking blokes like the Jimson boys. Out back of the dance, Brenda Ferguson willingly submits to Jimson's desires, but afterward he doesn't feel so good. Too much beer. He feels that faint sweet nausea, looking at Brenda's pale wet body in the half light that spills from the hall. Insatiable cow. There is the click of contracting metal round about the parked cars and trucks. She lies there on her spread dress between the cars, her body relaxed, reeking, breathing deeply. *If I get pregnant you'll marry me won't you Ernie? You won't get pregnant Brenda. I whipped him out just in the nick of time. Good ol' Brenda, she's always so understanding. Seems to know what it is to be a man, to feel the way a man feels.*

Driving back across the plain the headlights pick up kangaroo bounding across the road, their eyes flashing red and green. For miles the air is full of moths and flying insects, white in the white light.

Some weeks will pass without him leaving the station. Forever, it seems, he is destined to ride the endless fences, repairing, checking on stock, moving the flocks from pasture to pasture. He has finished high school. Soon he will leave, he tells himself. He has spasms of hating the place. Then he forgets, sinks back into that heat-soaked inertia, that state of half-dreaming, that basic bedrock Australian indifference to everything, even his own thoughts and feelings.

The white cockatoos fly up from the dry grass. They sit in the tree branches and watch him as he rides along.

When he's thinking, he's thinking of other places, wondering what they're like. He sees the glow of a distant city on the plain. It is dusk and he is approaching the city. And as he approaches, and sees the lighted streets, he can hear music.

Back at home the old man is having a coughing fit in the outhouse. His older brother is killing snakes. WHACK. Like a rifle shot. WHACK WHACK. The snakes flee from his big freckled hand. Some of them hiss and try to coil around but he is too quick. WHACK. Disembodied snake heads litter the ground, their mouths open, their tongues out. His brother has a fierce, feverish look in his eyes, like some snake-killing bird. An eagle or a kookaburra. The same look he has in the slaughterhouse, straddling a lamb and dexterously slitting its throat. Or blasting the tail of a kangaroo off with a shotgun. Or shooting parrots out of the sky. Or shooting dogs he claims have been running sheep. Or breaking a rabbit's neck.

Jimson's memories of his mother are vague. The old man doesn't seem to remember her at all. Never talks about her. Keeps no pictures. The only reference Jimson can recall is that of the dust storm. The woman who disappeared in the dust storm. Who was his mother.

Old Lyle and his older brother simply don't get along. Never have. They fight a lot, sometimes physically, throwing each other around the house. Those two are too much alike to get along. Old grievances. Bitter memories. His older brother remembers his mother. Claims the old man drove her out. The mean old bastard. Everyone knows Lyle is a hard man. Some nights the two of them fall into sullen drunks on the veranda. Fight like cat and dog. Their thin red hollow faces, their dark incensed-looking eyes. Australian eyes. Peculiarly Australian faces. In the bush, in the vast and empty darkness, the mournful cries of the moepoke and curlew, marking the time.

AFTER THE STORM had passed, the land was covered in a heavy rippling blanket of red dust. In places the dust was yellow. The dust powdered the leaves of the trees and built up against the telephone poles and against the houses. A brown haze hung in the air, and through it the people could see the sky was blue. The willy-willy had passed and the dry continued. Several people saw Lyle drive into town, his truck spraying dust, the day the storm passed. He drove straight to the railway station. They watched him park and get out and walk slowly and deliberately onto the platform and look down the long glinting and vanishing stretch of track into a vast emptiness. And they all knew somehow what had happened. That the mysterious and yellow-haired woman that none of them knew and who they would all soon forget had gone. No one saw her get on the train, which had left that morning, not two hours before, but they all believed that they had, for suddenly, as Lyle stood there squinting on the platform, they saw it all clear as day: saw her in her blue dress and her blue hat and her blue high-heeled shoes get out of a taxi and get on the train. When Lyle finally walked across the street to the pub to drown his thirst, a few of his mates were so convinced they had seen her leave on the train that morning that they told him it was so.

So Lyle returned to Rumbalara (End of the Rainbow) alone to raise his two sons—one six, the other two. He took everything she had left behind—her clothes, the magazines she had lived out of, miscellaneous cosmetics, and burned them. He said nothing to the boys. When, after several days, his eldest asked him what had become of his mother he simply told him she had gone—that she was no good and no more and that he might as well forget her. Soon the farmhouse took on the distinct appearance of a dusty barracks for men as Lyle quickly reverted to his old habits of a drover.

People watched the Jimson boys grow from a distance. They came to town rarely, and when they did, always accompanied by their taciturn and severe father with his long naked wooden and impassive face, they were able to note the growing changes in the boys, as though they were growing daily under Lyle's influence, being molded in his image. Quickly they recognized the bitter spirit in his eldest, and they took sympathy on him, knowing his circumstances, hoping he might be changed. But their effort meant very little. In the end they could only stand back and watch him grow in the old man's persistent and merciless shadow, knowing that he was a member of an isolated and impenetrable household.

LYLE PUT his sons to work young. First in the simple maintenance and care of the farmhouse. He showed them how to cook crude meals and how to repair things. His tolerance for childhood inadequacies was low, and these boys whom he loved were living proof of the woman he was trying so hard to forget, living proof of the fact that he had undressed her and seen her naked, that what he had experienced was not just some abstract identity. So it was necessary for him, if he was to forget, to make his boys into men as quickly as he could; to eliminate, if he could, the very fact of their childhood, the very fact that they were not simply external phenomena in his life but his own flesh and blood and evidence of his sorrow. So it wasn't long before he had them both in the saddle, trained as jackaroos.

A good pair of boys, Lyle thought, when he realized that their mother's milk had quickly turned sour on them. *If they grow like me they'll hate weakness and love practically nothing.*

In the mortal silence of the heat, young Ernie, twelve years old, rode his horse along the sandy road between the fenced paddocks. The red sand was in small ridges on either side of the pale road, and coarse sharp grass grew out of it. Directly ahead he saw the long shimmering and slowly moving streak of a black snake. It glistened fiercely in the sunlight, like metal or ice. He pulled his horse up and watched it slide across the pale pink clay of the road and up over the sand. Then he pressed his heels gently into his horse's flanks and the horse walked on, Ernie swaying in the saddle, raising his hand occasionally to brush the flies from his eyes and nose and mouth. After several yards he looked back over his shoulder to take one last look at the snake. He could still see it. It was coiled between two small ridges of sand, a shimmering black pool, a dark lake between two red hills.

The boy and horse plodded on. Something fluttered on the fence ahead. As he drew near, what looked at first to be the image of a dark crucified angel was in fact a large wedge-tail eagle, its wings extended, pinned to the fence. It was the custom of the farmers to shoot the eagles and pin them to the fences, believing that the birds took small sheep. Ernie had seen three strung in a row, all with a wing span of six feet or more. This eagle was also a big one. He stared at it, fascinated by its reddish brown feathers, the fierce beak and talons, by the noble head that now hung limp, remarkably humanized in death. A tiny whirlwind blew its feathers in passing, and they made a dry, papery sound. The willy-willy spun a narrow cloud of dust that got into Ernie's eyes and mouth and stung his face and then was gone. He stared at the eagle in the resumed and hot stillness. And then he nudged the horse with a forward thrusting of his thighs and immediately it began to walk its slow plodding sleep walk along the road.

When Ernie rode up to the house, his older brother Tom was sitting on the wide veranda, in the deep shade of the corrugated iron roof, cleaning his rifle. He looked up and his small pale eyes seemed to flash silver, rat-like, and he stood up and his thin lips smiled. He squinted at Ernie out in the yellow light.

"Hey, nippah," he said in a loud nasal voice, his tone and the look on his face eager. "See the eagle I just nailed? Put him out on the fence."

"Yeah, I saw him."

Ernie dismounted and led his horse around to the stable where he unsaddled her then led her into the pen with the others where there was already water and hay. He walked across the yard, past the windmill and the water tank that smelled of slime and rust, toward the kitchen.

The kitchen was dark after the outside glare, and comparatively cool. It smelled strongly of soot from the wood stove and kerosene lamps, and soot had blackened the roof beams and colored a couple of the windows a urine yellow. His father, dressed in singlet and dungarees, was asleep on the wooden table, and snoring loudly. His two dogs lay sprawled under the table. One of them grunted when Ernie entered and got up and walked over to him, sniffed him and wagged its tail. As Ernie crossed the room toward the sitting room door the white cockatoo, which he had not seen perched in the corner, suddenly let out a squarking effluvium of obscenities that startled Ernie and woke up Lyle, who sat up and swung his legs around, blinking at the frozen boy.

"Where've you been?" Lyle asked, still half asleep, not looking at Ernie but eyeing the cockatoo with a sideways glance. He stood up and yawned and stretched his arms. His arms and neck and shoulders had been darkened over the years by the sun, but beneath the singlet the skin never was exposed, and was a ghastly gray-white color, as were the undersides of his arms.

"I've been down along the river," said Ernie in a dry cracking voice. Lyle had caught him down there with a young dark girl from one of the shanties, and he had told him he was not to go to the river by himself ever again; and now, by telling Lyle that he had been down there, he was being openly and remorselessly defiant.

"I thought I told you, you weren't to go down there by yourself." Lyle looked at Ernie with moist, bright green eyes. He lifted his hand and scratched the back of his neck, and the boy, anticipating a blow that did not come, stumbled back against the rough red-gum boards of the kitchen wall. The man's stern immobile face crinkled in laughter.

"Still frightened of Old Lyle, hey. That mean ol' bastard. Well I reckon there isn't much I can do. I can't keep yer away from the riverbank forever. I'm just tryin' to keep you pure." He laughed and then had a coughing fit and spat on the floor and rubbed the spit into the dirt and wood with the sole of his shoe. The cockatoo, bouncing on its perch, imitated the laughter and then the retching sound of the coughing and spitting. Both the man and the boy laughed at the parrot. "Look at that cheeky bastard," said Lyle. The cockatoo leaned way forward, his tail in the air, and bobbed his head up and down. Then he stuck out his thick hard black tongue and swung around on the perch and hung upside down, obviously quite amused.

A lizard flickered beneath a warped floorboard. A wasp, point-blank and blond, tapped against a windowpane. There was a moment of fly-buzzing stillness in which the man and the boy simply stared at each other, the boy seeing an image of what he might become and the man amazed by the fact that the boy was really his issue, was in part an image in miniature of himself, of what he might have been. Lyle seemed to be constantly startled by his sons. Often he found that he had simply stopped what he was doing and was gazing in mindless incredulity at one or both of his boys. The boy Ernie had his father's eyes and jaw and his mother's yellow hair. Tom was short, square, muscular, and dark, and his eyes were blue. They were his mother's eyes, but it was the youngest who reminded Lyle of the mother. Not that he truly remembered her. Not in his mind. It was his body, the muscles with which he saw and heard and felt, that remembered her, which reminded him of her when he looked at the boy.

Sometimes the sensation in his body made him irritable and uneasy. Sometimes he felt like he lived in a haunted house, that each time the wind blew through the house she was somehow present, that she came and went with the wind. A specter. A woman he could not quite see in his memory but whose presence he could still often feel. No one had seen her leave. She had disappeared during a dust storm, and for all anyone knew she had simply crossed the border into some other dimension.

Ernie caught the familiar look in his father's eye; that stare in which he saw a mixture of shock and disbelief and recognition and regret. This time it startled him, and blushing he turned and left the room without another word, confused by his own hurt feelings. One of the dogs trotted after him, and the cockatoo, sitting upright, stretched his wings and bloomed his yellow crest.

In the late afternoon Ernie went out with Tom to check the rabbit traps in the hope of scoring for the evening meal. The first trap they came to, buried in the sand and marked by a stick, had been set off. The second had a rabbit caught by the hind leg, and Tom instantly took its small head in his fist and twisted it around until the neck popped. Then he gutted it and flung the guts away. The third trap had caught a red fox by the front paw. A vixen. She snarled and snapped as they approached, and pulled at the trap. Then she whined and crouched down, curling her nose and showing her fangs. The two boys stood several yards from her, fearful and astonished, seeing her dark eyes that looked directly up into theirs. The great red brush of her tail, the white of her paws and buttocks. The fox made a low steady growling sound, muted now, her mouth close to the earth.

To Ernie she was fierce and beautiful, and instantly, in his childish heart, he loved her. He wanted to set her free, to see her bound away. He loved her russet color, the way the sunlight gleamed on her fur; her dark eyes that seemed to look right into him. And he knew that Tom saw none of what he saw, that Tom's only thought was to kill the fox.

Tom found a heavy stick beneath a tall gum tree. As he started to walk toward her, the vixen flattened to the ground and snarled, and Ernie could see the red fury glow in her eyes, as he could see it in Tom's. The fox tried to pull away, gnawed frantically at the metal trap, biting her own foot. Ernie yelled No at Tom, and then sprang at him, grabbing him around the neck. But Tom was too big and strong for him, and easily threw him aside, calling him a little fucker and backhanding him across the mouth. Ernie landed flat on his back. The vixen whined and growled and leapt up snapping at the air as Tom brought the stick crashing down on her head and then kicked her in the chest with his heavy boot. She let out a short yelp and lay still. Blood flowed from her muzzle.

When they got back to the house, they had collected three rabbits. Lyle quickly skinned them out, as was his pleasure, and both Tom and Ernie stood and watched him out in the golden dusk. The skins peeled off like little Lyleets, exposing the naked pink carcasses. Lyle looked up at his two boys. Ernie stood in the background with his head lowered, but Tom stood close, watching. They hurriedly ran their eyes over each other, like curious but bashful strangers. In Tom's eyes flickered sparks of hostility; in Lyle's eyes there was a light ironic astonishment.

Ernie went alone into the house and lit a lamp on the kitchen table. In his mouth he experienced a bitter taste like iron. He sat down at the table and buried his burning and dust-streaked face in his arms. His bottom lip was broken and swollen. His back ached, and he felt defeated, and all the bitterness of defeat. For a while all he heard was the hissing of the burning lamp. He fell asleep and dreamed about the fox.

It was the loud voices outside that soon awoke him. He sat up abruptly and opened his eyes. It seemed to him that he had been pulled violently, wrenched, from the still comfort of sleep. And now he could hear their angry voices clearly out in the yard. The room was dark and through the screen door the sky looked a peculiar tender blue, almost turquoise. Black swans were honking in the distance and their voices, although remote, were for a moment louder, more real, than the voices that were yelling outside. He became aware of the white shape of the cockatoo sitting silent and immobile on the perch, listening and watching, its head cocked slightly to one side. He sat straight backed in his chair, his hands flat on the table, blinking at the bird, who opened its beak and stretched its wings and dilated its eyes. The cockatoo was his friend, his only friend in this isolated place. He sat still and concentrated on the cockatoo's eye as though it was a crystal ball, seeing the images of dark, indiscernible shapes flicker back and forth within the perfectly round eye, which glowed with its own mysterious light.

He found a box of matches on the table beside his hand and relit the lamp, which had died inexplicably. He saw that his hand was trembling. The bird made a hissing sound, as though impersonating a snake, as he lowered the glass over the quivering flame. Outside his father was yelling: "Put that bloody axe down. I'm not gonna stand for this! Tom!"

And Tom was screaming in a high dry voice: "You lousy fuckin' bastard. I hate you." Crying so that Ernie could hear the sobs. "You drove her away."

The house shuddered as the axe was hurled against a wall. The old man erupted: "You young ratbag, I'm gonna show you that I'll have no argument. No fuckin' argument."

Even now this was an old contest, and Ernie knew to stay inside. It seemed to him that his older brother and his father were inexorably bound in a relationship and purpose to which he was extraneous, a bystander. Perhaps a witness. He heard Lyle's heavy footsteps on the veranda. Heard the pause in which he knew the old man was reaching for the stock whip, and the loud vicious sharp whip-crack, like a rifle shot, and the instant yelp and wail of his older brother.

The cockatoo took up the wail, and Lyle, appearing in the door with the whip still in his hand, heard it and started to laugh. "He just got stung, that's all." Outside Tom cried harder, and the cockatoo cried harder with him. Lyle roared with laughter, and Tom ceased abruptly and the cockatoo continued to cry.

"That kid was born mean and contrary," Lyle mumbled. He coughed and turned around and spat out into the yard. Then he looked back at Ernie sitting stiffly at the table, and although the old man was smiling his eyes looked haunted and lonely.

"I didn't even touch 'im," said Lyle, tossing the whip onto the table. "I didn't even touch 'im. Just listen to that boy carry on." He sat down opposite Ernie and leaned his elbows on the table and looked at his hands in the lamplight. Bats flickered around the door. Tom appeared in the doorway, his knees dirty beneath his baggy shorts, holding the rabbits in his left hand and looking in at them with glittering, unseeing eyes.

Lyle's eyes rested on his eldest, held him with that long dark lingering gaze of his that now seemed full of wonder and sadness.

"Boy," he said. "I really don't want to fight with you anymore. We're all stuck out here together for the time bein', an' we might as well try to get along. Now bring those rabbits in an' we'll cook supper an' sit an' eat it as though we was a family."

Tom entered silently and tossed the rabbits onto the table and stood glaring at Lyle. The cockatoo muttered and then laughed, and Tom's eyes shifted from Lyle to the bird. "That fuckin' stupid parrot," he mumbled petulantly. "I'm gonna kill that bastard."

Ernie leapt from his seat. "You won't touch him," he hissed. "You kill everythin' an' you ain't gonna touch him. He's my friend."

"Nothin' but a stupid bird," said Tom.

"You two shut up!" Lyle bellowed, rising from his chair. Then he sat down again, gaining his composure, aware that things were very close to a second eruption, could get that way before anyone knew what was happening.

"Okay, now, you two calm down." Lyle's voice was lower now and seemed to tremble in his throat. "Let's cut the crap and get these rabbits cooked."

Ernie said quickly: "You better not touch that cockatoo."

"SHUT UP!" roared Lyle, cutting him off.

ERNIE, on horseback, rides along the river in the early morning. Cockatoos fly up into the trees. Kangaroos hop nonchalantly away. The day is bright and clear and the heat has not yet begun and there is little dust. Ibis fish in the reedy shallows, and the smoke of several campfires hangs stationary over the sparkling water. The white sand shimmers. He rides by some shanties, and yellow and brown dogs run barking at the horse's feet. There is a young girl there, about sixteen. He has seen her before, and now he pulls his horse up and watches her walk languidly through the gum trees, in and out of the bright shafts of morning light. The sun shines on her dark skin, making it glow like the upper side of the leaves of certain tropical plants. Lovely little black gin. Pretty dark sheila. He watches her through the heat, the air thick with the odor of eucalyptus. As the heat rises the cicadas start up. His ears are like amplifiers and he can hear the river, the soft gurgling and splashing of the current. He dismounts and tethers his horse and sprawls on a log in the sun, thinking about Brenda Ferguson. He is bathed in heat. A lazy delight drifts up his body. He looks up and sees the girl standing on the riverbank, watching him. He feels that warm familiar pulsing in his loins. She walks away, looking down shyly, and her bare feet stir tiny clouds of fine gray dust. Her loose, pendulous breasts look very full and soft beneath the thin cotton top. Her hips roll slowly, easily. Lovely. He sits up and licks his lips, thinking the unthinkable. *Gotta get some of that before she goes to fat, hits the booze, and gets her teeth knocked out. Boy, I'm glad I was born a man. A white man, that is.*

IN THE WINTER the wind rips in off the Great Divide. There is snow in the mountains and the cold wind pierces the lungs. The mornings are white and brittle with frost. The river swells with the rain and the roads turn to mud. In the spring, with the thaw in the mountains, the river floods. Snakes and rats invade the farm, driven to the higher ground. Kangaroos and rabbits eat down the grass. Foxes and packs of wild dogs take sheep. There are red-breasted robins and green and red parrots.

HE WALKS down the main street of town in the spring, eying the girls. Italians gather in small groups on the street corners and outside the pool hall, talking quietly, furtively. There is an

Italian greengrocer directly across the street from an Anglo greengrocer. D'Agostino's and McGuire's Fruits & Vegetables. McGuire has a big sign out that reads: SHOP HERE BEFORE THE DAY GOES. It gets a lot of laughs from the passersby. A few Aborigines sit around on the benches beneath the town clock, in the shade of some palm trees. The clock has been stuck on one-fifteen for as long as he can remember.

One hot slow Saturday afternoon in town he is witness to a vendetta. Right in front of D'Agostino's. The long afternoon quiet of the bright flat empty town is suddenly broken. A car roars around a corner and screeches to a stop, and short brown men in singlets or brightly colored shirts fly out of the doors into the dust like a pack of dogs let out of a cage. Windows are broken. Women scream. And people have appeared out of no-where, fighting, yelling. Women tear at each other's hair. Men draw knives. Some are clubbed to the ground and then kicked, and there is the sound of splintering bone. And apart from this concentrated skirmish, around which dust hovers, the town is quiet, still, blank. The dull-faced men on the pub veranda watch the women roll around in the gutter. See the men stab each other. Those bloody dagos are mad. Shit! Look at those sheilas. Vicious, I say. Just plain vicious. Another carload of men roars by, screeches to a halt, and the men explode into the street. Dogs are barking now, and the men on the veranda, including Tom and Ernie, order another round of drinks. This is better than cricket on a hot afternoon.

Later Ernie walks along the street, down the center of town. He sees blood on the pavement and long strands of black hair pulled out by the roots, with bloody tips. A police car crawls by, the fat constable leaning over to take a good look at Ernie. The dusk is settling over the town and there is a smell of cooking an-imal fat and the last bright rays of the sun are reflected in the windows of the flat brick suburban houses. There are old houses too with overgrown hedges and deep verandas, some of which possess a certain old-style raffish charm. Ernie thinks about escape. About hitching out or jumping a train. About simply taking off. The world seems huge and he feels very small. Standing at the edge of town looking out at the wide horizon of sky and dusty savanna he is overcome by the feeling of being on the edge of the world, by being doomed to obscurity, to an existence that is peripheral.

ALL THAT NIGHT Ernie lay in bed unable to sleep because of the warm shame he concealed. It was partly the need to cry at seeing his brother kill the fox. It was partly his growing awareness of the lack of a woman in the house, and of his own hunger and dreams. He knew he had had a mother, but that she had done some terrible or shameful thing and that she was not there, in God's own country, because of her own fault and doing. Unlike his brother, he did not blame his father for the lack of a female in the house. Rather it seemed to him that she had been rejected by the place, by some force or deity that had judged her unsuitable; not-of-the-land. And so she had been spirited away by invisible hands on a day filled with omens, and Ernie accepted it all without explanation but with hidden understanding, the way an Arab submits to the will of Allah.

Even in his own mind there was to be no real accounting as to why his brother actually killed the cockatoo, even though Ernie half expected it. He did not understand it, and it was at that point that he reached the same conclusion about Tom that his father had reached, that he was born sour and mean. Yet there was affection between the two boys, and it was because of this affection, and because Ernie's emotions were still innocent, that he did not comprehend at all the meaning of the dead cockatoo.

He found the bird on the kitchen table. He did not cry. Instead he simply picked it up gently and held it in his hands and stroked the feathers. He opened the crest with his fingers. He felt the strong hard feathers of the underwing. He was at once filled with rage, a need for vengeance, and with fear. The stock

whip was still on the table from the night before, and was a re-
minder of what Tom's fate would surely be if Lyle was to find
out about the cockatoo.

Quietly he took the bird out into the yard and buried it. Tom
was not around. When Ernie came back into the kitchen, silent
tears had started to well up in his eyes. He saw the whip on the
table, and remembered the sound of it and Tom's fear of it. He
had never fought back. To him his older brother was a superior
physical being, gifted with strength and brutality, not to be
challenged or even compared to himself. But he remembered
the whip, and before he knew what he was doing he had it in his
hand and was draping it across the floor, dragging it slowly and
sensually back and forth, feeling its long weight, the worn
leather in his palm. It was more than a whip. It was a scepter of
power. A punisher. With wide eyes, a cruel and excited smile on
his face, Ernie let out a sudden yelp of glee and ran from the
house with the whip.

He came twirling like a dervish into the dusty yard, the whip
singing like a bull-roarer above his head. And then he cracked it.
And again and again. It was a frenzied, almost ritualistic dance of
hatred, of muscular fury. He twirled and twirled, cracking the
whip, until he fell on his knees, exhausted and out of breath.

Lyle came back to the house toward noon and asked Ernie
first if he knew where Tom was and second did he know what
had become of their pet cockatoo. To the first question Ernie
said he did not know and to the second he said: "He's dead. I
found him on the kitchen table. Looks like a cat got him."

"A cat, you say." Lyle pushed his hat to the back of his head
and stood thinking with his hands on his hips. He bit his upper
lip and breathed deeply through his nose and looked down at
Ernie with weary distance-seeing drover's eyes.

"Shit," he muttered and nodded his head and turned a full
circle on his heels and then walked once around the room.

"And you don't know where Tom is?"

"No," said Ernie.

"Did Tom kill the bird? Tell me!"

"I dunno. Looks like a cat got it."

"You shouldn't cover for him. He's done a despicable thing."

"I'm not coverin' for him."

"Where is he, then?"

"Gone, I reckon. If he did kill cocky then for sure he's gone."

"He thinks I don't love him, and I'm afraid he's right. He makes it very hard."

Tom was gone for over two weeks. Lyle promised a flogging when he returned. He spread the word at the pub, and eventually it trickled back to Tom, where he had made a camp in the company of a pair of swagmen under a bridge across a dry creek not ten miles from the Rumbalara station. That was at the end of his first week, and he stayed one week longer than he had planned. It was the swagmen who drove him out. One night they came into camp drunk and molested him as though he were a woman. He managed to escape into the darkness. Rage came to him later, when he was alone in the bush; then fear; then a terrible shame, a feeling of unwholesomeness and death.

He spent the next three days and nights in the bush, wandering around in circles. Driven by hunger, he finally relented and found himself on the long, straight, and lumpy clay road that was the driveway of Rumbalara. He appeared in the kitchen door in the morning as Lyle and Ernie were eating breakfast. Ernie saw him first. He looked up from the fried lamb chop he did not want to eat straight into the eyes of his brother, and immediately he noted the change. That this being he had been afraid of and for, whom he had loved and hated, now looked to him like a scared rabbit, had the look in his eye that a rabbit has when it's in the trap. He stood there staring at the food; it seemed to be nothing more than base instinct that had brought him back, neither love nor humility nor contrition seemed to be present. To both Lyle and Ernie, it seemed that Tom felt nothing but hunger and cold.

"Why don't yer come in and sit down." Lyle's tone was cordial and casual, indifferent. Trembling, Tom stepped into the kitchen and took his place by the table. His eyes were fixed on the lamb chop on Ernie's plate.

"I reckon you must need some tucker," said Lyle.

"He can have my chop," said Ernie.

"No." Lyle stood up, grabbed Ernie's plate and put it on the floor and the dog immediately ate the chop. "I'm gonna fix this bloke his favorite dish."

He walked heavily and deliberately, not quite a strut, to the far corner where his shotgun rested. He picked it up, broke it, saw that it was loaded and snapped it shut.

"Now you just wait here, me boyo. Yer ol' dad'll be right back."

He stepped outside and walked off into the glare. The two boys sat silently. Tom seemed to have gone into a state of shock, for he sat catatonic in his chair, his eyes staring blankly at the greasy wooden table. Watching him, Ernie was filled with foreboding. It seemed that within two weeks Tom had changed into a different person. He was brown with sunburn and his hair was wild. The bush had done something to him. Ernie wanted to ask him straight out why he killed the pet cockatoo. Was it that he really wanted to kill him, Ernie? Or was it because of what his father had said. But he felt unable to speak in the heavy atmosphere of Tom's animal silence.

Outside there was a sudden loud screeching of cockatoos, and then two thuds of a shotgun followed by more outraged screeching. The screeching got louder and louder, more frenzied. There was another gunshot, and the voices of the cockatoos persisted, only fainter now and growing more distant as they flew away. Lyle came into the kitchen holding his gun in one hand and a dead cockatoo in the other. Without a word, he sat down at the table and proceeded to pluck the parrot. Tom would not look at him and Ernie watched in disbelief. When he had plucked it, he gutted it and then cut it up into pieces. The bluish meat had a strong musky odor. Lyle fried it with bacon fat in a pan and served it up to Tom on a tin plate with tomato sauce and bread and butter.

"Now eat it," he commanded. "All of it."

Tom ate slowly, but he ate it all. And then he was sick out in the yard. And for the rest of that day he was out repairing fences. He fell asleep without taking a bath and without saying a word. And the next morning he was gone. He left no note. A wind had come up during the night, and Lyle had awakened early to that awful and familiar sensation of emptiness he had whenever a strong wind blew. He found Tom's bed empty and his clothes gone. He stepped out onto the veranda, and in the half-light, way in the distance, he could see the blurry figure of his son vanishing gradually into the flat landscape. He stood there and he watched him and he did not go after him.

SIX MONTHS passed before the first letter arrived. Tom had gone north to Queensland and had a job as a station hand on a place east of Rockhampton. He talked of emus and big red kangaroos. Further north he had seen water buffalo. His main job was killing dingos. "It's better up here," he wrote, "as there are fewer dagos and it doesn't get cold."

Secretly Lyle hoped that Tom would never return, that he had truly struck out on his own. The boy was barely sixteen. Within a year he was home again. He had grown a good four inches, his hair was lighter, and hard work had developed the muscles in his shoulders and arms. He was taciturn, and seemed old for his age. His voice was deeper as well. He was shaving regularly now, and his chin was covered in pimples. And whereas before Lyle had been pleased to see him leave, he was now pleased that he was back. He had returned the same, but instead of a boy he was a man, and suddenly he was a useful and necessary hand on the station. He plowed fields and planted wheat and herded sheep. And he did it all quietly, and without contention. Rumbalara was at peace, although set in its ways. People watched the boys grow, commented on their development. Everyone knew that Lyle was a hard man and that Tom had a mean spirit. Tom was a hard worker. As he grew older he earned a considerable reputation for himself as a "good" drinker and a bar brawler. When he got into fights, often with Italians, the other men in the bar would make bets and Tom usually won. One day a stranger pulled a knife. And then Tom pulled a knife. He had carried one ever since he was molested in the bush. Everyone was startled. Tom was arrested and locked up for the night. And when he was let out in the morning there was a group of men waiting for him, to escort him home. They put him in a truck between two of them, and drove out to Rumbalara and told Lyle exactly what had happened, knowing that Lyle was a hard man and would certainly do the right thing.

A flight of zebra finches flew by the barn and then settled in the dust of a barren field beyond the homestead. Sheep had gathered around a square pond of mud-colored water in the middle of the field, and crows flew back and forth. All this Ernie could see from the loft window, and below him, in the dark interior of the barn, he saw his father and his older brother Tom and the two men who had brought him home. They were both friends of his father, Wally Creeley and Murray Scott. And in the name of that friendship they had brought Tom back to his father.

The two men spoke in low mumbling voices, slow, lazy, Australian voices. They told Lyle what they had seen. As they spoke their eyes became incensed, their throats tight, their voices outraged. That was no way for a white man to behave. Tom was a mad dog, a disgrace to the community. He would probably be banned from the golf club and the new swimming pool. And when Lyle became furious and humiliated, and threatened to whip the devil out of Tom, the two men immediately denied everything they had said. Surely it was a nasty business, and without doubt Tom demanded punishment, but all in all he was a good kid with a fiery nature and they understood the way he felt about that dago with the knife. Tom didn't pull his first, it was the other fellah. And then they left, their minds and hearts at ease, feeling that they had done the right thing by Lyle and by themselves and last of all by Tom, whom they had defended in the event that he should receive a flogging.

After they had gone, and while Ernie could still hear them out in the yard, opening the truck doors, the engine starting and the doors closing, Lyle stood staring down at the frowning, dark, petulant and dangerous-looking youth. The man only had an inch over his son. The boy was closer to being his rival. Lyle took a good long look at Tom and he saw that indeed the boy was now a man, violent and strong. He saw too that inside the man there lurked a devil, almost a monster, that was of his own making. And he realized with a grave finality that he did not and could never love him, and that he never had. But he did not hate him; rather he felt a cold and tolerant indifference, as though Tom was simply what Lyle had always wanted him to be, just another hired hand. A good worker. Somewhat ornery. A type. One of many sunburnt and dusty and faceless jackaroo.

Grasshoppers clicked in the dry grass; the ground itself, cracked and dusty already in December, seemed to have a buzzing sound of its own under the blazing sun. Crickets rasped. The cicadas gave a shrill twanging voice to the trees. Ernie's eyes glanced out of the dark loft into the yellow sunlight. The truck was driving away and the red cabin glinted in the bright heat. A funnel of red dust rose and grew behind the moving truck.

Ernie looked back down at his father and older brother. He had the feeling that something was passing between them of which his senses were unaware, but which he detected nonetheless. Again that feeling of being a third party, that he did not share in the manhood that his father and brother and the men who had brought him home shared. He would have to show that he too was a man, was one of them. But how? He wanted their acceptance, to belong. To share in that peculiar bond of masculinity that united all of those around him. Yet part of him despised their brutality and was repulsed by their unnatural lack of female influence or concern. The men around him seemed coarse and weak. He yearned for another kind of strength, a female strength. Without a woman to look to, he yearned for a rich and aromatic life in exotic places. An exotic place was in Ernie's mind, any place where there were women who were sweet smelling, pleasant, available, and full of laughter. Already he had cultivated sexual fantasies that would've seemed advanced for his age to the adults around him.

He was in the midst of one of these fantasies, images spun from books, movies, and magazines (this time it was Tahitian maidens), and busy manipulating himself in the secret nest he had made in the loft, when his father came in searching for a tool to work on the engine of his truck. And not ten minutes later the men had arrived with Tom.

He watched the proceedings below him with interest. When the men left, and Tom and his father were alone in the barn, and the truck had gone, he thought: This is it. Tom is full-grown now and they're going to have at it.

Ernie suddenly felt despair, the same despair he felt when he saw Tom kill the vixen in the rabbit trap. A frightened sorrow closed around his heart. A curious silence had taken hold of the barn, and of the people in it, a silence from the place itself. There was no sound, no movement. Even the crickets and cicadas had ceased. And they all felt the silence as a living, palpable presence; Lyle spoke deliberately, nervous and self-conscious, reluctant to speak, to hear his voice against the silence, but straining against it, wanting to break it.

"So you carry a knife?"

Tom nodded his head, his eyes looking up into the eyes of his father. His neck was thick and muscular and his hair was short. His thighs bulged in his jeans. He stood with his feet apart, bent slightly forward, his fists clenched by his sides. He was ready to fight, waiting for the blow. But it didn't come.

"Show it to me," said Lyle flatly.

"I don't have it," mumbled Tom. "The coppas took it away. Said it was a concealed weapon."

"What's the matter with you that you carry a knife?"

"You gotta learn to cut. Anyone messes with me, I'll cut."

"What's wrong with yer fists? You prefer to fight like a dago, is that it?"

"I'll cut anyone who messes with me."

"What happened to you, lad? Tell me. What made you like this?"

"What do you reckon, old fellah. You tell me. You tell me why I'm like this."

Lyle looked down into the cold and furious blue eyes of his son, and his own eyes became watery and blank like a sleep-walker's. He spoke without emphasis or modulation, pronouncing each word flatly and carefully, as though he was speaking a language he did not understand. "My wife left me," he said.

"Shit!" snarled Tom. "Boo hoo. You poor miserable old bastard. You're piss weak. I've watched you for years mopin' around here an' coughin' your guts out an' feelin' sorry for yourself because some bitch left you. You make me fuckin' sick. What about us, who never had a mother?"

"I don't know about you. I've done what I could. You've got a lot more than I ever had."

Tom looked theatrically around the barn. He turned around and looked out the open door at the dry land. "Well, Lyle," he said, turning back to face the old man and smiling sardonically. "You're welcome to all of it."

"If you leave now, don't come back. We can get by without you. You're a mean petty little ratbag. I had no idea. No understanding that you had grown this way. I reckon you were just born with the taste of bile in your mouth and you've been spittin' it out at the world ever since. Even before your mother left. Even then."

"What was her name?"

"What?"

"Her name. My mother. Your wife. What was her name?"

"Claire." Lyle's voice caught in his throat. His voice went dry. The name slipped from his lips without his willing it to, as though he spoke from a deep trance.

"Claire," Tom repeated. He had never thought of her as having a name before. Neither had Ernie, listening and watching from the loft. Suddenly the mysterious specter of a blonde woman who haunted all of their dreams now had a name, had been made somehow real. And as though sensing the effect of the name, Lyle added, "But that is only the name of a ghost. Of a woman who used to be."

The flat tone of his voice of a dead man, a voice that seemed to speak words it did not understand, the image of their mother as a ghost, put a chill in both boys. Ernie shuddered involuntarily. It seemed to him that there were ghosts everywhere, that the house had been haunted for as long as he could remember. Often, in the night, he heard strange knocking sounds coming from inside the walls, as though someone was straining to break out.

A flock of green parakeets cried out as they flew over the barn. It seemed to Ernie that his father and older brother stood as still and as silent as statues for a remarkably long time; for such a length of time that they became more like cats than men. And like cats their combat was swift, sudden. The wild youth sprang at the man, and the man smashed him to the beaten earth floor with his fists.

Tom landed heavily on his back. He rolled onto his side and touched his lips with his fingers and then looked at the blood on his fingertips. Then he stood up slowly, pulling himself up to his full height and bouncing on his toes. He drew his fists up and leaned forward, grinning now, his feet spread and blood flowing down over his chin. He danced around Lyle, who did not move a muscle. Lyle looked at his son with cold, hard, perceptive eyes, eyes that burned with an inner fury, with a hatred and anger that he had never before known. He fought against it, terrified, not really believing it, like a man who looks at himself in a mirror or a photograph and cannot really believe that the face he sees is his own.

Tom came at him again, bobbing and weaving. He threw out a couple of wild punches and Lyle blocked them both and caught him on the jaw with an uppercut and Tom stumbled back, panting, blood continuing to flow from his mouth.

"Alright boy," said Lyle. "That's enough. I don't want to fight you."

He lied. He wanted to fight him more than anything in the world, to pound him with his fists. The violent and unexpected hatred he felt for the boy frightened him.

"I could smash you into the earth," Lyle said flatly. "Perhaps that's what you want. But it would only make you worse. Would give you the excuse you need to be a bastard for the rest of your life. My old man beat me into the ground, you could say. No. I'm not gonna do that. Not yet. You're not old enough or big enough or smart enough to take on old Lyle yet. When you're a man. Don't come at me. I won't fight. You can beat the shit out of me, but I won't fight. Not yet."

Lyle turned and walked out of the barn. Tom stood panting, his stomach muscles heaving, his head hung limp and his fists clenched on his thighs. He appeared to be weeping, but no sound nor tear came. Ernie stood at the head of the wooden ladder that led up to the loft. He looked down at Tom, who once again seemed rigid, frozen like a statue. Ernie coughed and the statue came to life. The head jerked around with a sudden wild movement. The blue glazed eyes were those of a confused and frightened animal. Tom looked straight up at his younger brother. His lips began to tremble, and then he forced a smile and gasped.

Ernie was silent. Outside a dog began to bark. Then there was the muffled, distant sound of a man's voice. Tom seemed as though he was trying to speak. He mouthed a word and it stuck in his throat. He squatted on his haunches, buried his face in his fists, and started to weep. Tears flowed silently. Ernie went to the loft window and looked out to see what the dog was barking at. Out across the flat land, blurred in the shimmering and throbbing heat waves, a man astride a camel floated toward the homestead.

THAT YEAR, same as every other year, Ernie and Tom attend the Wallangirrii Show. Lyle has entered his prize merino ram. Hopes to win a ribbon. They see all the same animal parades and sideshows. The fire eaters and boomerang throwers, the freaks and misfits. All the carnival people. Tom spends some time in the snake pit, where the man lets him handle the snakes. Shows Tom his hands. Look at all the holes. Been bitten so many times I don't even feel it now. The snakes slither and coil on the canvas, twist around each other. The tent reeks of the odor of snakes. The little snake man in his dusty green suit, with his small pointed dark face, his black glistening snakeeyes, his thin dry snake lips, grins knowingly at Tom.

Ernie floats in the two o'clock in the afternoon heat past the pens where the sheep and the cattle doze.

In a hot and dusty and man-filled tent, Ernie watches a strip show. The dancer hardly seems to move at all, an awkward, great-thighed girl with a hard blank face. Her hollow eyes are smeared with cool blue. Her pale skin is covered in pearl-like beads of sweat. A clarinet whines from a crackling loudspeaker. She moves without any rhythm or poise, as though she does not hear the music at all. Removes a bracelet. A glove. A thin red nylon veil. A coiled snake is tattooed on her round white belly, right above where her black G-string forms a capital V in her thighs. The men's eyes hang on her hungrily as she drops another nylon veil, this time a green one. The men whistle and applaud, and she smiles faintly, seeing the drooling faces, her eyes impersonal, strangely animal behind the abstract mask of the face.

The music grows louder. Suddenly she turns her back on the audience and unclasps her bra, her large overspilling buttocks swaying heavily. The men begin to yell with excitement and push forward. The music erupts into a long crescendo of drums and the woman turns quickly and reveals her chest and runs from the stage before anyone knows what is happening. The music ceases abruptly. A withered man in a dark wide-brimmed hat and a brown pinstriped suit comes out applauding and praising the spectacular beauty of Jasmine, Princess of the Condamine. "Now you blokes wait outside while we get the ring set-up. We're gonna put on quite a show. Just wait outside and we'll let yers all back in, in a jiffy."

Outside, fighters are already lined up on a high platform. Dust hangs in the air above the crowd. A midget with black curly hair and wearing an orange suit bangs a bass drum. The thin man in the hat and brown suit barks at the crowd for challengers. "Pick ya own man. Ten dollars if yer last three rounds against any of my boys 'ere."

Ernie looks along the row of fighters. Four Abos, two whites, and one Islander, a large Maori covered up to the neck in intricate swirling blue tattoos. The Abos are all very dark and small and electric. Their black eyes flicker over the leering red faces of the crowd.

Ernie feels a tingling in his stomach. His heart beats in his throat. The pounding drum fills his head, reverberates throughout his entire body. There is a thick smell of bodies. He could certainly use the ten dollars. And none of those blokes look too bad. If anything they look small and frightened, except for the Maori.

He decides to enter the contest. He picks one of the Aborigines, and together they go into the tent. The Aborigine says nothing, and he keeps his face and eyes down. Without looking up, he hands Ernie a pair of gloves and togs and shoes and then points to a curtain at the back of the tent. Behind the curtain other contenders are changing. No one is smiling. They are all nervous and silent now, like soldiers before a battle.

Outside the drum is still pounding, flat, monotonous, and brutal. He can hear muffled shouts from the crowd. Raucous male laughter. The reek of sweating bodies mingles with the oppressive and hot smell of dust and animals. The other fighters look at him; some furtively and some dangerously, a couple seem sympathetic and curious. They are all town boys, all white. The persistent dead flat boom of the drum, the shrill and nasal squawk of the man in the brown suit, the noise of the crowd wanting blood. He hears it all, and for the first time wonders what he is doing, why it is necessary for him to put himself through all of this. For ten dollars. So he can show his bruised and battered body to his father and older brother. *You see what I done? You see what I put myself through? You didn't know I had it in me, did yer? Today in the ring with the strange black fellah I picked I'm gonna find more truth about myself than on any dreary day out there on the land.* Stimulation of his passion for risks.

The first fight is a featured event between two members of the troupe. The Kraut and the Maori. The Kraut is lean and pale, with a small red face and pale rat-like eyes. His blond hair, cut in a flattop, is like a short wire brush. A cluttered sea of faces, some hostile, some amused, some shouting impatiently, ring the fighters. Already the air is filled with racial insults. C'mon Fritz, smash the black bastard.

The Kraut jumps up and down on his toes, making whimpering sounds like a small hungry dog, his eyes wide and rolling back in his head. The bell sounds and he shrieks and leaps out at the Maori like a wild cat, covering him with a savage tattoo of blows. The Maori, huge, scared, clumsy, slow, recoils back into the crowd. He seems incapable of defending himself. The crowd reaches out hands like an octopus and hurls him back into the ring where the Kraut dances. The Maori turns, confused and dizzied, and the Kraut smashes him in the face with a right hook. There is a loud crack as the Maori's nose explodes beneath the glove and blood spurts over his cheeks and mouth. Another uppercut to the jaw and the Maori, the tattoos rippling as though alive on his wide torso and thighs, buckles at the knees and turns a complete circle once before he drops onto the floor. He lies crumpled and unconscious on his side, his chin and throat covered in a thick wad of redness like a deflated rubber balloon. There is hissing and booing in the crowd. This upsets the Kraut. He bares his teeth and pants and holds his fists up, and the crowd roars, angry, mocking. He cries out, and leaps into the mob, swinging wildly. The man in the brown suit and the midget rush from the back of the tent and drag him back into the ring. The man slaps his face. The midget takes hold of both his wrists. He calms immediately, hangs his head, and starts to cry. The midget takes him by the arm and leads him out of the tent, while the man throws a bucket of water over the Maori and then slaps him awake.

Ernie is next. He hears familiar voices shouting encouragement through the general uproar. Sees the keen, eager, and ruthless faces. Spots his brother in the crowd. Their eyes meet and then he quickly looks away. Looks across and for the first time sees the eyes of his opponent. They are fierce and shining. Point blank. The man in the hat yells the Aborigine's name. Jimmy Ruffles. "And you, young fellah, you 'ave a name?"

He hears his name only faintly, a name that doesn't sound like a name at all. The crowd cheers. Good on yer, Ernie. Kill the bastard. Way to go, Ernie. He feels sluggish. The gloves drag his arms down like lead weights. His feet slip on the canvas tarpaulin that is the floor. There is an oddness, an unreality, about the entire scene. He is fascinated by the violence of it all, the mad clutter of passions. The referee, the man in the hat, calls the fighters into the ring. They stand toe to toe, their faces nearly touching. Ernie smells the Aborigine, sees him as though for the first time, looks into his face, while the referee makes a speech about observing the rules and fair play. He detects a meanness in his opponent that he had not noticed before. A ruthless animal cunning. And he seems bigger now, expanded. It is his ring. Ernie looks down at the floor. He is startled to see a column of red ants moving across about six inches from his left foot. He looks up and notices the ants climbing the tent poles. One climbs onto his foot. The tent has been pitched right on top of a large ant nest.

The two fighters touch gloves and return to their corners. Ernie has not quite reached his when the bell rings. He turns quickly to see Jimmy Ruffles closing on him fast. He is caught off guard, and Jimmy hits him in the stomach and ribs with a series of short, accurate jabs, punching swiftly and scientifically. Ernie dances backward, leading with his left. Jimmy hangs in close, punching him the whole time, not hard, but swift and accurate, while Ernie jabs at him, hitting his face and shoulders and slowly driving him back. Jimmy goes into a huddle, covering his ears with his gloves, while Ernie pounds his head. As he tries to bull his way out, Ernie drives him back and down into a squat. The referee swears out loud, curses Jimmy, and springs snarling at Ernie. "Okay, that's enough. Let him up." He grabs Ernie's arm and pulls him violently back. The crowd hisses and boos. Jimmy shoots forward, butting Ernie hard in the jaw with the top of his head. Ernie feels his breath burst. A splintering crash shatters through to his brain. And he is sitting on the floor, hearing the crowd faintly, seeing the dusty brown shoes of the referee, the green canvas of the floor, the red ants darting back and forth, colliding with each other. The referee speaks in a sharp, rapid whisper. "Quick! Finish 'im off!" Ernie falls onto his side and rolls away and up onto his feet as the bell sounds.

The crowd is shouting and angry. The referee takes no notice of them, but is intent on abusing the young Aborigine. Ernie tastes blood in his mouth, but he feels nothing. An ant stings him on the knee. The bell sounds. Jimmy comes hopping out, dancing and smiling. He works in close like before, his blows hard, precise, going for the kill. A gloved fist squashes into Ernie's face, hard and stinging. He feels himself going down and then his back hits the floor. Bones crack. He feels himself bounce and settle, and then his back goes into spasm, pain takes his breath away. Lying there, he remembers the day he fell off a horse while leaping a ditch. His foot twisted in the stirrup, and the horse dragged him for several yards. When he finally got his foot free, he lay in the grass, in the absolute stillness, thinking he had died. And then the pain flowed up his back, into his shoulders and head. He looked up and he could see the grass tops and the thistle heads waving in the breeze. The blue of the sky. The horse looking down at him, its head shaped like an ironing board and its yellow eyes blinking beneath dark curling lashes.

"He's out!"

He turns onto his side at the shrill and vicious sound of the referee's voice. Then he is on his knees. Then he is standing. Someone yells: "Ring the bell, ya no good bastard." Others join in, shouting and threatening. The bell rings. There is loud applause. Hands reach out and slap Ernie on the back as he stands with his feet wide apart, his arms hanging lifeless, swaying like a sapling in the wind

"Fight dirty," a thin, high male voice advises. Tom kneels in front of him, rubbing his thighs. "You're doin' just great, nippah. This is the last round. Kick that black bastard in the balls."

The bell rings. Jimmy comes straight for him. He stomps on Ernie's right foot and then slams the side of his face with a hard right. Ernie's knees buckle, a dazzling light fills his skull, his head feels huge, as big as the tent. He staggers back, fighting the impulse of his legs, and then he collapses in a daze onto his knees. He hears the referee.

"As soon as he moves to get up, you bloody well nail 'im."

Voices in the crowd. Give 'im his money. Ring the bell. You better let 'im up. Yeah, you better let 'im up or else, you no good mongrel bastard. We ain't kiddin'. We know this boy. He's from around here. He's one of us. You better let 'im up. Let 'im up.

Loud applause as Ernie slowly rises. He has the town behind him now. He can feel their concentration. They'll talk about this for weeks, about how young Ernie Jimson refused to go down, how that boong hit him with everything he had, every muscle and every dirty trick, and still he wouldn't go down. He lurches toward Jimmy, throwing punches loosely, feeling a new surge of faint strength. A new rage. He hears men and boys calling to him by name, telling him to smash the black bastard, noting the excitement and fury in their voices. And Jimmy seems to feel it too, for he shrinks from the collective rage of the crowd.

"Finish 'im," hisses the referee.

Jimmy's face floats balloon-like through the smoky air toward Ernie, where he floats on a sea of dusty green canvas. He is experiencing a strange euphoria, aware only of the vast outpourings of his own sweat, a permeating odor of horseshit from the racetrack, the now distant voices of the crowd, the remote music of a piano-accordion, the bellowing of cattle, the crying of horses, and the acute sensation of shards of broken glass piercing his lungs.

Jimmy suddenly cries out and lunges at Ernie, his teeth bared, swinging wild and frantic. He covers Ernie's torso with a savage tattoo of blows. Ernie stumbles back, his feet slip on the canvas. Then he is kicked hard in the Achilles tendon. He falls with a moan and rolls onto his stomach. The referee stands over him, tries to kick him in the face. Ernie sees it coming, and catches the foot with his gloved hands. He holds it tight, then he twists it sharply. The man screams as Ernie hears the ankle pop. And instantly he is amazed at what he has done. He is mean after all. For a brief moment he is filled with self-pride. He has conquered something in himself. He feels relief. Something opening up inside. Three men leap into the ring, and two of them hold the referee by the arms. The third quickly searches the referee's pockets, produces a roll of notes, peels off a ten-dollar bill, and holds it up for the crowd to see. They cheer and applaud when he bends down and tucks the note into the elastic waist of Ernie's shorts and then pats Ernie on the shoulder. Ernie stands up and unlaces his gloves with his teeth and lets them fall off. He looks at Jimmy Ruffles, who stands off by himself in a corner, watching.

Two policemen enter the tent. They step into the ring and tell the crowd to leave. "Alright, you blokes. Move out now. Come on, move along."

Ernie starts to walk away.

"Not you, mate. You just stand right there." The policeman hardly looks at Ernie. He looks at Jimmy in the corner. Then at the man in the hat, still supported by the two townsmen. "That vicious young bastard," the man mumbles. "He just snapped my ankle."

The townsmen interrupt, explain things as they see them. And besides, Ernie is one of their own. Tom stands a couple of yards away, watching. The policeman asks the man if he wants to press charges. Ernie now hears a buzzing in his ears, and his body is starting to stiffen up. His shoulders and arms are badly bruised. The policeman looks at Ernie with dull mud-colored eyes out of a thin acne-scarred face.

"Okay, mate, I reckon you can go. Don't think this fellah has any more argument with yer."

Ernie nods his head, and goes back behind the curtain and changes. The tent has been cleared, and now bright sunlight enters through the wide doorway and dust hovers in the stale hot air. Outside Ernie sees the other boxers waiting around, huddled in a group. On the other side of the tent he sees the midget in the orange suit standing beside a camel. The camel is tethered to the back of a pickup truck. He feels the midget's eyes upon him. The little man's curly black hair is heavily oiled and it glistens in the hot afternoon sun.

The Interview

THEY FLEW low over the mountains, which were still partially covered with melting snow, glistening brightly under the clear blue sky. The range was low in comparison to what she knew, its shapes rounded and worn. From the sky she had a stunning sense of the endless breadth of the land—it was like nothing she had ever seen before. It was subtle and strangely terrifying, not in a dramatic way, but in a slow, narcotic, and dwarfing way. In the Sierra Nevada or the Rockies or the Swiss Alps, one was intimidated by size, by sudden, jagged peaks, by impenetrable passes, by the violent, vertical upthrust of the land which now seemed in her memory strangely human, strangely comprehensible. The mountains gradually gave way to rolling tree-dotted grasslands and then flat parched plain, a dry seabed as vast as an ocean and like an ocean mysterious and terrifying, filled with dark, hidden forces that could rise suddenly without warning—a place where the unconscious ruled, where consciousness, as she understood it, could go mad and easily lose itself. But to what? The question, from the air, eluded her. Now the great plain spread before her, beyond it nothing but the hugeness of sky.

They veered down, the now familiar roar of the engine filling her ears. She had had little to no conversation with the pilot because of it, although he had maneuvered the plane constantly over landmarks—the peak of Kosciusko, the horn of Mount Buffalo, the headwaters of the Murray—she had studied the map, and was having fun referring to it and recognizing the names and shapes of places. "That must be," and she was always right. She'd point her finger to the map and then look down and the pilot would nod, impressed. He smiled at her. And then, in the flat vastness filled with secret colors, he had pointed out other things—clumps of trees, a large elongated hill rising abruptly and alone out of the plain that to him seemed of immense significance. And then there were water holes, brown and glistening in the sun, and game trails, and a herd of cattle spreading out in fingers that left clouds of red dust as the shadow of the wing came across them. The cattle turned and scattered, tiny now, round shouldered, their heads down. There was what seemed like a moment of rapid moving blurred emptiness of land, and then she saw the kangaroos. They darted below her, remarkably swift and buoyant. Their poise as they moved, their slender shoulders and erect but forward-leaning heads and their tails like curved, stiff rudders made her think of the spry elegance of gazelles. And then abruptly they were left behind. She turned her head and saw the last of them. It looked like they were bounding after her, swift and fragile, athletic and strong. The plane veered upward. The pilot smiled at her again. The landscape below him was his way of talking to her. It was nothing personal. It was just something to be shared.

The plane tilted sharply and veered down, and she saw the river, a green glistening ribbon belted with a thick line of trees. It twisted ridiculously, like a tortured or angry serpent. There was obviously a line to it, a direction, but in that direction it repeatedly meandered back on itself, as though constantly rejecting its purpose of reaching the sea. The land itself offered no tangible obstacles. What the river wound around, she concluded quickly, was deep and hidden. It was something in the land itself, something that resisted the river, something that had made the water's course difficult and perverse. But the river had won. It had made it as an act of nature in spite of the dry conspiracy that constantly plotted against it.

They came down swiftly toward a dusty airstrip, and the heat of the land rose up and enveloped them. Suddenly it was very hot and there was a smell of dust and eucalyptus mixed with the smell of exhaust fumes and burning rubber as they hit the hard earthen runway and bounced along with a violence she had not expected. The pilot looked at her and smiled again. He turned the plane abruptly and brought it to a halt but kept the engine running.

"Well," he said, taking off his earphones. "We're here."

She took a deep breath, jolted by the landing, and removed her own headpiece.

"I guess—I reckon—we are. Thank you."

"Don't mention it. It's my pleasure. You've been great company."

"I have?"

He offered her a meaty, gnarled palm. She shook hands. His hand told her he meant what he said. She opened the door and climbed out of the plane. The pilot reached back and handed her her briefcase and bag. This time he didn't smile at her, but his look was sincere and gentle.

"Good luck," he said. "You better step back."

She did so and he immediately started to roll forward, the propeller erupting in a swirling, coughing roar that cloaked her in a whirlwind of red dust. She retreated backward as he spun the plane around and took off.

She turned, dazed, and looked at what now lay before her as the dust settled.

There was a tin-roofed hut, and a yellow wind sock on a pole, rippling in a breeze that she could not feel nor see in the distant line of trees. Scattered round about there were other buildings, abandoned and dilapidated—what looked liked airplane hangers and corrugated iron Quonset huts and long institutional shacks overgrown with weeds. They were all set far apart, between expanses of broken concrete pockmarked by dense clumps of coarse grass. Dust drifts were piled up against the walls of the buildings, and flimsy doors and overhang signs creaked and flapped in the breeze. She felt surrounded by the bawdy, reckless ghosts of seasoned farmers and soldiers laughing raucously in their mockery of her as a newcomer. She had an acute sense of vast space and desolation. A hot wind abruptly blew against her, full of hidden particles of sand that stung her cheeks and eyes. A Land Rover was coming toward her. It pulled up alongside her and the driver immediately got out. He was tall and lean and oddly dressed in a white shirt and tie and suspenders, the shirt sweat-stained and the black tie loose around his neck. His face was long and lean and very sunburnt, brown where it had tanned over the red and freckles. His coat lay across the passenger seat and he picked it up and tossed it in the back so she could sit. His dark blond hair was conservatively cut but still wild and unruly. The spectacles he wore did not correspond with his demeanor nor with his eyes, which, when he looked at her, did not seem to need them. He took her bag and briefcase and tossed them in beside his coat and climbed back behind the wheel and looked at her. She looked back at him and said nothing and climbed in beside him.

"So you're the hunter," he said.

"Yes, I'm the hunter."

He shifted into gear and started to drive toward the trees.

"I reckon that makes me the tracker."

"I suppose it does, if you've found our prey."

"That's for you to decide."

"Yes, it is."

He saw her look around.

"It's a World War II American Air Force base. It was a supply line to New Guinea. You buggers saved our asses and left us with an airstrip."

They drove out onto a potholed black tar road, following the river. She welcomed the trees and their shadows, the cool vision of the river passing before her, meandering and disappearing and then reappearing, white sandbars gleaming in the sun, the eucalyptus forest growing thicker, suddenly trees rising on either side.

"It's beautiful here," she said. "There's something—biblical about it. The sky. The . . . "

He smiled.

"How will you know?" he asked her.

"I'll know."

"How?"

"History. Questions."

"Are you a good shot?"

"Yes, I'm a very good shot. But I'm not here to shoot anyone."

"What will you do, then?"

"He has agreed to the interview?"

"Yes, he's agreed. But what choice does he have?"

"He could refuse. But the interview is his chance to talk his way out of it before he is arrested. To lie. To charm. To be old. This is only a preliminary to a preliminary investigation, but you never know. Have you ever done this before?"

"No."

"How did you come upon him?"

"A teenage boy befriended him. The boy has problems with his family. The old man lives alone down on the riverbank. Anyway, they fished together. One day the boy found some things in the old man's hut—photographs, letters. The boy saw some pictures and recognized the uniform he was in from the war movies he's seen. He told his father. His father told him to shut up, to let people be. Outraged, the boy went to the parish priest. Showed him the pictures."

"He stole the pictures?"

"Yes. You have them, don't you?"

"Yes. I have them."

"The old man was very upset about the theft."

"Not to mention the betrayal."

"The boy isn't rejoicing. The old man is well liked in the town. Seen as a character. And there is a strong immigrant community here—a very significant number of Eastern Europeans, Czechs and Yugoslavs and Poles and Germans and what-have-you, with small but guilty histories. This is a naive country. Full of space and New World euphoria. After the Second World War we welcomed everybody. Listen to that boy's father—a prisoner of war who can't use his right hand because they destroyed it with one of their sophisticated tortures—and he tells the boy to leave the fellow alone!"

"Who did?"

"Who did what?"

"Who destroyed the father's hand?"

"The Japanese."

"Back to the priest."

"Right. The priest, himself an immigrant, persisted through a long bureaucratic process, eventually getting to us. I was sent in to investigate. Now you're here. I hope we get this bastard."

"Why? Are you Jewish?

"Do I look Jewish?"

"No."

"Are you?"

"Only on my father's side, but that doesn't count."

"Why not?"

"It comes from the mother—being Jewish."

"Interesting people."

"Why do you hope we get him?"

"Because I can tell he's a bastard."

"How?"

"I can smell them. I don't like his smell. He has the stink of history on him. He reeks of bad deeds."

"Don't we all?"

"Some of us have the stench of direct participation."

"We have to be impartial."

"As I said, there is a strong immigrant community here. They have their own little town down by the river. All the houses are the same—little gray brick cottages with gardens out in front. It's called German Town by the locals. But they're mostly Slavs. A few Germans and Italians mixed in. Anyway, these 'new Australians' are now as nervous as a warren of scared rabbits. I've been questioning them. They thought they'd left their pasts behind."

"If I believe he is who we suspect he is, I will authorize you to arrest him—on suspicion of crimes against humanity."

"I'm only an investigator, and unofficially at that."

"You can't make an arrest?"

"Technically, no."

"Then why are you here?"

"To pick you up. Otherwise you'd be standing out in that dust for days."

She took a breath of hot air. Through a line of trees she saw orange groves and then rolling vineyards. The country she had thought so hostile and arid was now meticulously cultivated and ordered, watered and green.

"Would you like a shower?" he asked. "I can drive you to the hotel first."

"No," she said. "Let's get on with it. I can wash later."

They drove through a small hamlet. It was on a wide bend in the river and there was a cultivated lawn that looked like a park along the riverbank, overlooked from the other side of the road by a hotel, a single-story building made of whitewashed brick with a wide, curved green corrugated iron veranda roof. On the opposite bank there was a shimmering white sand beach with thick eucalyptus forest beyond it—a wall of trees, nothing like she had expected from the air. Huge pepper trees and a few date palms shaded the town—a row of eight buildings, about half of which appeared deserted, with scattered houses in the fields behind them and an iron railway bridge, on which a train was crossing the river.

"Is this the town?" she asked.

"This? No. It's a few miles up river from here, on the Victorian side."

They passed through the town quickly and crossed another bridge and continued to follow the river, invisible now because of the trees.

Eight hundred and fifty thousand people died in the Treblinka camp. The retreating Germans destroyed the camp and its records in 1943. At present, there are a number of pending cases and suspects at hand who may or may not be former SS guards at Treblinka and other camps. Outstanding among these cases is that of the sadistic SS guard at Treblinka known as Ivan the Terrible, who has been tentatively identified at large in the United States. However, evidence has begun to surface that a number of suspected war criminals entered Australia in the late forties, the fifties, and early sixties, either under aliases or beyond the reach of investigation by the Australian authorities. Ivan may be among them, along with a small number of his compatriots. The Australian government has formally expressed its outrage and is offering assistance along with a guarantee of complete cooperation, hoping to cast a wide net.

THEY HAD FALLEN silent together. Now he was more like the pilot, easy and familiar with silence, and she had a chance to study him more closely. Like her, he seemed anxious to do justice, but something about it disgusted him, in spite of what he had said to her; it was not only the association with horror, with the atrocities of the past, but the hunt itself. It was apparent the entire matter left a bitter taste in his mouth—it was written all over his face, in his manner, in the way he moved. It was something he was instinctively uneasy with, this hunting of a man, no matter who he was or what he had done. She tried to share in this feeling—it was the kind of individualistic and silent and very human disgust she innately understood but had never before fully, honestly, encountered. It was there, immediate and mute, filling the seat beside her in the Land Rover. After the initial burst of conversation he had become remote, his eyes removed from her, not even daring to look. She realized she had become overly aware of his presence.

"By the way." She heard herself speaking, her voice catching in her dry throat. He glanced at her quickly, allowing himself a brief but intense examination. It seemed that he focused on the tiny mole on her left cheek just above the corner of her mouth—her old-fashioned beauty spot. "You haven't told me your name."

He looked back at the road and said: "Reardon. Phil Reardon. Didn't they tell you?"

"Yes, they did. I'm Rebecca Newman."

"I know."

"Are you from around here, Mr. Reardon?"

"Not anymore. But I grew up here, and the place is pretty much the same."

"You know him, this Marczenko?"

"He's been around for years, since I was a kid." He looked at her briefly again, the sunlight flashing on his silver-rimmed spectacles. "But no, I don't know him. Ah, here we are."

They turned off the road and headed into the trees along a winding bush track that was in parts overgrown with dry grass. They crossed the flat, cracked clay pan of a dry swamp and went up over the embankment on the other side. The track continued on, deeper into the forest.

Looking at his crinkled and dusty clothing, she felt self-consciously overdressed. She was wearing jeans and a safari jacket and a store-bought bushman's hat and boots—all newly purchased. And she was hot, her body aching. Once this initial interview—it would really be only an encounter, a short formal meeting, a chance to get a look at him and he at her—was over, she would go to her hotel and change into a light cotton summer dress and sandals. In fact, she would do it here. The boots made her clumsy. She wanted her feet flat, her legs bare. She had her bag and she could do it in the trees, do it anywhere, really, and forget this outback nonsense, be herself.

They had warned her to dress this way because of the mosquitoes and the snakes, and she had taken their advice. But upon being with him in the Land Rover, and perhaps upon seeing him, she had started to feel ridiculous—like a vacant-eyed model in some dress-for-adventure catalog, the pressed unblemished newness of her clothing an embarrassment. He glanced at her quickly just as she was having these thoughts, startling her with the idea that he was reading her mind. She saw the quiet smirk on his face as he looked back at the trail. His smile both pleased and angered her. She sat up and turned and faced him directly, reaching up and tugging at the lapels of her jacket.

"I was advised to dress like this—for comfort."

He looked at her and smiled and the faint wrinkles at the corners of his eyes grooved merrily. She looked away and then sat back and faced the windshield.

"You do make that gear look glamorous," he said, without looking at her.

She turned her head sharply and glared at him. He looked back at her quickly, catching her gaze, and then returned to his driving. She sat back and reached into her jacket pocket, withdrew a golden-cased lipstick, opened it, and started applying it to her mouth. The track was now bumpy, full of potholes and trenches. As they bounced along she saw him watching her as earnestly as he watched the road, but now there was no road. He was navigating an obviously known and winding path through the trees.

"Lip balm." She held up the lipstick and smiled at him with rouged moist lips. "It's all I've got. I forgot the real stuff."

He looked at her. At her lips. At the lipstick in her hand. Then back at her.

"Want some?" she asked. She looked directly into his eyes.

"Your eyes," she said.

"My what?"

"You have sad eyes." She realized immediately what she had said. She had overstepped the mark. She couldn't believe her own brazen flirtatiousness. It was her way of getting back at him for his comment about her clothing, an attempt to put him off balance. The remark was spontaneous but presumptuous. She put the lipstick back in her pocket and looked straight ahead.

"I don't know why I said that," she told him.

"We're in a sad business right now," he said flatly, unperturbed.

Ahead of them the river once again flickered through the trees. As they drew near she saw crude huts scattered along the riverbank, which was high on this side. The air, suddenly, was filled with the heavy ashen smell of the camp, a rancid and smoky odor that cut through the all-pervasive aroma of eucalyptus.

They stopped a short distance from the huts and climbed out. Immediately a swarm of flies tried to settle on her, and she waved them away with a strong and irritable motion of her hand. The smell of the camp was now even more intense—a miasma of primitive human settlement, of the smoke of repetitive cooking fires that clung to the trees and the shanties, the rotting burlap and the piles of rusted opened cans. She reached for her briefcase and they walked toward the camp, the crackle of dry bark and twigs and leaves loud beneath their feet. Something slithered away under the leaves. A few dogs moved lethargically about, ignoring them, but there was no movement within the shadows of the huts and no sign of any people.

"Is this it?" she asked, somewhat amazed.

"Kind of," he said, and pointed beyond the huts to where another building stood, separate and distinct, several yards from the camp. "Let's see if anyone's home."

It was a cabin, made of the same crude materials as the shanties, but unlike the shanties it was neat and substantial, built to last. It had a pitted roof and even a blackened stone chimney. There was a rough but aligned picket fence around it and a garden in front, filled with daisies and poppies, with a stone-lined path leading from a small gate up to the door. As they approached, she saw a bicycle leaning against the wall by the door, and what looked like wire crayfish traps.

He opened the gate and she followed him up the path to the door and stood beside him as he knocked. There was no reply. He knocked again, waited, and then slowly pushed the door open and entered, indicating for her to wait. Then he called to her.

"There's no one home. Come on in and take a look."

The interior of the cabin smelled of wood smoke and burnt kerosene. There was an old, rain-warped wooden table surrounded by four battered chairs. An iron cot in the corner supported a thin mattress wrapped tightly in tattered woolen blankets. A small brown bottle dangled over the table, hung by a cord from the roof. A note stuck to it read "Achtung. Pills," scrawled in dark pencil by a shaking, frail hand. Rustic as it was, the place was clean and orderly.

"Neat, isn't he?" said Phil Reardon.

She took hold of the bottle and shook it and studied the label.

"Heart trouble?" she asked.

"I wouldn't know. Why don't you wait here while I take a look around? I told him to expect us."

"The note," she said. "It's in German."

"So?"

"His name's Marczenko."

"Maybe that's not his real name, or maybe he prefers the language of his former masters."

He left, and she stood holding the briefcase with both hands in front of her, gazing up at the roof and around at the sparse interior. Her eyes fell on a pile of brittle smoldering ashes and particles of unburned paper in the fireplace. There were answers to be hewn out of the silence, out of the smoke-stained timbers of the cabin, in every object and detail she could quietly, clearly, focus her attention on. She put her briefcase on the table.

The ashes were still warm and smoking. Their presence was inconsistent with the swept orderliness of the place. The fire had been made in haste after he had cleaned the fireplace. Apart from the pile of ashes, it too was swept clean. There was no evidence anywhere of any messiness overlooked. He kept his house neat and clean; it was an outpost in the wilderness, his own monument to himself, to civilization, to memory, to some crude and stark dignity that he battled in fugitive isolation, in exile, to preserve. Had she come to find a Mr. Kurtz among the natives, to expose the heart of darkness? Perhaps. It had been done several times before, in places far more wild and remote than this. And yet somehow this was the most obscure place to hide, the most cunning, the place least thought of in the great international centers where the hunt for his kind was planned and coordinated.

She got down on her haunches in front of the hearth, picked up a blackened metal bar, and sifted through the ashes, lifting out the small fragments of paper and examining them. She could partially make out bits of words written in faded and browning blue ink, but nothing of any meaning. There were what had been photographs of various sizes, but they were burned beyond recognition and crumbled at the touch. Still squatting, she looked around the room. Metal thumbtacks remained in a couple of poles and in one of the walls. There was an empty picture frame on the stove. She rose and walked over and picked it up. A torn dark fragment of the corner of a photograph remained between its metal edges. He had cleaned the house and he had forgotten about the pictures. Then he had seen them and burnt them in a hurry, maybe even in a panic.

There was nothing under the cot; on the shelves only some tin plates and mugs and cans of food. A wooden fruit crate in a corner contained an elaborate array of fishing tackle and hooks and leaden weights. Other than the basics of his existence, he had made a concerted effort to rid the cabin of any further clue to his identity.

The door creaked open and Phil Reardon looked in at her.

"No sign of him. Old black woman in the camp says she saw him early this morning, but that's it."

"We'll wait," she said, and put the frame down where she had found it.

"Suit yourself. Maybe you'd like a swim."

"A swim!"

"There's a beach around the next bend. It's a short walk."

"We're on official business, Mr. Reardon. I hardly think taking a swim right now is appropriate."

"Why not? It's hot, we're bored. We could go traipsing after him into the bush, but I doubt it'd do any good. And somehow I doubt he'll be back before dusk. He cleaned this place out pretty good. Did you bring a swimsuit?"

"No. I didn't."

"Too bad. You don't mind if I take a dip?

"Well, I don't know."

He turned and let the door swing shut. She picked up her briefcase and opened the door and stepped outside, where he stood nonchalantly waiting for her with one hand on his hip. She stood and looked at him and then at the trees and the shanties and then out at the river with its shimmering white-green glare.

"We'll go and come back in the morning," she said. "I'll leave him a note telling him we'll be here at ten o'clock. Is ten o'clock alright with you?"

"I reckon he'll be well gone by ten in the morning. He's caught your scent. You frighten him. We'll leave nothing and come early. Come on, I'll take you to the hotel."

"What about your swim?"

"I can do that later. If you want to join me, you can buy a suit in town. There's a nice beach close by."

"Actually, that sounds like a good idea."

SHE BOUGHT the swimsuit, a turquoise bikini, at a women's boutique in the town, not far from the hotel. She changed in her room, putting on a light cotton shoulderless dress with a button-down front over the bikini, and a pair of wood and leather scandals. She was happier, cooler, and suddenly refreshed and excited by the novel idea of going to the beach out here, so far from the sea. Her host, if she could call him that, was also staying at the hotel. His room was at the other end of a long, dark, linoleum-smelling corridor, and he met her outside in the Land Rover.

"Nice hat," he said, grinning, seeing that she still wore the bushman's hat.

"Thank you. I like it."

They drove down to the river, into the cool scented shadows of the trees and then the wide, gold and silver sparkle of the beach and the water. When she disrobed she felt immediately saturated by the light and heat. It was intense but soothing, joyous with the water lapping against her ankles and the gentle throbbing buzz of the forest filling her ears.

She entered the water slowly, wading out over a sandbar; the water seemed to swallow her, coolly devouring feet, ankles, knees, thighs, sex, waist. Suddenly hundreds of tiny fish exploded all around her, flashing like metal filaments, blunt needles brushing her skin. The water was mineral rich with silt, marked by tiny swirling eddies. The mosquito bites from the night before—in Sydney, of all places—stung pleasurably. A large green fish hung by her legs, mouthing. It was an ugly, lugubrious creature—slow, ponderous, and ancient. A school of fingerlings, swimming as close as gnats, darted away. A pair of kingfishers squabbled, a blue whirling disk in midair, and plummeted again and again. She turned to call to him on the beach, but he was already out in the middle of the river. He waved at her and started to swim toward her, his arms rising in broad, powerful strokes.

That night they dined together in the hotel dining room. It was formally decorated with a chandelier and starched white linen tablecloths in an almost absurd juxtaposition to the raucous shouts that came from the bar.

Over dinner she found the impulse for mild flirtation irresistible. It was harmless; it added spice to what would otherwise be a tedious evening spent in the middle of nowhere, and the attraction between them, inhibited as it was by circumstances, was real enough to warrant casual speculation and some playfully pantomimed recognition. She was aware that the afternoon on the river and now the warm night and the wine had brought out her natural insouciance, and she was enjoying it, relaxing into it. It was an easier way of dealing with him, and with herself, given what she believed to be their shared disposition. If anything, it was a refreshingly sanguine change to the usual formalities of her work, and she could trust him to understand its silent language without allowing things to get out of control.

He was a handsome-looking man.

As the evening progressed she started to wish that something would happen—that in some gentle way he would act on it, drug her with his will and guide her to his room, like a sunflower that blindly follows the sun. She was flushed with sunburn and wine, her skin pleasantly on fire. He continued to meet her gaze, unflinchingly direct, his eyes smiling. With each new stare she felt more drawn to him, felt herself trying to pull back while fantasizing different ways he might approach her. It was the journey, she thought, the place. It had made her feel lonely while realizing how lonely she had been. Here, in the midst of vastness, he offered an intimate and exciting comfort. *It's been a long time*, she thought. *Too long.* She sat back, as though catching her breath. *And it will continue to be a long time*, she told herself, in a half-hearted attempt to break the spell.

She put her napkin down on the table and stood up.

"Well, it's been very pleasant—the whole day. But I am tired and we have to be up early." He smiled up at her and didn't move.

"Good night, then," he said, raising his glass slightly.

"You're staying?"

"For a while. Finish my drink and relax."

"You're not relaxed enough already?" she said, laughing.

He downed the last of his wine in a purple gulp and stood up and held out his hand. She took it and squeezed it firmly. The air seemed to swing solidly between them, like their hands. There was a moment's stay of uneasiness.

"Well, good night, then," she said, holding the hand, not yet wanting to let it go.

"Good night. Do you want me to wake you in the morning?"

"If you're up before me, please do."

She hesitated a moment, and then leaned forward and kissed him lightly on the cheek. She was slightly drunk, and pressed the side of her face against his and drew his hand gently to her hip. She lingered that way for a moment, his cheek, with its stipple of roughness, fused to hers.

"Don't worry," she whispered. "Where I come from everyone kisses good night."

She stepped back to arm's length, still holding his hand, and looked glowingly into his eyes.

"It's just a pleasantry," she said, smiling languidly. "Good night, again."

IN HER ROOM she thought: *What will she do next? The girl just can't help herself.* They had touched hands and exchanged smiles— signs of recognition. They were grateful for each other, at least for now, out here. If only gratitude could be allowed to fully express itself. She smiled wistfully and sat on the bed and looked at herself in the dresser mirror. Her skin was already tanned to a rich ocher, her copper hair streaked with yellow. All it took was an afternoon at the river to make her glow. It was the Spanish blood, inherited from her mother. She had almost completely forgotten about the old man, the reason she had come to this small point on the map. Within an afternoon and an evening that reason, and even her past, including the day before, had grown remote, a faint mirage in the dazzling light. Everything, even her own assured existence, was swallowed by an immense explosion of sky and sun in which she in turn had grown immense and physically free.

She undressed and turned out the light and pulled the blankets back off the bed and climbed in under the sheet. "Mr. Reardon," she whispered softly. "What are you doing now, Mr. Reardon?" As the day—sky, earth, water—fell away before her.

SHE WAS ALREADY up and dressed when he knocked, having collected herself from the night. The day, the old man, were once again before her, waiting. As was Phil Reardon in the hotel dining room. As was the river, opalescent, a pale and tender green in the morning light, the trees full of white cockatoos that screeched above their heads as they drove toward the camp.

"They weren't here yesterday," she said.

"They're around here in the mornings, and we're disturbing their breakfast. That's what all the ruckus is about."

"Well they certainly let you know when you're not appreciated."

She wanted to reach out and touch him, but the specter of the old man, looming forever nearer, made her hold back. Many disturbing and opaque thoughts began to filter through her mind. All the warm sensations she had from the night before were now tainted by that singular, invisible presence.

People were squatting around their breakfast fires when they pulled up at the camp. This time dogs ran barking to greet them and the camp dwellers, a small group of ragged blacks, watched them silently as they walked toward the cabin. The cockatoos had stopped their screeching pursuit, and were now nowhere to be seen.

They found the cabin empty and undisturbed from the day before. The picture frame remained on the stove, the scattered ashes in the fireplace, the cot unslept in. But the bottle of pills was missing from the string.

"He's bolted," said Phil Reardon. "I'll be damned if the bugger hasn't bolted!" He shook his head and looked at her, truly surprised. "What do you think of that?"

"Where would he go?"

"Who knows? His bike and gear are still here. He's gone bush, hopin' to hide out 'til we go away. Let's take a look around. Then we'll go and call in the police."

"You mean stage a manhunt?"

"Right. Dogs and all. He can't have gone far." He grinned at her. "I hate it when people stand me up."

"I can't imagine who would," she said as she turned and walked out the door.

"That evil old illywhacker," he murmured.

In spite of his humor, she could tell that he was far from amused. His words the day before, when they met, were a ruse, masking his true feelings. The old man, in his eyes, had revealed a horrific truth about himself that up until now Phil Reardon in his heart had hoped would prove false. The raw truth, with all of its evil implications apparently now exposed, was shocking to him, and the bitterness of its taste made him grim and determined. The old man had betrayed them all in their innocence, beguiling them with his great deception. The ugliness, after all, had proved unavoidable. He had, indeed, been dealing with it all along, face to face, while refusing to let his imagination admit that, in this place, it could even be possible. He walked around the camp asking questions with the indignation of a man who had been swindled and was now out for revenge.

She saw him turn suddenly from an old woman standing by her fire and track off into the bush, heading up river.

"Phil. Mr. Reardon. Wait!" she called, and ran after him, but he was quickly gone.

Now she was alone in the blue-gray forest, walking cautiously through knee-high yellow grass. The morning light streamed in hard, bright shafts through the trees, making leaf-dappled shadows. She looked around and called again. Her voice was bounced back at her off the ironbark trunks. For some reason her heart was pounding. She stopped for a moment and caught her breath. Her lower legs were scratched and stinging from the grass. She made her way out onto a clear path along the riverbank.

The last of a small morning mist was rising swiftly off the river and the slight chill that had been in the air was leaving. The sun started to gently burn her shoulders and the forest to release its eucalypt aroma. She followed the path, the river glittering below her beyond the shadow of the high bank. Talc-like dust powdered her feet, and ahead of her, on the path, large red ants swarmed over the drying carcass of a red and black snake.

The heat descended quickly. She followed the rim of the bank down onto a small sandy flat. Behind it a creek had formed a gaping mouth in the high clay bank which was cluttered with branches and logs. The sand was moist and cool. She took off her sandals and tied her dress up above her waist, exposing her underwear, and waded into the clear shallows. The current was swift, and the bright water pressed against her and swirled around her knees.

The sandbar extended several yards out into the river. At its far edge, a huge snag lay half submerged with a heavy broken branch extended skyward. It reminded her of some giant swimmer stranded and frozen in the act of battling the current. She waded deeper, wishing to make it to the snag, beyond which the river's broad and rapid flow had the smooth surface of liquefied green glass.

She did not, out in the river, expect to come face-to-face with anyone. The water was now up to her breasts. She climbed up onto the snag and crawled on hands and knees along its slippery surface toward the jutting branch, careful not to fall off the other side into the deep. Suddenly, her knee slipped, and she lunged forward, hitting her chin and clinging to the wide trunk with outstretched arms. Something bright caught her eye. She glanced down into the water and saw him looking up at her through a tiny whirlpool. He was only a couple of feet below the surface. He hung there, his waist and legs stuck beneath the log, held by the current, which tugged at his short silver hair as it did the green beard of the snag. She reached down and picked up the small brown bottle from where it lapped against a rotting branch. She did not feel shock, but recognition, and stayed there, on her hands and knees, looking down at him for some time, studying his blurry face.

When, finally, she looked up, Phil Reardon was standing on the riverbank, looking down at her. She saw that his clothes were wet and that in the heat he was drying off quickly.

Mastering the Inner Leap

LATER HE WAS to be rich and famous, a cult leader in America, and author of several books. But when I first knew him he was at high school in a small country town on the Murray River in the southern part of Australia. He was never big and strong, but even then he quickly became famous throughout the region for his remarkable ability to leap over obstacles with the effortless grace and style of a kangaroo.

He was high-jump champion. He neither straddled nor rode the bar, but simply hopped over it, easily clearing seven feet and landing with both feet on the ground. They tried to make him jump conventionally, scientifically, and he couldn't. Their choreographed athletic techniques, their understanding of the dynamics of human movement, barely lifted him into the air. But left to himself, to his awkward leap, he seemed to be not only in defiance of his teachers but of gravity itself.

His name was Russell Gill and he always insisted that his middle name was Mary. He lived with his mother and a de facto stepfather and a younger sister and an older brother in three wagons in a vacant lot that was actually part of an abandoned sawmill down on "the bottoms." Not far from the wagons were a few humpies made of corrugated iron and bark where some half-caste Aborigines and a few poor whites lived, and beyond the humpies was the levee and the river and the bush.

I met him during my second last year at school. He was my age but three grades below me. His family had been wandering around the country like gypsies for years. He hadn't been to school for quite a while, and as a result was somewhat retarded in his reading and writing. Since I was considered bright and advanced, the headmaster assigned me the task of teaching Russell these skills when he brought him into the class on that first day and introduced him as the new boy. Russell stood before us, in baggy short pants and short-sleeved shirt, the obligatory gray uniform of the government schools, and looked at his shoes, which were polished but split and falling apart. He had thick, carrot-red hair. His face was small and round and covered in orange freckles, as were his bare skinny arms. Occasionally his bright, furtive blue eyes looked up from his shoes and swept over the class as the headmaster spoke, and I saw that he had the kind of boyish face that somehow reminds you of an old man. He certainly did not look like one marked by fate for great success.

He was the poorest white person I had ever met. That very same day, after school, he invited me down to his "new home." It was in the dead of the heat of the afternoon, and the lumpy unmade road that led down to the bottoms was bright and dusty. We walked along in silence, our school bags over our shoulders, watching the little clouds of yellow dust that were stirred by our shoes. And soon the town, the brick suburban houses with their neat lawns and hedges and the sprinklers turning and hissing in the heat, was behind us, and we were in the bottoms, walking between vacant fields and random shacks and abandoned rusting automobiles. Occasionally there was a section of rundown picket fence, or an old windmill or an outhouse, sagging and alone, in a desolate field.

The bottoms always had its own curious odor, which was partly the slime mud and eucalyptus smell of the river and partly the permeating odor of the nearby garbage dump. And there was a third smell, which was an odor of wood smoke, of cooking over fire, which for me was the most distinctive smell of all: the odor of poor people.

Dogs ran barking at us from all directions as we walked along. We stooped and pretended to pick up stones and they ran away immediately. Cockatoos screeched overhead as we turned in the gate to the yard, where the three wagons were arranged in an L. The houses on the wagons were square, with pitted roofs, and made of corrugated iron. Two were painted red and the third was green, and they all had big iron wheels with wooden spokes. Chickens pecked about the yard, and off to one side were stacked several wire cages in which were pigeons and ferrets. Smoke issued from a small chimney on the roof of the green wagon, and in the yard was a heavy odor of frying animal fat. A dog was tied with a long rope to the wheel of the same wagon, and it started to jump around and bark frantically as we came in the gate. Beyond the wagons were the sheds of the old sawmill, and in these sheds there was now hay, and from what I could see, a cow and a camel.

A woman in a gray dress came to the door of the green wagon and yelled at the dog to shut up. She was short and thin, with black hair tied in a bun on top of her head. She wore spectacles that flashed white in the sun as she turned and looked in our direction.

"That's me mum," said Russell, pointing at her with a nod of his head as he closed the gate behind us. "Reckon Mr. Jones is havin' his afternoon tucker."

I followed him across the yard toward the second red wagon, the woman, in the dark yawn of the doorway, watching me the whole time, her face long, gaunt, and blank beneath the spectacles.

"Mr. Jones don't like to be disturbed while he's eatin'," Russell continued. "He likes to eat, then sleep 'til sundown. And we're not allowed to disturb him, so stay away from the kitchen for now. He'll be out soon enough, then we'll go an' get a bite an' I'll introduce yer to me mum."

It was the most I'd heard him say all day, and it was apparent that he was relieved to be out of school. We reached the wagon and he sat on the steps and took off his shoes and socks. The woman disappeared into the green wagon, from which now came the muffled sounds of a man coughing. Russell looked up at me and grinned.

"That's Mr. Jones havin' his after-dinner fag while me mum makes a pot of tea. Any minute now he'll appear in the door and have a spit. Queer lookin' bugger. Hello. Here he comes."

I looked around to take a look at Mr. Jones. He was tall and thin and wearing a brown suit and a brown bushman's hat which hid the upper part of his face. He leaned out from the wagon door and spat at the dog tethered below. Then he laughed and spat again and the dog crawled beneath the wagon. Mr. Jones looked up and saw us watching him. His face was long and brown, the eyes pale, small, and piercing.

"Mr. Jones provides for us," said Russell flatly. Mr. Jones held us with his lingering gaze and I felt a sudden wave of apprehension about being there. Russell seemed to detect this, and tried to put me at ease.

"Don't worry about him," he said. "He won't hurt yer, as long as yer don't go near him. Come on, I'll show yer his ferrets. I take 'em out meself. We practically live off rabbit."

He took hold of my arm and led me directly to the animal cages, Mr. Jones watching the whole time.

"I ain't ever brought anyone home before," said Russell. As he spoke another face appeared, turkey-like, out of the door of the middle wagon. It belonged to a girl about fifteen, and she had the same carrot-red hair, only it was down below her shoulders. Slowly she emerged onto the steps. She wore a light pink cotton dress which fitted tightly over her swollen and protruding belly. Her bare feet were pale and dusty and her face and arms were covered in freckles, giving her skin an orange glow.

Her eyes were very blue, but had the dark intensity of a frightened animal.

I just had time to catch a quick but complete look at her when I heard a man's voice yell shrill and harsh across the yard: "Ruby-Mae get back inside! Where's your shame?"

The girl turned pale and faded back into the dark interior of the wagon. Mr. Jones had stepped down into the yard, and now he stood staring at the two of us while chickens pecked all around him. One rooster in particular, a large Rhode Island red, was circling him ominously. He appeared not to notice, but instead wrapped the two of us in the awful climate of his look.

Russell ignored him. He opened up one of the cages and reached in and pulled out a ferret by the scruff of its neck. The animal was covered with soft yellow fur and looked up with moist, round, pink eyes. He let it run up his arm, and when it tried to leap away he caught it in his hands and it lengthened out, stretched like elastic, in order to get out of his grip. He grinned, very pleased, and put it back in the wire cage.

"You see that? A ferret can get through almost anythin' by stretchin' himself," he said. "Slips down a rabbit hole without any trouble. This one here's no good, though. Keeps killin' 'em in the hole. The others chase 'em out an' Mr. Jones grabs 'em by the ears an' slits their throats. Real quick. Mr. Jones loves to eat rabbit."

As he spoke there was a sudden squark and a wild fluttering of wings. We turned to see the rooster, the Rhode Island red, flying at Mr. Jones's face and Mr. Jones fighting him off with his hands, which were scratched and bloodied. He managed to fling the rooster to the ground and retreat up the steps into the middle wagon, where Ruby-Mae was hiding her shame.

Russell wiped his lips with the back of his hand. "Reckon we can go and 'ave a cuppa now, an' maybe some biscuits."

He started immediately toward the kitchen. I followed close behind, cautious to avoid the red rooster, who now strutted about in front of the middle wagon.

Now I could see the mill sheds clearly, the cow and the camel, and some of the derelict machinery that remained from the old days. Beyond the mill were some half a dozen small wooden houses, all of them very run-down, and beyond the houses was a swamp of tall spartina grass and bulrushes and a plant known as a "black-boy." The river was right behind the swamp, and between the swamp and the houses was a narrow pale clay road. A truck was coming slowly down the road, making a lot of noise because of a broken exhaust, and a cloud of red dust and black smoke billowed behind it.

I followed Russell up the wooden steps into the wagon. It was dark inside, after the glare of the yard, and smelled strongly of burnt kerosene from the lamps and of soot from the wood-burning stove. A flock of parrots screeched overhead and Russell turned around and pushed past me and scrambled down the steps back into the yard, his face lifted skyward.

"He just loves them stupid birds. Says they got magical powers. Poor bugger's sun-struck."

The woman's voice, dry and nasal, came from the far end of the wagon. Dusty pencils of light pierced the gloom, and I couldn't see her at first. Then she moved. A ray of light flashed on her spectacles, and I saw her sitting with her back against the far wall, upright on a stool, straight and lean and gaunt like a stick, a ghost in that close, hot, and hollow and human-smelling darkness.

"Maybe they do," I said. "You never know."

"Don't tell me you're as mad as he is. What's yer name?"

"Frank Mills."

"Nice t' meet yer."

Outside Mr. Jones was having a coughing fit, and then I heard him curse and spit, both at the same time, and then the dog let go a yelp. Russell came back inside, looking wide-eyed into the gloom, his blue eyes shining.

"I'm starvin'," he said and sat down at the table and attacked a loaf of stale sliced bread, stuffing it ravenously into his mouth.

The woman didn't move, but sank back into the darkness, vanishing like a chalk outline on a blackboard being quickly erased. From outside came a loud squarking, violent fluttering of wings and the sound of Mr. Jones's harsh and snarling voice. Russell was momentarily distracted from his meal; he shot bolt upright in his chair and looked at me, laughing and talking with his mouth full of bread.

"Sounds like Mr. Jones is 'avin' another run-in with Ben. Gettin' 'ard for that ol' bugger to take a shit without that rooster goin' for 'im."

"Better not let Mr. Jones hear you laughin' an' talkin' like that." The woman's voice was flat, and sinister in its flatness. Russell, his head pulled into his shoulders, lowered his eyes and continued eating.

"Sit down," he said. "Me mum's made some tea. Wanna cuppa tea?"

"Yes, thanks," I said and sat down at the table, resting my elbows on the greasy soot- and lard-soaked wood. I poured a cup of the strong black tea and spiked it heavily with sugar to counteract the bitter taste. Russell ate and drank loudly and said nothing. His mother, sitting in the darkness, watching us, I supposed, also remained silent. She was a strange, weary, silent, frail bird of a woman, anonymous and beaten down by the world. We had just finished our tea and were rising to leave when Mr. Jones appeared in the doorway, his face and hands scratched and bleeding. He held a bloodied axe, and he was smiling, his long gray face looking as malicious as a mule, his pale eyes flashing bright and rat-like, a curious mixture of pink and silver.

"Russell," he hissed. "I got a job for you, boy."

Russell didn't look at him. He kept his eyes lowered, looking at the tea leaves in his cup, cringing as though waiting for a blow that didn't come. There was a heavy silence in the wagon, punctuated by the sound of flies buzzing and the sound of Mr. Jones's heavy breathing, which came in harsh, asthmatic whistles. He was tall and thin, a brown man in a brown suit and brown hat, with large, bony hands, the fingers stained heavily with nicotine, like his teeth. He bent down toward the boy, who remained frozen at the table. Bent down slowly, but with what seemed the speed of an express train. I smelled his breath, which was warm and sour, as he brought his face level with Russell's, close enough to kiss him. I could see the blemishes on his skin, cancer from too much sun and dirt that was ground into the folds and wrinkles.

"I got a nice job for you, a real labor of love—pluckin' chicken."

"You didn't kill Ben?" His mother's voice was a quavering whisper. Mr. Jones didn't move and didn't answer. He kept staring closely at Russell, his eyes full of a cruel and unaccountable glee. Russell seemed paralyzed. He didn't move for what seemed a full minute. Then he said, mumbling: "Ben was my friend. He hated you for what you did to Ruby-Mae, and for what you did to her dog. You had no need to kill him. He was a good breeder, and he was too old to eat."

"You watch your mouth, son, you hear me," Mr. Jones snapped, his lips turning to string. "An' that dog was no good. Was just a no good mongrel cur. Now you get out there an' pluck that chicken."

Suddenly Russell's paralysis was broken. He let go a wild but accurate punch, short and hard and scientific, that landed squarely on Mr. Jones's long, pointed jaw. The man howled and fell backward, landing on his rear on the floor, still holding onto the axe. He struggled to get up, and as he did so Russell leapt from his chair, over Mr. Jones's head and out the door, landing on his feet in the yard. I sat, rigid and immobile in my chair, staring down at Mr. Jones and not wanting to look at him, wanting to get out, and wondering if I, too, was capable of such a leap. But escape, for me, was out of the question.

Mr. Jones, panting, rose awkwardly. He seemed completely unaware of my presence. He stood, stooped, holding onto the axe, and started to cough.

"You won't catch 'im. He's gone," said the woman. Still, she had not moved, and although my eyes had grown accustomed to the dark, I still could barely see her. Could barely see her in light or darkness. Mr. Jones drove the axe into the floor, splintering the old boards, and was gone, out into the heat and light.

I sat for a moment in a kind of shock, waiting for the woman to say something, but she didn't. I saw the outline of her spectacles reflecting invisible light, saw that she was completely rigid. I stood up and went outside. The beheaded rooster lay in the dust at the foot of the wagon steps, and Russell was nowhere in sight.

HE DIDN'T APPEAR in school for over a week. He had fled downriver, sleeping nights in Aborigine camps, as a result of which he received a blackened eye and a cut lip, as he waited for Mr. Jones to forget, which he evidently did, his beer-soaked brain incapable of recalling events beyond two or three days of their happening. Such explosive confrontations between the man and the boy were common, and they lived through them and forgot about them in the name of simple and tedious habit, thrown together as they were on the free-spinning world of a vast and empty and mindless continent, aware only of the dust they stirred with their feet as they moved across it.

He possessed a recklessness that was as much a point of concern as it was admiration. He did crazy things, like running out directly in front of the school buses as they drove out of town full of farm children. He would stalk a particular bus from a peppercorn tree where he waited, watching it approach and calculating its speed. The tree was a place where the buses were just starting to speed up as they approached the edge of town and the open road. Right as the bus reached the tree, he would dash out in front of it into the red dust stirred by its wheels and the choking black smoke of crippled exhaust pipes and take a running leap, landing, sometimes on his face, on the other side of the street. The bus drivers were all nervous wrecks. They learned quickly to watch out for him, but never knew when he would strike. When they finally identified him with the pepper tree, and began to slow down upon approach, he simply changed his location. Some of the drivers grew irritated and vicious, and tried to run him down, which only increased his sport and that strange, reckless joy, the bus like a ponderous but deadly bull and he an agile and splendid athlete dancing in the dust of the Minoan arena.

The drivers eventually complained about him to the school, and he was reprimanded and put on probation.

I'd walk home with him often. I was his only friend, his teacher, and although I felt rather paternal toward him there was something about him that eluded and fascinated me. It was his wild, curly red hair and the sparkling blue eyes that revealed an otherwise hidden and keen intelligence. No one else seemed to understand him or like him, and it was obvious to everyone that he would not be in school long, maybe two or three months at the most, before he moved along. To most he appeared to have no more than the simple destiny of a chicken thief. It was inconceivable that he was capable of taking giant leaps out of obscurity.

For a while he watched the buses with hungry eyes. He'd stop and stare at them as they passed, his mouth shut tight. Then he'd spit on the ground and start to walk. Although when we first met his face had shown a spark of humor, there was no humor in it at all now.

He became surly and withdrawn, and the other students in the class, boys and girls alike, began to dislike and ostracize him for his look and manner of a beaten and mean dog. A couple of teachers actually appeared to hate him, and were wary of the wildness they sensed in him, his hidden propensity for extreme and reckless acts.

But after the annual sports day at school, they all changed their minds about Russell. At practice he had performed moderately, well enough to make the high jump team, but nothing spectacular. It was believed he had demonstrated the limit of his awkward hop, which was always the target of a lot of laughter.

The girls, especially, would shriek with mockery and amusement, which in turn made the boys laugh louder. Everyone
laughed. Even I laughed. But mine was a laugh of delight at the
comical defiance of his being, at the physical act, which in spite
of everything achieved its purpose.

It was a bright day in winter, clear sky and long shadows,
cold and dry because of a drought. There was a wind, and it
sang in the lip of my Coke bottle as I sat on the grass watching
them all prepare for the final high jump event. Yellow and red
dust rose off the road beyond the green sports field. The bright
winter afternoon made everything—the flat, white faces of the
school buildings, every shadow of every blade of grass and every
tree, the boys and girls in their sports costumes and the flapping, brightly colored flags—unnaturally precise. Joe Phillips
had cleared six feet, five inches. Now Russell stood, staring at
the bar, breathing deeply, and already some of the boys were
laughing, anticipating the clumsy spectacle of his leap. Some of
the teachers were shaking their heads. Russell seemed like an
athletic Don Quixote. He let go a wild shriek and flung his arms
into the air and ran at the bar. It seemed that he was about to
run into it when his feet left the ground. He shot straight up
into the air, bringing his knees to his chest, and sailed over it.
There was a stunned silence, then a gradual, reluctant applause.
When he did it again, this time clearing seven feet and being
declared the uncontested champion of Wallangirrii High, the
applause was loud and spontaneous, for it had suddenly become
apparent to everyone that Russell possessed intangible qualities
that were nonetheless worthy of appreciation.

I went home with him that afternoon. He told me not to say
anything to his mother or Mr. Jones. We went into the wagon
where his mother had made tea, and sat at the table feeling the
warmth from the stove. The tea was there, fresh and hot, but
there was no sign of the woman, nor of Mr. Jones. His older
brother was out working on a nearby farm. Why Russell had
been set aside for schooling, even if it was only for a few
months, was a question whose answer eluded me.

The bottoms were cold and dank in the leveling sun of the late winter afternoon. The evening was approaching, the quick winter dark, and a mist was rising off the river and there was a sweet smell of wood smoke from the cabins and of cow dung. The gloom came down fiercely on the bottoms, the dusk gloom of the gum-tree forest. Far across a field, a man was chopping wood in front of a small, run-down cabin. The cabin looked like a gray, swaybacked beast, lower in the middle than at the ends, and smoke came out of a brick chimney, all of it gray, including the man, against the gray-blue forest. A girl with very blond hair came galloping down the road on a large brown horse. She rode bareback, but with the strength of her thighs she held herself as though she was standing in the stirrups and leaning over the neck of her speeding mount. From the vineyards at the other end of the bottoms came the faint voices of Italians shouting and laughing. There was a man on the road, a tall, thin, hunched silhouette in baggy trousers, a ghost in the near dusk, walking home. And not far behind him a woman, a young Sicilian peasant, moving languidly and straight-backed into the abrupt dark. She turned into the gate of a small, pink, square cement bungalow, and I watched her open the door and go inside from where I sat at the table. Dogs were barking, and from behind us, in a shack I could not see, a man and a woman were having a violent argument.

Russell slurped his tea loudly, smacked his lips, and belched. He searched the cupboards for food, but there was nothing.

"Wonder where the ol' sheila is," he said. "An' good ol' Mr. Jones." He went to the door and looked out. He stood for a moment, staring wide-eyed at the dusk. He seemed far away, and I could've sworn, at that moment, that he glowed in the dark, something kinetic and inexplicable, only seen, vibrant and iridescent. He turned around and looked at me, his face impassive, looking that queer, flushed combination of youthful and old.

"She never goes off by herself. Mr. Jones won't let her. Scared shitless she'll run off. One time, when he went away, he kept us all locked up in a cabin for five days. Woulda bin six if I hadn't busted out, an' I woulda done that sooner 'cept the ol' sheila kept tellin' me not to. Then he came back and roped me to a tree. Beat me bad and then kept me there three days. The old girl couldn't do nothin'. She's scared shitless of Mr. Jones. Says if it wasn't for him we'd all have nothin'."

"Why don't you want to tell them?" I asked.

"Tell 'em what?"

"About your victory today. Your triumph. You're high-jump champion!"

"Me triumph! That little hop? That was nothin'. I can do that backward. The old girl says I'm part kangaroo. No. I'm goin' on to bigger and better things."

"You defied them all. You showed them."

"Showed 'em nothin'. I can jump like that 'cos a somethin' inside meself, somethin' that wants to take off."

"Only one other man I know of ever had that gift. He's dead. You're his successor. It could really take you somewhere."

"Oh, it will." He smiled. He was glowing with renewed radiance, was full of a deep, inner, personal glory. He told me he could go even higher if he didn't succumb to certain urges to deplete himself—a personal act that the health manuals of the time for adolescent youth described as "self-abuse."

"You can do it, too," he said. "Anyone can. You just gotta know it."

I was flattered by this remark, by his inference that I possessed dormant qualities that he, an accomplished flier, was able to recognize.

"Maybe you can teach me," I said.

"Maybe. It's just a question of masterin' what's already inside of yer. People can fly, or could, an' just don't know it. It's a part of man's nature. The Abos know that. They used to fly in the Dream Time. Then somethin' happened. They forgot how to. Maybe they just got lazy like the white people."

He had shown a subtle, silent contempt for his jeering competitors, hearing their laughter, seeing the leering, mocking, wind-reddened faces of the girls. He had strutted about alone on the track, saying nothing as he waited to jump, his pink thighs as skinny as his calves and covered in short, bristling, orange hair, his eyes haunted, brooding, watching them with that look of a hunted and cunning animal, his hands on his hips. And then afterward, walking away, indifferent to their astonished applause. Perhaps more contemptuous and supercilious than ever. It was hard to tell. He simply turned and faced them with that look of a fierce old man, spat on the grass, and retired from the field. He wasn't even there to receive his trophy, but sat melancholy and alone in the locker room reading a book I had given him, a copy of *Huckleberry Finn.*

I realized, as we sat there in the wagon drinking tea, that I was finally getting to know something of him, that he was directed inwardly toward great eternal things. Within him was a deep flow of loose energy waiting to burst through.

He said something about going out to cut firewood, and then I heard a cough and then a soft voice sobbing. Ruby-Mae stood in the doorway. Her soiled red dress was bulbous with her shape and torn around the shoulders, showing her pale, freckled skin. Her round blue eyes were wide and red with crying, her bare knees dirty and bruised. She reached out a trembling hand toward me, sobbing the whole time, and then let the hand drop listlessly to her side. Apart from her pregnancy, she was really thin.

"What is it, Ruby? What's the matter, love?" Russell was on his feet. She shook her head and bit her lower lip and looked down at the floor. She started to cry, her chest and shoulders heaving in deep, gasping sobs.

"What is it? What's the matter?" Russell bent down and took hold of her hand.

"Mr. Jones," she whimpered.

"Where's Mum?"

"Gone . . . Mr. Jones."

She pointed toward the shed. We went outside and it didn't take us long to find Mr. Jones. He was in the shed, lying on his back just inside the door. A chicken, perched on his chest, picked away at the bloody wound on the side of his head.

Russell turned and ran back to the wagon. I stood there, staring down at Mr. Jones. His eyes and mouth were wide open, his features frozen in death. He was cut deep into the temple, a killing blow, and the side of his head and neck were covered in now congealing blood. Blood also coated the chicken's beak. A pair of sheep shears lay in the dust just a few feet from Mr. Jones's head. I chased the chicken off just as Russell came back in carrying a shovel.

"Me Mum did it. Bugger startin' messin' with Ruby-Mae again and this time she did it. She really did it."

He took a long look at Mr. Jones and then started digging.

"You're not going to call the police?" I asked.

"No."

He dug in silence, concentrating on his work. He worked hard for some time then stopped and looked up at me.

"You have to promise me you won't say nothin'. I'll bury 'im, and he'll be forgotten. Gone. That's all. No one of any account will know the difference."

I nodded my head, amazed at what had happened, amazed at Russell, amazed at myself. I could see that he spoke the truth. Mr. Jones's disappearance would barely be noted by the town, if at all. And I felt instantly in league with Russell, bound in conspiracy, protective and secret. There was no way I would bring myself to tell. Outside, flying high in the purple and black of the oncoming night, came the faint voices of swans honking.

I hardly slept at all that night, thinking about Russell and Mr. Jones and what Mr. Jones and Russell's mother had done. A cold wind blew dust in off the Old Man plain, which sprayed the corrugated iron roof of the farmhouse like a fine but persistent rain. The wind put me on edge, along with a bittern that called all night from the gum trees near the house.

Russell was not at school the next day, nor the day after that. So I went down to the bottoms in the late afternoon.

They had abandoned their wagons. A small group of half-caste Aborigines, three men and a woman, had taken up residence in the kitchen. The men sat back inside, in that boxed-in gloom that smelled now of stale, cheap port and tobacco and that other smell, that Aborigine smell. The woman stood up and moved slowly to the door. She had a wide, plump face, with big round eyes, and although her brown hair was streaked with yellow her eyes and skin shone with a dark, lustrous quality in the pale sunlight. She was not too old nor too far gone. She had not thickened around the waist and neck, and her breasts did not sag.

"Those white people 'ave gone. They jus' up and gone." She gestured with her hand. That was all I could get out of her. She folded her arms and leaned her shoulder against the doorway and relaxed into a grave, animal silence, looking at me while the men shuffled about and murmured inside.

I walked over to the shed. The camel was gone and there was no sign of a grave. The ground looked dry and undisturbed. Only he had left the shears. I picked them up and put them in my jacket pocket and walked out onto the road, heading for the river. It was just about dusk. I climbed over the levee and stood at the edge of the high bank, looking out at the wide, dark river, flowing steadily, but unseasonably low. The beam of an old wrecked riverboat, half buried in a sand bar, was now above water, the weeds hanging from it dry and brittle like paper. Exposed snags, once hidden reefs, cluttered the shoreline on both sides, looking like crocodile or hippo in the fading light. I hurled the shears way out into the middle of the stream, marking where it splashed in the deep water near the edge of a sand bank. Then I turned and headed upriver toward home.

Carter's Creek

"WHEN I WAS younger," she said to him, "I kept a diary. But I don't anymore."

Carter had been talking to her about something else entirely, talking, as usual, with the enervating feeling that she was not listening, that discussing anything with her did not help at all. Her listening which was not listening only served to drain him, leaving him tired and empty. He sat at the table watching her self-absorbed examination of her skin—she was perpetually worried about skin cancer, the new plague of the nation.

"You," she said, her eyes now on the backs of her wide-spread hands, "are indestructible. I see you standing alone out here in your own brilliant desert, bathed in sunlight and the clumsy contentment of your flesh. I know you love it here. You love it because everything is yours. I could love it too, if I thought I had something. Lately I feel like we've both lost our old luster. You even think and speak slower now."

He looked at her somewhat bewildered by her comment. He could only think that it had something to do with what she was currently reading. She shrugged and smiled at him.

"I'm sorry. What is it you were saying?" She ran her fingers through her thick yellow hair and then along the back of her neck, feeling for some new evidence of the sun's detrimental effects on her skin.

"I was saying I'm going to swim the river. I know you'll think I'm mad, but I've decided."

"I don't understand the big deal. You do it every day, practically."

"No, I mean—not across it. To swim its length, as far as I can, to the sea, if possible."

"You're talking about a couple of thousand miles of river—a big river. And who'll take care of the place while you're gone? I'm certainly no farmer."

"Bergman will. He's more than capable."

Kris Bergman was a Swede he had hired on as a foreman a year before. Bergman loved the river, the wide open country, strong drink, and women. The place seemed to suit his temperament. It was both harsh and carefree, like Bergman himself. Bergman had managed to add the role of Carter's wife's secret lover to his list of duties on the property. Carter had come upon them in the orchard one night after an evening of drinking together on the veranda. He had retired early, leaving her to indulge in the company of the Swede's drunken charm. Unable to sleep because of the heat he had gone for a walk in the moonlight only to discover their tryst in the red loam furrows between the orange trees. He had said nothing. Bergman did not interfere with marriages or make any private demands. His lighthearted and even humorous womanizing was notorious, and only the stringently pious disdained him for his apparently insatiable appetite. In fact, he managed to make it a part of his irresistibly pagan appeal. For Bergman, life's meaning and joy lay in sedulously following the path of his addictions, and he simply provided his services of a robust and jovially intoxicated satyr to any woman, married or single, who came under the spell of his priapic allure.

It was a one-time affair, as far as Carter could tell, although he preferred to think of it as ongoing. Carter himself had a sloe-eyed Italian girl with long black hair and an hourglass figure who smelled of smoke and catered to his need for exotic and mindlessly voluptuous distraction. A haughty creature who seemed to disdain the company of the other immigrant workers, she was a strange and forbidden fruit that he had immediately wanted to taste when he first laid eyes on her working in the vineyard. Her full breasts swung loosely beneath her white cotton singlet, her dark, ripe olive skin glowed in the sunlight, and he saw the splash of wet black hair in her armpits as she bent over a gnarled and twisted vine. She, also, demanded nothing, allowing him to come and go through the back door of her blue stucco bungalow as his mood suited him, her desire piqued by his prolonged absences, the clandestine nature of their meetings, and the fierceness of their lovemaking.

His wife, Jessica, rapidly crossed and then uncrossed her legs the way she did when they were at some local grower's lawn party, sitting poised and self-conscious, aware that she was an anomaly among the women and that the eyes of all the men were surreptitiously upon her. But they were alone on the veranda, it was morning, and her fragile-looking face, balanced delicately on her slender neck, was looking out across the garden at the distant trees with a weary, blank-faced intensity. Once again she was not listening to him; she seemed to be imagining voices and people who were not there but who somehow held her full attention.

"You must think I'm mad," he said. "It is mad."

"Oh, I'm used to it," she said. "It's your madness that brought us here in the first place. If you want to swim the river then swim the river, but it'll take some managing."

"Managing?"

The listlessness and distance vanished from her eyes.

"You'll need to rest, eat, you could get injured, in trouble, bitten by a snake, things like that. You'll need someone on the shore, ahead of you. And there are those locks that you'll have to get around."

They were miles below the big dam but he had forgotten about the locks, and the resurrected steamboats that plowed the river downstream, catering to a dawning tourist trade.

"You amaze me," he said. "I haven't figured it out logistically yet. It's just the idea."

"I can take the Land Cruiser. It's a good excuse to see the country."

"Do you really want to see it?"

"I'm here, aren't I?"

"But what about the farm?"

"Bergman can manage it. You just said so yourself."

Carter saw the amiable Swede walking up the drive toward the house. Bergman smiled and waved to them, and Carter could see that he was in a jolly mood, probably because of a wild night in town. It was when he abstained from drinking and fornication that the Swede became depressed, his manner surly. A successfully debauched evening always left him merrily assured of his luck, no matter how bad his hangover.

He was hard with the constant exercise of walking over the estate, and red with sunburn. He took his tattered hat off and wiped the sweat from his wrinkled forehead and squinted up at the two of them on the veranda.

"Good morning," Bergman greeted Carter with a self-satisfied smile. Then he smiled and nodded at Jessica, who crossed and uncrossed her legs as she turned toward him in her chair, a teacup poised in her hand.

"How are you, Bergman?" she asked.

"Fine. And you?"

"The same, as always."

"That's good to hear."

"Bergman, I need to talk to you," said Carter, rising from the table. He stepped down from the veranda and for a moment Bergman looked apprehensive.

"We're going away for a while and we need you to run the place. Do you think you can handle it?"

"I don't see why not."

"You can stay in the house, if you like."

"That won't be necessary. I'm comfortable in the cottage."

"Yes," said Jessica. "The cottage is nice."

Bergman flashed his mischievous, blue-eyed, satyr-like grin, and Jessica's face turned bright red at this instant suggestion of some gambit between them. She continued, stumbling, trying to find a way out.

"I mean, it's perfectly livable and all your things are there. I used to stay there myself from time to time—before you came."

Bergman said nothing. He smiled at her mild uneasiness, unperturbed and pleased with himself.

"Have those Italians started on the bottom rows?" asked Carter.

"They're already there—started at dawn."

"Good," said Carter. "Let's go down and check on them."

"I've already been down there," said Bergman.

"Well," said Carter, "it certainly wouldn't hurt if I went down and said good morning. How was your evening?"

"Oh, it was very interesting. I'd almost call it anthropological."

"You can tell me all about it on the way down."

"That's life for you, isn't it Bergman? Anthropology?" said Jessica. She chuckled and drank the last of her tea.

Bergman put his hat on and offered her a departing grin as the two men started off together toward the packing sheds.

In the vineyard Carter watched the Italians work. It was a transporting Mediterranean tapestry against a backdrop of eucalyptus forest broken by the early morning screeching and flight of cockatoos, bathed in a light that was fierce and bright but different from Mediterranean light. There was more of it, like the stars in the nighttime Southern sky. Having lived for a time in the North, he could see the difference distinctly. This was where he belonged, in this realm of minerals and ocean and sun-filled sky. But he was a long way from the ocean, on an isolated vastness of floating land, an inconceivable island that was also a realm of fire. Fire here was like water in a Northern forest; it appeared with the same frequency and naturalness as streams do in a redwood valley, flowing through, something to be crossed. Fire was more than an event; it was a source of renewal, a vital element of the living earth, like rain.

And that much scorched and ancient earth, arid against the sea that surrounded it, beckoned with the offer of riches. It was, in his mind, like an alluring woman who quickly became cruel, giving and then holding back, turning the hard labor of courtship into a sensual punishment of enticement and denial, and even betrayal; an addictive combination that Carter found irresistible. It made an idiot of him while offering a path to wisdom.

More than anything, he wanted, now, to be recognized as a country man, to walk in a way that anyone seeing him would instinctively know that there was something burnt and renewed about his body and posture, something he had merged with that was greater than himself but which gave him a recognizable shape, an integrity and even a certain aura of mysterious knowhow—the aura of a man who had wrestled, like Jacob, with a mystery and survived.

The Swede had left to supervise the laying out of aluminum pipes for watering the trees on another section of the property. More than likely, Carter suspected, he had dropped by the house, was at this very moment performing his duties. It didn't matter. Friendship, Carter had decided, was a stronger bond than connubial fidelity. If Jessica was to leave him for the Swede—well, then, that would be her mistake, and it would never happen. Perhaps it would all lead to a crime of passion, a murder on the farm, the revelation of a scandalous affair. He smiled as he envisioned Jessica as Bette Davis in *The Letter*, shooting Bergman off the veranda and then sending for her husband, who would naively believe in her innocence and protect her virtue—but that, too, would never happen. And it was Carter, not Jessica, who was flirting with danger and dark passions in his affair with a wild and foreign girl.

Would he succeed in going to the very end of the idea—the river? Perhaps it would kill him, the river would take him, swallow him, annihilate him. There were one or two drownings a year, on average. A swimmer would vanish in the current, sucked down in a whirlpool or under a snag. The police would drag the river with a net, sometimes pulling up the body. Sometimes the body was found downriver, washed up. Sometimes the dead had simply disappeared. The locals lived in fear of the river; visitors were warned of its hidden perils, its deceptive force.

That was the challenge, on the surface, but there was a lot more to it than that, but what it was, exactly, he did not know. He would only know when he had done it.

A swarm of bees passed noisily over the vines and disappeared behind the rim of the slope. He could hear the sprays clicking in the distance—Bergman had started watering the trees. He heard the pump start up down on the creek; more of the clicking sprays started up, closer this time. He turned and gazed down toward the creek and the forest directly beyond it.

The creek was a deep inlet formed by the river where it cut around a long island. The island was tree-covered and infested with snakes. Some foxes and a small herd of wild horses also lived there. The water was dark and swift and cluttered with snags. It was named after the property's previous owner and already, in his mind, it had been renamed Carter's Creek in perpetuity.

"Carter!" A lilting female voice called across the field. The other workers, men and women, looked up as the girl, Claudia, strutted toward him, the bangles on her dark wrists rattling and glinting in the sunlight, her naked sandaled feet covered in red dust. She was, for Carter, a consistently remarkable image. She stood with one foot forward and to the side, a hand on her hip, and gazed at him fiercely, her face in a petulant frown.

"You said you were coming last night, and then you never came."

Her voice was raised but hushed, even though the others were out of earshot.

"I fell asleep."

"By yourself?" Her bracelets shook, emphasizing her exasperation.

"I always fall asleep by myself."

"Will you come tonight?"

"Yes. Now go back to—"

He broke off before finishing the command.

She stood there gravely. The heavy eyelids drooped slightly, and she flashed him a sidelong look, keen and sharp like steel. With her head poised and half-turned away, her nostrils distended, she had a look of wild and resentful defiance. She took him in from head to toe in one sweeping glance. Then, suddenly, she smiled, turned, and sauntered away. Some of the men watched her as she passed them, glanced at Carter, and went back to their work. The women began to chatter among themselves. He watched her work at a distance through the shimmering heat waves, as he did every day.

That evening, not long after sundown, Carter left the fields and drove straight to Claudia's bungalow. It was on the edge of the town, down by the river, and surrounded by similar dwellings where Sicilian and Calabrian immigrants lived amidst their trellised gardens and vines on small plots of land.

In the shadows of her house, a single room lit only by a solitary kerosene lantern on the table, she waited for him in her usual manner, her strong back pressed up against a wall, facing the door, her breathing deep and slow, beads of sweat glistening on her skin. She fell upon him as soon as he entered, crushing his mouth with her lips and scratching his neck and tearing at his clothes.

She seemed to have lost all restraint, and he realized it was in keeping with her overtly defiant display in the vineyard that morning. She had virtually made a public announcement of their affair before her coworkers and countrymen, and seemed delighted with the results, however covert. She had punished him for his failure to come to her the night before, and she had brought him back on line. Her pride, as well as the voracity of her feelings, demanded it. And she had defied the traditions and taboos of her people, a tribal enclave with whom she lived and worked by accident while keeping herself contemptuously apart from their tangled allegiances of blood and custom.

The confrontation in the vineyard and the increased wildness of her passion surprised him. She had taken him unawares and astonished him with her unpredictability. It was as if she had invented the whole thing deliberately, for the purpose of playing it out. And she did it with an all-consuming fury and conviction, waiting for him and then pouncing, panting, her eyes glowing out of the darkness like the eyes of a cat reflecting the small flame of the lamp.

She showed, now, an avid and rapt and tireless curiosity for the possibilities of physical love, her body gleaming in the slow shift from one erotic posture to the next. He left her still whimpering for more. Exhausted and empty, his back and neck marked by her nails and teeth and her smell still on his skin, he drove home through a haze of dust and flying insects.

What he saw, as he drove, was not the road but the river, winding before him, dark and wide and cool. That was it: cool. He was thinking to himself, *It's time for me to take the plunge, to move. It's time for me to swim the river.*

Jessica was sitting on the veranda when he returned. Her hair was wet and brushed back and she sat with a burgundy-colored towel wrapped around her bare torso, sipping a gin and tonic, her blue swimsuit in a wet tangle on the floor. She now rarely ventured out during the heat of the day, and these night swims had become routine.

"Bergman was here. He was looking for you." She smiled that small slow smile that, as long as he had known her, men always brought to her lips.

"Did he stay long?"

"Long enough for a drink—and a swim." She grinned and rattled the ice in her glass and then pressed it to her flushed cheek and watched him as he sat down. He smelled the sweet coconut odor of her skin lotion.

"You're lucky you didn't drown," he said.

"Let's hope you're so lucky."

"Let's hope."

He poured himself a gin and tonic from a pewter ice-bucket on the table and added an olive to it. He had to admit that she was civilized, effortlessly maintaining the small details of her standards, even out here.

"I told Bergman what you're planning to do." Her pale green gaze was fixed on him, coolly alert and strangely hungry.

"Oh, what did he say?"

"He said fine, why not. Only he thought you should find someone else to drive the Land Cruiser—that the journey is long and hot and that ultimately I wouldn't like it."

"He may be right."

"I told him that he was absolutely wrong, that I was going to love it. You are serious, aren't you?"

"Yes, I'm serious."

"Good. It's been a while since we had an adventure together."

"You'll be alone all day."

"What's so new about that?"

"Nothing at all."

"I've been looking at the map, and there are some nice little towns where we can stay together."

"How do you know they're so nice?"

"By their names. And I can make camp along the river. Have it ready for you at the end of the day—waiting."

"It's an interesting concept."

"I can do it if you can."

He sipped his drink and sat back and listened to the sprays clicking and hissing in the orchard directly behind the house. She uncrossed and crossed her legs and turned sideways in her chair, showing him the smooth muscular curve of her thigh outlined by a horizon of short, fine golden lanugo, her skin lightly bronzed by a cautious tan and unblemished except for a small bruise just below her hip. She saw that he was studying her and smiled and reclined languidly back, shifted slightly, and held her glass poised in front of her lips.

"Did you have a good swim?" he asked.

"Yes. It was wonderful. But I'll tell you, for a Viking, Bergman is hopeless in the water. I think he might even be a little afraid of it."

"Perhaps that's why he's here—because he's a Viking in disgrace."

"Perhaps." She laughed and rattled the ice in her glass and looked away from him, out at the night, while she took a slow drink.

HE HAD WANTED IT done quietly, secretly. He had calculated the journey on the map and she had agreed to meet him at or near various towns along the way. At times she might be able to follow him along the river, but for the most part she would be on main roads and he would be alone, isolated in bush country, relying on the river to deliver him to the appointed destination. If he didn't arrive she would wait, and then go looking. It was not without hazard or risk, but it was a risk he insisted on taking. It was the way he wanted it done—alone. He would go as far as he could.

The lower portion of the property bordered a strip of gum tree forest and a narrow white sand beach on a bend in the river. It was from here that he entered the water. Jessica stood on the sand, her eyes hidden behind dark sunglasses, and watched him from beneath her white cloth hat as he swam out into the middle of the stream.

The river was smooth and flat, the current swift and green. It swirled around him and then it grabbed him, pulling him into it and carrying him along. He looked back over what now seemed a vastness of dark sparkling water and saw her standing there, and then she disappeared behind the trees as the river swept him steadily and rapidly around the wide bend. He saw the pumphouse of a neighbor's farm, and marked the spot on the high bank from where he had seen the sunken wagon during the last drought, the old wooden-spoked wheel bearded with streaming weed and barely visible beneath the surface, and entered a long straight stretch of deep water known as the Dead River.

The midstream of the river was wider and darker here and the current immediately gained momentum. It was here that many of the drownings occurred, and it was his first test, full of dangerous eddies and hidden snags that created unexpected whirlpools and crosscurrents.

Gradually he got used to its speed, to being propelled so hastily forward while learning how to avoid being sucked under. He allowed the current to take him, swimming, gliding, and then riding it almost like a horse while he concentrated on staying afloat.

The current, as he rounded the bend, had swept him in toward the bank. He passed quickly over a hidden log, missing its surface by inches except for a minor scrape to the knee. He had barely cleared it when he was seized by an eddy and spun around and thrown sideways into a protruding branch. The fallen tree was enormous and as treacherous as any maritime reef. He hit the branch hard, scratching his ribs as the current gurgled and frothed around him and then grabbed him once again, whipping him around the branch and sucking him forward, tumbling as he struggled to regain control.

The great sinuous mass of moving water carried him relentlessly onward. It had looked, when he first laid eyes on it, almost perfectly motionless and flat. It looked like you could walk on it, and it wasn't until you were in it that you realized it possessed motion beneath its deceptive and almost demure surface. It was green like clouded jade, darker here, lighter there, its smooth skin creased and wrinkled and billowing in places like a huge silk cloth unraveling and twisting before him. He stretched out in it and started to swim, feeling its soft and cool embrace as he became one with its flow and tried to overcome the river's instant surprise. He had swum across it almost daily for the last three summers, and believed he had come to know it. But this time it had greeted him with something other than his daydreams, immediately humbling him with the serious business of learning to ride it.

He was now directly in the main stream, holding a steady course and moving easily and swiftly with the current. He turned onto his back and spread out his arms, and thus suspended, a piece of the river's flotsam significant only to himself, he floated down and away, rounding the next bend and leaving the Dead River and his old world behind.

He passed a black camp—a series of shabby huts between the trees. A woman in a mud-fringed faded yellow dress spotted him and watched the river carry him by, her eyes squinting beneath her bat-wing hand. He heard her call out as he turned into the next bend. He saw occasional cattle lumbering through the trees. A flock of white cockatoos screeched as they flew directly over him and a black swan spread its wings and took off low over the water, gliding into the shadows along the opposite bank. Then he was alone once again. In the insect-buzzing stillness of the deep forest, a dog started barking. By the end of the day he would be thinking of the gum tree forest as a wall of trees that shut the river off from the world, and then, later, as an endless tunnel of trees (already he was starting to feel that first strange inkling of suspended time, of trance), but that was not yet. A dog was barking, strangely alone and plaintive, echoing across the water. The barking became shrill, excited. And then he saw it on the bank, a yellow dog like a dingo. It seemed to sense or see his eyes and immediately the barking stopped and it started running along the bank, following him.

By mid-afternoon he was waterlogged and tired. The sun glared off the water, and he needed shade and rest before continuing on. A beach presented itself directly around a bend and he swam toward it. He had not yet reached the first appointed stop with Jessica, and he did not know how much further he had to go before he found her.

The dog was still with him. He saw it standing on the bank where it sloped down to the beach, looking down at him as he swam slowly for the shore, the current carrying him sideways.

He reached the muddy shallows at the edge of the sandbar. The water here was still and tepid and brackish and cluttered with weeds. He stood up, knee deep in the water, the sun burning his shoulders and back. He was almost blinded by the river's glare. He felt totally saturated by the heat and light, floating in it like a mirage as he had floated in the river. Fingerlings nibbled his ankles as he walked toward the shore.

He saw the red-brick ruins of a large farmhouse through the trees, set well back from the water. It was a broken and desolate monument to persistent, harsh struggle and eventual failure. The thick crumbling walls, built as a Victorian fortress against the heat and the land, were now toppled and abandoned. The early settlers here had described this country as a place of glaring heat, impenetrable bush, deadly snakes and giant lizards. Homesteads like this were constructed as stark and solid outposts of colonial civilization, erected as stone buttresses against the harsh and overwhelming countryside. Settlements and communes had risen in successive waves of obscurity, one after the other, and one after the other had vanished, leaving behind remnants of their secret history, naked testimonies to the alien and fearsome nature of the land to these early pioneers.

There was a sudden, almost indiscernible motion in the water all around him. It shuddered, disturbed, and then a loud, high-pitched whining filled his ears, shattering the bright stillness, and a thick black cloud of mosquitoes rose up and enveloped him. He was blinded by the whirring mass. A thousand needles immediately pierced his skin. They stung viciously, much larger than ordinary mosquitoes, biting even his lips and nose and eyelids and ears. He staggered back and turned and dived under the water, swimming out toward the cool deep of the river.

He emerged panting at the far end of the beach, where it narrowed and dropped away beneath the shadows of some large, drooping gum trees. He collapsed onto his knees in the shade and lay down and almost immediately fell asleep, his breathing heavy, the bourdon of cicadas ringing in his ears and filling his brain like a narcotic.

He was awakened by the frenzied yapping of the dog. He opened his eyes and sat up and saw it, only feet from where he lay, engaged in a mongoose-like battle with a large tiger snake. He sat there frozen in rigid disbelief and fear. The snake was coiled back, its head high, poised and swaying, hissing as it lunged. The dog darted back and forth, throwing up sand, fighting skillfully, with knowledge of its enemy. The snake lunged and the dog caught it between its teeth and shook its head vigorously, breaking the reptile's neck.

It dropped the still writhing serpent at its feet, sniffed it, pawed at it, jumped back with a short, spry leap, and then edged cautiously forward and sniffed it again. Then it stood there, panting, its tongue out, watching him with intense curiosity. He reached out and called to it. It growled and lowered its head and shied back. Then in one swift movement it snatched the dead snake up in its jaws and bounded off into the forest.

It was only after the dog had vanished that he was startled and then amazed by the fact that it had saved his life. He became mildly elated and stood and plunged back into the river.

He swam into the brightness of the afternoon, the forest casting a band of shadow along either bank, the main channel glimmering green and golden. The river twisted and turned, winding endlessly so that except for the current he lost all sense of any direction. He knew that he was basically headed southwest, but the river's wild meanderings created a sense of confusion, like a maze. The sun would suddenly shift at any given point, moving all over the sky. He imagined that he was in the coiled intestine of some huge primordial beast, a leviathan lying dormant in a glittering sea, its back scarred by the wind and sun.

The wall of trees on either side gave him no sense of change or distance. Not even the occasional camps of bush shanties and itinerant settlements and a bridge he passed under near the outskirts of a small town broke the monotony. There was only the ceaseless and steadily forward motion of the river through the gray-green forest. His body submerged and engrossed, he knew the river would take him where he needed to go. He was one with its implacable and irresistible flow. If he so desired, it could even determine his fate. He could submit totally to its omnipotent force. But he was not just drifting along. The river was now his chosen path to happiness or disillusion, to success, failure, or extinction. The outcome, he realized as he swam, was up to him. He stretched out to his full length, his strokes became concentrated and vigorous but timed, even, swimming now as he would in a prolonged race, bent on maintaining a sustained effort of athletic power, form, and grace.

To ride the river, to swim with the stream, to be carried along while navigating its hidden reefs and avoiding wrongful turns, took an equal match of skill and strength. He was in the midst of paradox, physically and mentally absorbed in a secret drama of both action and contemplation, concentrating on his breathing and the flow of energy through his body. It was as though he knew what would happen, but was obsessed with the question of why it would happen, which made what would happen unforeseen. It was a delusion of thought, he decided, brought on by being so long in the water.

Now memories of growing up on the river and of the people he knew then and of leaving came to him in flashes as he swam. As a boy he had always felt that he was not one of them, but was a spy in their country. He lived among them covertly. There was nothing outwardly about him that could justify or rationalize this feeling; it was just there, always. He left. He became a wanderer, in an exile he freely chose, a spy wherever he was—in Europe, America, Asia. There were special women he had loved, all different, who had unknowingly conspired and abetted his secret mission. There were those who were conscious of their role and who delighted in their mystery. Each one had taken him somewhere, had been both portal and guide into some complex and foreign region of habit and place, flesh and blood manifestations of a greater passion for both geography and culture. Those who provided no map, no insight and challenge, no language or bridge, no secret possibilities, were quickly forgotten. Carter the traveler, the adventurer, became the passionate but ruthless connoisseur of women and the people and settings in which he found them. With each one—there were five important ones before Jessica (his homecoming)—he had had the firm conviction of settling down, of plunging in, that he was now spoiled for all other women. But the realm of possibilities was always greater than he realized. Always he had moved on, ultimately freewheeling and restless, unable to linger or turn back.

It was years before he returned and there was much in between, much that he now was, and there was Jessica and the orchard and the vineyard, and then there were those others he was swimming away from. But he was also swimming toward something, back toward where he had started.

Then suddenly the current had him, was pulling him toward something. He looked up and saw that he had been swept in close to a high perpendicular bank and was in deep, dark, and swirling water that was dragging him swiftly toward a giant snag. He slammed into it, the water boiling against him. He clung to it with his arm and reached out for a branch. The wide smooth trunk was coated in green slime and weed. He slipped and was instantly dragged under, his feet in front of him, looking upward at the thick, solid shadow looming above him as he was sucked beneath the massive log. His feet hit a submerged limb. He turned sideways and twisted around and reached out and grabbed it. There was still enough room to clear the snag. He slipped between the trunk and the branch and immediately the current pushed him forward, hurling him along as he struggled to the surface, passing over still more logs and tangled dead branches that formed spiraling eddies and hidden undertows in the dark torrent.

His head cleared the water and he gasped for breath, gulping wide-mouthed at the air. He seized the overhanging wooden root of a large tree and hung clinging to it, exhausted, the current dragging his legs. He held on for a moment only, just long enough to catch his breath, and then let go, submitting to the current but bent on deliverance.

He was swept rapidly down and around, spinning in the sudden vortex of a whirlpool as it congealed into the main current and carried him back into the great steadily moving aggregate of the river.

It had made him terribly weak, but slowly he felt some surge of strength returning. He started to swim, just enough to steer himself, and rounded the next bend well out in the middle of the stream. The sun was setting behind the trees, outlining dark twisted shapes against a red sky. A ribbon of orange and gold broke the encroaching twilight gloom of the forest upon the water.

He saw a small fire flickering in the shadow of the bank, straight ahead on a thin pale stretch of beach, and there was a welcome smell of cooking smoke. Dusk was departing and the river was quickly becoming engulfed in deep shadow. The evening sounds of frogs and crickets and calling birds erupted all around. A fish splashed in front of him, and then another, off to the side. Something slithered by his face and then he saw a black snake swimming quickly away, winding furiously for the bank. Another fish jumped, flopping heavily and slowly as it turned in the water, not quick and flippant like the two before it and he knew it was one of those possible giants of the river, a large Murray cod. He knew its sound, different from the smaller fish, from another dusk on the river, when the Big One had taken his line and he had felt its weight and heard its voluptuous splash.

He turned and started breaststroking for the shore, still upstream from the fire, calculating the flow of the current as it carried him toward the beach.

Jessica was waiting on the sand, squatting barefoot on her haunches and feeding the fire with sticks she had gathered. There was an iron skillet on the fire, and the sound of sizzling meat. She stood up as he rose from the water. She was dressed in an unbuttoned khaki shirt and wide short pants.

"Well," she smiled, and brushed a stick at some insects darting around her face. She was radiant and fresh in the firelight. Her skin gleamed beneath the loose shirt and her hair was wet and still unbrushed. "You finally made it. Did you see any platypus?"

He told her that he had seen very little.

IF SHE HAD been apprehensive, worried, and then earnest, as she proceeded to tell him she had been, it had all immediately vanished at the first sight of him. It was not in her nature to express surprise where he was concerned. She listed her emotions as she had waited for him with a blithe and almost careless detachment, insisting that he know about them while avoiding any display of anxiety or relief. Although she pretended to be simply glad that he had arrived in time for dinner, tenderness was returning to her with humility and her weakness was delectable. Human relationships for her, and this one in particular, demanded daring. And here was the little fire she had made, the comforting camp in this lovely spot on an elbow of the river. It was a very human fire filled with sympathy and warmth and brilliance, a marker that had brought him safely to her. She had gotten lost at one point along a bush track and then came upon this beach and decided to chance it and bivouac in the hope that he would surface. He did not tell her about the current or the snags, nor even about the dog and the snake, remarking only in passing that there had been a few tough stretches, it was his first day, tomorrow would be better, he would be ready, he would swim with that third eye of alertness forever open. He didn't say anything about being lucky.

Lying on his back he was dazzled, if not in the end delirious with stars. Her hair swung down in his face, smelling of the river, and her dark slender shape, shuddering in a spasm of flexing muscle as she mounted him, was crowned by this glittering firmament. The nighttime scent of eucalyptus cajoled the air; a mere touch of light lay on the water, a faint shimmering membrane upon the darkness. Jessica's soft, steady panting mingled with low calls and whoops, the muffled noises of the river's secret life.

An eternity of days seemed to open before him when he awoke to nothing but the river, and he felt a new, diffident respect for his surroundings. Most personal hopes and fears had been quickly reduced to little account, and the past had been forgotten. The last stars clung to a white sky. Light had fallen upon the river, but the beach remained in shadow.

The sun rose above the tree tops, its warm rays slowing flooding the sandbank. Jessica stretched and awoke beside him and immediately threw off the blanket and scrambled to her feet. She appeared rested and full of vigor. She put on her shirt and hat and scrambled up the beach to the trees, where she squatted and urinated in the sand. She smiled at him, her chin rested on her hand, her elbow on her knee, and then stood up and ambled back and set about rebuilding the fire. He sat up and looked at the flat surface of the water, smooth and shining like glass, flowing steadily by, and his body shivered and ached, reluctant to move. The night, remarkably, had passed without incident. Nothing had intruded upon his sleep, not even a mosquito, and it was that sleep that he longed to return to.

But she had lingered in this place long enough, and was anxious to be on her way. They ate breakfast in silence, filled with the day's anticipation. Slowly his strength returned; his body became fully conscious and flexible; the soreness and fatigue subsided. They bathed together, washing their bodies with soap, then took a short swim before he helped her break camp and load the Land Cruiser, kissed her goodbye, and dived head first into the water where the shallow bar was cut away by the deep emerald current.

For a time he could see her, following him along the bank, trailing a cloud of dust. Then the track veered away from the river and he saw only a thin haze of settling dust beneath the trees and heard the whining and grinding of the Land Cruiser in low gear grow faint and then disappear entirely.

It was replaced almost immediately by the drone of a small outboard motor that came and went upon the water, softened by distance. Then it came again and he saw the boat appear around the bend, coming toward him in the middle of the stream.

It was a small, flat-bottomed skiff of a type common on the river, the motor spewing curling threads of black smoke. An old man was at the tiller, seated low in the stern. That is, he assumed the man was old—from the distance it was impossible to really tell his age, nor for that matter if the figure was a man, white or black—but something in his dress and the way he sat

upon the river told him that he was old and that he was a fisherman and that he was in his familiar and regular haunts. Carter
had not yet gone far enough downstream to meet any steamboats or other river traffic. The river had been his solely, alone,
suspended in its dream and the dusty gold of distance. Once in
the water, he had abandoned, temporarily, the middle regions of
the human. He was testing his powers, caught in a wavering
flight above the depths, neither in the whirling blue sky above
nor in the field below. So the old boatman coming toward him
was, in his mind, a shadowy figure, more spectral than real,
some sentinel of a guarded realm emerging out of the morning
brightness upon a wandering intruder.

The illusion did not last long. Soon the boat, the prow sitting flat in the water and cutting a gentle glittering wake, was
slowly bearing down on him.

"You alright?" The old man was leaning sideways and peering over the gunwale as the bow slid by within feet of him. He
cut the engine and pulled out an oar and allowed himself to
drift, looking at Carter with a mixture of curious concern and
mildly hostile astonishment. His heavily lined face was long and
gaunt and the color of a burnt brick beneath the wide haggard
brim of his brown hat, his cheeks stained with tobacco-colored
blotches of benign skin cancer. His pale blue eyes were small
and round and close together, staring down at Carter like an
ibis stalking a fish in the shallows.

"Yes," said Carter. "I'm fine. How are you?"

"As good as I can be."

"I'm glad to hear it."

"Whatchya doin' here?"

"Swimming."

The old man nodded.

"You're not from around here."

"I might be."

"No you're not. You're not from here. Be careful in the
river."

"Thanks. I am."

"You better keep an eye out for Old Billy. He's been causin' trouble with people down here lately."

"Who is he?"

"No one knows. That's his trick. A very clever bloke. Some think they've seen him. He's like a bunyip. He haunts these parts. They've been lookin' for 'im ever since he killed a young Abo girl with an axe."

"Why is he called Old Billy?"

"That's what he's called, like namin' the devil. Anythin' bad 'appens down 'ere, you can bet it was Old Billy."

The old man stood up and leaned down and pulled the engine's starter chord with a steady jerk. The motor coughed and then started, propelling the boat forward against the current. He sat down and turned his back and took hold of the tiller. The two parted company swiftly, moving away in opposite directions, the flat swirling water glimmering like a sheet of mica.

Carter turned and swam on. He passed a large group of sagging tin huts and the rusted shells of several wrecked cars and then what looked like the gray mounds of a rubbish tip through the trees. A mile or so beyond the tip a small town hugged the riverbank behind a levee, after which he passed beneath a high wooden bridge. Then there were orange groves and vineyards clustered on gentle slopes of red sand, after which the forest continued, larger and denser now, and he knew he had entered the great gum tree forest and that after it the river would gradually change, cutting a wide and high sandstone ravine into country that would grow forever sparser as it opened up into mallee scrub and desert. How long it would take to see the change, or if indeed he would last long enough to see it, he did not know.

He had thought, possibly, that he might have seen Jessica on the bank in front of the town, but there was no sign of her. He wondered about Old Billy and the bird-eyed boatman and the murdered Aborigine girl. The riverbanks were low here and the trees older and broader. The forest seemed to rise around him, casting long morning shadows that closed in on him from either side.

The country here was no different from the country he had passed through the day before. There was the same endless tunnel of drooping, sinuous trees—the same bush, the same water, the same sky, the same flocks of parrots, the same scattered camps and shanties along the riverbanks. But somehow it was different, imperceptibly at first, more a feeling than an actual vision.

He passed the ruins of an old sawmill, overgrown by the forest, and then a small settlement of wooden huts, possibly left over from the mill, where some people were still living, the dull routine of their existence sustained by the river, with no need for haste anywhere under the sun and a sense of days filled with things no more significant than the rasping of insects.

Rounding the next bend he encountered a group of bathers on a wide beach. They were mostly teenagers and women with young children from a nearby town, rollicking and splashing about in the mid-morning sun. They did not seem to notice him—to them he was just another swimmer, one who had ventured far from the shore—and their shrieks and cries quickly faded into memory as he was carried around the next turn. The bank here was lined with willow trees, bright green against the muted blue and gray-green of the forest, and he could see red-tiled rooftops and a few palm trees beyond the levee, and a pumphouse and jetty down on the river. And then silence, and once again nothing but the river, broad and sparkling, putting out his eyes as it flowed directly into the sun so that everything else looked black or blanched to near invisibility.

A speedboat appeared out of the glare, churning loudly and rapidly upstream, a water-skier in tow. He waved so that they would see him. The boat swerved and shot by him, swamping him in its frothy surge. The skier, a deeply tanned girl in a red bikini, came right at him. He dived, the current sweeping him along, as she passed directly overhead. He surfaced to see her back, her hair flying, strong brown legs stiffly apart, the water boiling in her wake. She swung out in a wide arc and disappeared around the bend, heading for the beach.

He started to swim, sliding swiftly through the water, buoyed and driven by the current. The sensation of the current, of gliding so smoothly and swiftly with it, was intoxicating. He swam steadily on, anxious to be away from the townspeople and back into the lonesome self-absorption of the river.

The sight of the girl, and perhaps even the near miss, made him think about Jessica. Last night, on the beach, they had become lovers once again, and now, suddenly, his body ached with the memory of her. He started swimming the river in earnest determination, lunging forward with wide, heavy strokes and kicking steadily, his whole body, head and neck and arms and lungs and feet, working as one. He kept it up for a long time. How far or how long, he did not know, but he was now in a marathon, swimming without pause or break toward the long shadows of the dusk and his appointed rendezvous. He felt that he was almost sailing along the water's surface. He rounded a bend and looked up and saw, ahead of him, the Land Cruiser parked in the deep shadows of the trees above the rim of a small beach.

It was the first time he had bothered to stop and drift and look around. It was the middle of the afternoon and the river was cloaked in a blanket of heat and light. He had been swimming in a tireless and uninterrupted trance for hours. Immediately he sensed remoteness, distance. And something new and strange that made him shudder with expectation. They were now deep into the bush, with nothing but wild pigs and cattle and emus and kangaroos for miles around. Jessica stood on the beach, near to the water's edge. She was in the full glare of the sun, the water sparkling at her feet. He wondered why she had stopped. As he swam toward her she was, for him, like a Siren calling from the shore. His feet touched a sandbar and he stood up, thigh deep in the water. She took off her sunglasses and parted her lips slightly, as though about to say something, but no words or sound offered themselves. There was only her look, waiting for him in this unanticipated place. She spoke as he started to wade toward her.

"There was this man, a few miles back."

"How far back?"

"I don't know. It doesn't matter, it was quite a way. Too far to remember." She put a hand on her hip and her body relaxed, bending one knee slightly. "I just decided to stop. It's time to stop, anyway, and enjoy the evening."

He reached the shore and put his hands on his knees and breathed deeply.

"Tell me about the man."

She looked at him and smiled.

"Just an old swagman in the bush, miles back. I don't know why I mentioned it." She looked around and sighed with delight. "This feels like the perfect spot," she said.

She would be there on the bank at every stop until he quit. He straightened up and turned and looked at her. She was still smiling at him, a soft, sad smile, her skin darker and her eyes brighter than he had remembered. Behind her the river flowed on into the sun, winding flat and shining, a long way down through this portion of Australia.

The Reign of Frogs

SHE DECIDED it was the old river spirits, with their shaggy and vaporous and sometimes twilight human forms, that tricked you and got you lost. She felt a cold weight on her abdomen. It shifted and she awoke, alone, on an old straw mattress that smelled of stale wet ashes and rotting leaves. It was raining—still raining, she thought. Somewhere in her mind it had been raining, it had started to rain, and she, they, were in the bush, near the river, and it was night. Someone had been with her, but then went away. She was alone. It had been warm at first, there had been a smell of dust in the darkness, clinging, dry. Now everything was wet and dripping. They had been together in the hut. Or had they? It had all started in the hut. They had gone there together, had walked through the bush along a trail in the moonlight. There was a lantern. Its light cast shadows on the walls, lit up sections of limbs, muscle, a face, like gleaming blotches of bright flesh-colored paint. Like those garish and fetishist paintings on black velvet she had seen on a wall somewhere. She did not remember the face she saw, coming at her like a mask. And now she did not really remember the path in the moonlight, the shadow breathing beside her. The shadow that suddenly covered the moon. The rain that fell abruptly, without announcement. The hut was the beginning, but of what she did not know.

Gray light fell in through the open door, the rain pelted the ground, and pale gray mud flowed in over the flattened dry leaves on the floor. She moved to rise and a large toad leapt from her stomach. She screamed and sat up and watched it hop out through the pool of water that stretched beyond the doorway. She felt empty, without memory, and had a nauseating sensation of having consumed too much alcohol. Her legs dragged off the mattress. She lay half across it, as though she had been flung there, and her dress was damp and muddied and torn open at the neck.

There was a wind, blowing hard against the hut, gusting across the door, howling in the trees. Why had she not heard it before in her sleep, or as she awoke? Somewhere in the distance, a long way away, she could hear the continuous lowing of cattle. Thunder rolled and cracked, tremendously loud. Sheet lightning flashed, filling the gray air. Her back and shoulders ached, and her face was hot, throbbing. She stood up painfully and looked out the door as it began to rain even harder. There was nothing but meaningless bush, thrashing trees, blurred in the rain. She turned and looked around the hut.

She was halfway between dreaming and daydreaming. The hut was a small, rudimentary wooden shack, with nothing but a stained and tattered mattress and a few rusted and blackened pots and pans scattered over the floor, along with a few black pieces of cutlery half-buried in the tan-colored leaves. The lantern hung from the small broken branch of a rough-hewn pole. It, too, was rusted, its glass grayed and blackened with soot. The corners of the roof were cluttered with ancient spider webs that were filled with dust and dry insects. She looked at the lines of her hands, trying to remember. There had been a room full of people. Dancing. A man, someone she knew. The intoxicating smell of a garden. Roses and frangipani, a strange and sweet mix, thick and pungent. The odors, she remembered, clashed. Sweetness commingled with sweetness, filling the air, each one fighting to overwhelm the other. Then the dusty beams of headlights on the wide gray trunks of trees. The dry metallic scrape of drooping leaves. The eyes of small wild animals flashing red and green and iridescent. A sudden jolt and turn. A thick swirling cloud of fine talcum-like dust. A fleeting vision of a kangaroo, the same color as the dust, materializing as it bounded across their path. The memory of a road. Large, dark, and hairy hands firmly clasping the black steering wheel. And then the road again, the trees, the overhanging leaves, the settling dust, the truck, but no memory of getting into it nor of her destination. He was someone she wanted to forget, had forgot. There were only fragments, dismembered parts of him, glowing, floating out of the darkness; faceless, male.

Somehow she knew that she had been betrayed, that being here was part of the betrayal. There had been a scene of monstrous delight and jealousy, secretly played out, that was now only a feeling, a lingering sensation in her body. The rain, so unexpected and torrential, was portent of the change, the crisis, and it had left her stranded without knowledge or memory of where she was or what had happened.

Another toad hopped in by her feet. She froze and looked down it at with fascinated horror, seeing its gray and green mottled skin, the black onyx eyes full of thin jagged yellow lines, the sound of the rain filling her ears. It blinked, its body swelling, and turned and hopped out again. She watched it as it leapt away into the bush, wondering if it was the same one as before. The raindrops were thick and heavy, and she heard them splashing loudly below the wailing of the wind.

Where had she been? The road grew dim in her mind, and she tried to remember it, to hang onto it, in order not to lose it and forget who she was. There was somewhere the vague memory of terrible pain inside her chest, of breathless anguish, but it passed into numbness. She shivered, feeling the wind blow cold through her damp dress, and put her arms across her breasts and moved away from the door. She backed into the center of the hut and then stopped and looked all around her, glancing quickly at the roof, the walls, the crooked, broken-toothed yawn of the window. She had to get out of there. She couldn't stay in this place, but she was trapped. The rain had caught her, come down on her, vengeful and grieving. It had shut her off in a netherworld, a damp limbo that made her think that perhaps she had died and was dreaming.

After a while the wind died down, and then the rain stopped as suddenly as it had started. She stood perfectly still and listened to the dripping silence of the bush. The lowing of the cattle had ceased, and a terrible hush had descended. She decided to step outside, to see if she knew where she was.

All around the broken forest rose out of a shallow swamp that reflected pale light and long shadows. She thought she recognized the path along which she had come, a narrow winding gap in the trees, and decided to follow it. Suddenly, as she walked, she heard the scattered sound of frogs. Then their voices erupted in a deafening cacophony all around her, as though responding to her presence. She stopped and looked around. Her heart was pounding, her skin covered in goosebumps, and she didn't know why. And then she saw them, their moist round protruding eyes looking up at her, their throats palpitating softly. First one, and then two, and then what seemed like thousands of small, dark glistening forms leaping and splashing about in the mud, the earth convulsing with the unleashed deluge of their frenzied awakening.

They flowed through the forest in a wide, teeming river, their wanton and rabid croaking filling the air, reverberating through the trees and drowning out all other sound. The cold pulsating mass of amphibian bodies, a wild flood of burnished and tenebrous arms and legs and throbbing air-bloated torsos, covered the ground, moiling and blundering around her feet.

She was about to turn back to the hut when she saw the truck parked across the trail ahead of her, on the side of a road that was now a stream of liquid brown mud. It leaned sideways into a small ditch and its wheels were almost half-buried in the mud and water. A few frogs had leapt onto the cabin and were dark and clear against the red-painted hood. She started toward it, her bare feet splashing through shredded nylons, frogs springing away across her path, closing ranks behind her.

She had not quite reached the cabin door when she saw the man lying face down in a pool of water off to the side of the trail. Frogs hopped across his back and wallowed between his legs. Blood stained the pale yellow water around him and had started to mix in with the clouded silt. She stopped and gazed down at him, seeing him without face or hands or feet, but the rest of him, from the back, apparently whole except for the wound. She kneeled down and turned him over. He was heavy and lifeless, and flopped onto his back like a huge dead fish. She did not recognize his face, half-covered with mud that was almost the same color as his skin, and neither did she attempt to wash it off. The lips were visible, and seemed curled in an expression of disgust at the muddy water that flowed out of the corner of his mouth. A rusted carving knife was planted in the middle of his chest, and the rust, now, flowed from the blade and mingled with his blood.

She stood up and continued to stare down at him, at the object in his chest and at the unknown and only half-revealed face. He had been with her on the path and in the hut. There had been someone else before that, a woman emerging from a crowd, passing out of the light, coming near to them, not revealing herself but revealed. There was the smell of her perfume. The whirring of her transparent wings. The garden. Somehow she knew him, and that the woman was her enemy, hovering in the air like a giant hornet in her metallic green dress, menacing the boundaries of a secret place. She knew, also, that she and the man would be missed, and that her husband would be out looking for her. There was more light now and she could see the frogs clearly, swarming across the muddy road, hopping about between the shadows, perched on logs, filling the entire bush.

The Quiet Murmur
of the River

THE RIVER was bright in the late afternoon and we were blinded and burnt and tired from being on it all day. We came up out of the glare of the beach into the thick scented shadows of the great gum trees, walking home. I was with my sister. We had been silent together for most of the day, alone on the river, swimming and basking in the sun; and now as we walked through the trees she said she would be leaving tomorrow and that I would be alone with the two of them but that I was now old enough to no longer be terrorized by our mother and besides I had never been as terrorized as she had been. I was an afterthought, a latecomer, an outsider born on the periphery of the conflict that defined the lives of my older brother and sister and mother and father. She had protected me over the years as best she could, receiving most of the blows, although she admitted that I had taken my fair share. We both had scars to prove our point. She had high hopes for herself, and for me too, but now it was time for me to go it alone. She was leaving and I, five years younger, was going to have to stay for a while longer.

We left the forest and crossed the road and went up through the orchard toward the house. I stopped to let her cross the little bridge over the irrigation channel, in the deep shade of the poplar trees. The smell of newly watered red loam and fallen rotting oranges and the sharp aroma of eucalyptus coated our lips like the odors of a hot kitchen. We came out of the shadows into the last bright sunshine. The low rays pierced our skin and cast long, deep shadows. We both stopped for a moment, as though the dying sun's rays would cleanse and fortify us against the deep shadows of the house the dusk had now determined we must enter.

We came in out of the brown yard through the kitchen door, she first as always, ready to meet the evening. I was right behind her, suddenly nervous, all of my senses alert. The wire-screen door banged shut behind us. The colors of the kitchen were raw and vivid in the electric light. Our mother was at the stove, her face red, glistening with perspiration, her thick red hair fallen over her face. She was sweating and angry at her work, even as she took pleasure in it. Often, in her tirades, she called herself the little red hen. She seemed to suffer continually, not born for this land, a pale-skinned redhead, perhaps a beauty, but born for fog and rain and green, hilly country.

"Well, you're back," she said, looking up and greeting us. "I hope you're ready for dinner."

"Yes," said my sister, "We're ready."

"You've been gone all day."

"We've been on the river."

"And what do you think I've been doing, while you've spent the day on the river?"

"The day's long. What have you been doing?"

"You're just like your father."

"How could I possibly be like my father?"

"Being accepted into the university doesn't make you the queen bee, you know."

I left the kitchen and went into the living room and out onto the veranda, where my father was sitting in his chair. He would spend entire evenings out there, often not even coming in for dinner, especially under the circumstances of the woman-conflict within our household. He sat staring straight ahead, out at the growing dusk and the bush beyond the long abandoned and overgrown garden which was now filled with the ghosts of dead flowers. His eyes were iridescent, glowing strangely in the dark and seeming to see nothing human. It used to frighten me, that look, but I had learned to live with it, to sit with it the way you might sit with a large cat or some other beast of prey with whom you as a boy, and you alone, had made a friend. But you always sat on that tantalizing edge of terror, waiting for it to roar and spring, believing in your heart that it would never really harm you but always ready for it to do so and wondering why it ever would.

He was a sentimental man, both cruel and abused, and often betrayed, a nervous individual whose hands shook when he held anything or when he had to use them scientifically, like tying a spinner or baiting a hook. His physical nerves, he told us, had been shattered. A Japanese bomb had fallen on him in Darwin. It seemed, from the way he told it, that he had actually caught the bomb in his arms, like a football but also like some message from heaven, and somehow he had survived the explosion while all those around him, his command, were blown to bits. Ever since then his life had been fragmented, his soul rendered like the bodies of his mates. The shock to his system had been permanent. But we never quite believed it. We believed his nerves had gone after about two years of marriage to our mother.

He was a marvelous fisherman. The river was his lover. We would look in awe at the fish he brought in, and somehow try to deny that he had caught them. For a time we looked in disdain, along with our mother, at the crude river men he brought up to the house to entertain—bushmen who knew the river and the land religiously and with whom he was always happy and un-burdened and defiant, insisting that they be fed and honored as guests, which they inevitably were in spite of our mother's protests. They all had stories to tell and were very gracious to "the lady of the house." Although she disapproved of them they always won her over, because in their rough way they were very charming and even gentle, and when they told their stories she would sit happily, flattered by their attention, and laugh delight-edly at the simple but ironically profound conclusions that were the humorous yet tragic point of their real-life tales. They hon-ored her as the "queen," taking their hats off when they entered the house and greeting her with stiff formality and then later, as they were leaving, they would put their hats back on just so they could take them off and bow ridiculously to her as they re-treated into the darkness.

Our father was no great romantic white hunter, but he was always better than we could admit. Once I saw him drop a ra-zorback wild boar charging straight at him. He had to break and reload his shotgun twice before it finally fell at his feet. He was shaking all night remembering it, disbelieving what he had done, disbelieving that his nerves had not failed him. His wife, in a violent argument, had called him a coward, and unfortu-nately he had believed her and could never think of her as a liar.

I didn't say anything to him but sat looking out at the dark-ening bush, the silent wall of trees that in the twilight always took on a mysterious and almost sentient quality. Already the night sounds had begun, the last red was leaving the lower sky, and the treetop silhouettes were taking on the dark, shaggy forms of Aborigine Dreamtime creatures. The night, now, was completing itself, and I wondered if he was seeing what I was seeing or was simply lost in his thoughts, his mind closed to the world. I had the feeling that tonight, somewhere inside him, bombs were falling, voices were screaming—as suddenly they were screaming inside the house. He sat up and turned and looked at me and said, "How are ya?"

"Fine," I said. "And you?"

The screaming continued—my mother's voice. "She's on the warpath tonight," he said. "Your sister's leaving for a better life and she won't let her go in peace. She won't let anything go without a fight."

My sister came out onto the veranda. She didn't say anything or even look at us but stood and gazed out at the trees and the night. She started to take deep breaths, inhaling through her nostrils and rising up on her toes and then settling back down on her heels, swaying back and forth, breathing slowly, her exhalations long and slow. She was straight-backed, her arms firmly by her sides, her fingers straight and rigid against her thighs.

"What are you doing?" my father asked. She didn't answer, but continued with her meditation, rocking back and forth, her motion increasing, becoming more exaggerated and rapid, her long blond hair flying, her breathing faster, louder, as she moved like a human metronome, a mechanical doll pivoting rigidly from the hips.

"Stop it!" he shouted and leapt from his chair. I stood up and grabbed her shoulders from behind as she swayed back. She was gasping, making a high-pitched whimpering sound, and when I grabbed her she started to have convulsions, panting and shrieking as her body writhed, even as her legs remained firm, holding her.

"What's happening?" he asked.

"It'll pass in a minute," I told him.

I held onto her and felt her shuddering. He stood there watching. I pressed my fingers into her shoulders and felt the eruption subside. She tried to move and I wouldn't let her and I could feel the calm coming back. He took a step forward—one step, hesitant—and I looked at him and said, "Stay back! Just let her be." I think I shouted it. He hovered there, not knowing what to do. She became very still and then she gathered herself together. She opened her eyes and turned and smiled at him.

"Hello, Dad," she said, almost whispering. "Have you had a good day?"

He didn't answer, but stood staring at the two of us, his eyes wide, filled with fear, as though he had seen something haunting and terrible. Our mother came out onto the veranda. She said, "Dinner's ready. Are you going to join us, Murray, or sit out here and talk to yourself for the rest of the evening?"

The aromas of her cooking had followed her out into the night air. Although it was hot she had roasted a pair of rabbits in white wine and ginger and tarragon, the rabbits wrapped in boiled bacon and stuffed with wild rice, garlic, grapefruit, and walnuts. You could tell just by sniffing that it was a spectacular meal. There would be a simple but equally spectacular salad and three or four vegetables from the garden—steamed young potatoes, peas, roasted sweetened eggplant and stuffed tomatoes—to go with the rabbit.

I had shot the rabbits the day before and skinned them out. Three months before my father had given me my own shotgun, a twelve-gauge double-barreled side-by-side with ornate silver hammers that you had to cock with your thumb like a musket. It made me feel like a frontiersman in the bush. I loved the feel of the gun and the stiffness of the hammers and the click they made when you pulled them back that gave you the sense of slow, alert stalking and then shooting with sudden swift skill and accuracy when the game flushed. Not like a modern gun at all. One shot, really, to hit your mark and shooting in a way that you didn't ruin the meat. I am talking about rabbits, after all, and my own adolescence. And the fact that it was not only the gun that inspired me to hunt but the delectable way my mother prepared whatever I brought in and presented to her. She would take it from me proudly—her son, the hunter—radiant and smiling at my bloody hands and the meat I had skinned and cleaned to give her. The first time I did it she took the small gutted rabbit carcass and put her hand inside its abdominal cavity and then withdrew it, covered in blood, which she then smeared on my cheeks and across my lips, and said, "Look at you now, you're becoming a man." I sensed both delight and a strange fury in her eyes. I tasted the copper taste of the blood and stepped back, startled and even a little frightened.

"What's going on?" our mother asked. I was still holding onto my sister and our father was still standing in that abrupt, tenuous position of having sprung from his chair and never really finding his feet.

"She's upset," I said. "Why don't you just leave her alone!"

She came at me then, tears in her eyes, but her eyes did not look sad, only angry. She said, "Don't you talk to me that way, you insolent pup!" and slapped me across the face, stinging my cheek. Then she reached back and hit me again across the other cheek. Her hand sliced across my nose and it hurt and began to bleed. I tasted my blood as I had tasted the blood of the rabbit.

My father pulled a soiled handkerchief out of his trouser pocket and handed it to me.

"Wipe your face," he told me flatly.

I did as he said and handed the bloodstained cloth back to him. He didn't look at it, but immediately put it back in his pocket.

"Now go and have your dinner." He sat back down and leaned forward and looked at his hands.

He had been absent from our lives for several years; a tall, spectral figure with thick black hair and a handsome mustache who appeared occasionally in a greatcoat, the mantel of his fatherhood, to resume his ongoing argument with our mother. Then suddenly he had returned, or we had. We were once again a household, a family. And within that holy fortress they continued to resist and fight each other with stubborn strength that could quickly harden into anger and violence or sudden moments of raucous gaiety.

It is the same scene almost every night. Sometimes he joins us, mostly not. And now my older brother has gone, permanently, we hope. He keeps leaving, getting into some sort of trouble, and coming back. He is our mother's ally, her firstborn, her favorite, the one incapable of abandoning her. During our father's prolonged absences he would join our mother in her frenzied persecution of my sister, the verbal abuse, the physical attacks. He is her soldier, her attack dog. I am small at this stage. I am punished, often physically, for my hopeless attempts to intervene on my sister's behalf. It seems that there is nothing I can do. I secretly plot my older brother's assassination. I am convinced by my surroundings that fratricide is my noble fate and that my sister is the embodiment of everything that is pure and good. The last time he attacked her—yes, it was the last time—I was suddenly big enough. I laid him out with a very solid stick I had brought from the forest, where I had carefully selected and tested it for that specific purpose, much to his surprise. I stood over him and told him if he touched her again I would kill him. Then he left, and we have not seen nor heard from him since.

So now, tonight, our mother is alone against the three of us—my father, my sister, and I. At least for another day and a night it will be the three of us—and then it will be two, and then one, and then she will truly be alone, and then she will die alone, for by then her husband will be dead and the attack dog will have found another home and another mistress and my sister and I will belong to the world.

But that is not now, not yet. Time has not caught up with us yet. We are still on the river, in the house with its shadows and demons, the abandoned jungle of the garden with its smell of dead flowers, its dry odoriferous ghosts—the scene of a terrible slaughter, a killing field, my father's revenge.

It was because of the cats, you see. Two at first, that appeared one day in the orchard when we were very young and my father was away.

My mother suffered from a number of phobias, the worst of which was a fear, a horror, of cats. Her own mother had died of tetanus after a cat scratched her leg. She died in terrible pain, unable to speak because of a locked jaw. The sight of the cats in the yard was enough to reignite the torture of my mother's imagination, and she fled into the house and prepared us all for the feline siege she clearly saw coming. They were large, feral creatures, wild and unapproachable. Although they avoided us they continued to lurk, day and night, as though stalking my mother, stalking the fear they sensed in the house, ineluctably drawn to prowl the narrow perimeter of her life on the farm. Not even the locust swarm that blackened the sky and destroyed the crops for miles around and kept us inside for a day, filling our ears, the very walls and roof of the house, with its awesome and incessant reverberation, could drive them away. It seemed, instead, they were part of the same plague, or one in the series of plagues. The cats emerged from the mayhem with their numbers increased. Now there were eight, two adults and six kittens as untamed and as elusive and as predatory and as forever present as their parents.

Then came the flood. The river swelled, breaking the levees, and the water rose up to within about ten feet of the house. We were still on dry land but cut off, besieged now by mosquitoes and the snakes that appeared daily, fleeing to higher ground. It was then, for the first time, that we heard the cats in the roof, whining and fighting and mating beyond the stained white plaster ceiling above us.

We spent a lot of our time killing the snakes, sometimes ten a day. Our mother stayed in the house, listening for the cats. And the brown flood waters that threatened us were full of leeches from the irrigation channels and the billabongs. The mosquitoes were large and abundant and needled us through our shirts. In the night we were kept awake not only by the lascivious howling of crapulous cats in the roof but also by the teeming multitude of frogs brought suddenly and briefly to extravagant life in the torrid waters that all but surrounded us. We killed snakes on the veranda and even in the kitchen. We could do nothing but wait for the land, the dryness, to reassert itself.

Which it quickly did. Suddenly, one morning, the flood had subsided. The river, although still swollen and now carrying the bloated carcasses of dead cattle and the debris of the forest and washed-out homesteads, had returned to its familiar course, and the garden had become a tangled jungle from which it would never return, a haven for birds, rodents, and reptiles, and a feeding ground for wild cats.

In the summer heat the garden grew dry, tall, and impenetrable. Within its mysterious confines, as in the roof, the cats flourished and multiplied. We would hear them fighting in the night, hear them not only above us but in the unchecked brambles that now encroached upon us, see them in the daylight or the moonlight, stalking, fleeting, afraid to really show themselves as wild animals are but also bent on some perverse revelation of themselves, darting across our vision, wanting to be seen in their shyness and constantly, loudly, reminding us of their presence. Our mother looked to her children to protect her, and we looked helplessly back at her. In the night the cats howled and whined. Driven mad, she would beat us for the slightest transgression, or for no reason at all. By the time my father finally reappeared we had estimated the enemy's number to be around sixty.

It is raining the night he comes. His reappearance at first terrifies us. He is large, broad-shouldered, mustached, cloaked, a mysterious stranger. He stands there in the door, ridiculously tall in our eyes, the rain in his hair in spite of the hat he has removed. He looks up at the ceiling, as though he already knows there is trouble there, and then down at the children who have moved perilously close, gazing up at him. And then at the woman who stands beyond them, rigid and trembling, not knowing how to greet or forgive him. He senses our fear, our disdain, our anger, our love—and steps in to greet us—he tells us he has come back to stay—we are happy—he says that it is late, that the children should go to bed.

This is to be a long night, a night in which we lie listening to the rain on the tin roof of the house, drowning out the voices we hear like static on the radio. Out here on the river, on the plain, miles from anywhere, it seems that all relevant information, the things that you hear, come from across great distances, fractured and obscured by the elements that separate you from those voices you are trying to understand. The cats are remarkably silent, but the human voices are loud, although indecipherable, muffled by the walls and the rain.

In the early morning the rain has stopped and there is an eerie, loud dripping stillness in the bush. My sister comes to me. She is dressed in white calico, her hair is wild, tangled, she even has a strange smell, sweet but pungent and a little suffocating. I wonder why she smells this way, like dead flowers. I awake and find her beautiful and irresistible—I will do anything she asks—I see how she completely fills the world—and she is bent on some purpose.

She tells me we must hurry; we must get away from the house, get away to the river. When I ask her why, she has no reason, only a sense, an instinct, that has alarmed her. She is urgent, insistent. The sun is rising and we can hear the cats stirring in the roof, see them prowling in the garden through the broken mosquito wire that encloses my room at the far end of the veranda. She tells me to dress quickly and then leaves to dress herself.

Our older brother is still asleep at the other end of the veranda. We step down into the yard, cautious not to wake him. He is not part of whatever conspiracy we are involved in—most often it is a conspiracy against my mother or him or the two of them together—the two of them against the two of us—and whatever it is we are running from he is to be left behind. It is only we two, the chosen, who are to be saved.

It is then that we see him, our father, standing in the garden. He holds his shotgun across his chest and has a belt full of cartridges slung over his left shoulder.

"Hurry," she says. "They had a terrible argument last night. She blamed him for the cats. Hurry up and don't look back, no matter what happens."

A cat darts from the bush in front of him. Swiftly, he lifts the gun to his shoulder and aims and fires—*ka-boom*—shattering the morning stillness. The blast hurls the cat into the air, its legs dangling. Another appears, fleeing. *Ka-boom.* Its head is blown off. I watch him break the gun. The spent shells drop at his feet. Smoke wafts from the breach as he reloads. He snaps the gun shut and lifts it to his shoulder. She grabs hold of my arm and starts to pull me forward.

"Come on," she yells. I am transfixed, unable to move.

Ka-boom. Ka-boom.

He shoots into the bushes. Brambles and dry leaves fly. A blood-speckled cat rolls out onto the ground. Suddenly the creatures are everywhere, flushed from their hiding places, running for their lives.

Ka-boom. Ka-boom.

Our mother is on the veranda in her nightgown. She screams at him to stop. But he won't stop. She blamed him for the cats, for leaving, and he has returned with an instant solution, more than filling the void of his absence.

He fires at the roof above her head. A section of tin spouting and a dead cat drop onto the ground directly in front of her. She screams and runs back inside. He breaks the gun and reloads quickly as three more cats dart away in front of him. Snaps the gun shut and aims and fires, scattering the innards of two of them. Reloads. Aims. Blasts the third one as it scurries under the house. He drops onto one knee and reloads again. Swings around, the gun at his shoulder, and hits another on the veranda, blowing out the glass of one of the French doors and splintering the slatted bamboo curtain. My mother screams inside the house.

We run, holding hands. My sister runs in front, dragging me down the long driveway through the deep morning shadows of the poplars and tree ferns out the gate and across the red sand road. We scramble through the broken wire cattle fence and then we are in the forest. We stop to catch our breath. The shots continue. A cat bounds past us, and then another. Their feet make a soft dry whisper on the forest floor as they disappear into the trees, their tails high, leaping like rabbits.

The slaughter went on well into the morning. From the riverbank where we sat and waited we could hear the shots. They grew fewer and fewer as the morning dragged into noon. By early afternoon, it seemed, the killing had stopped and our father had retired. We sat in the stillness feeling the glare of the sun on the water on our faces, saying nothing. On the other side of the river there was an Aborigine camp beyond a white sand beach. We could see the smoke of their fires and the dark shacks and humpies amidst the trees, and, occasionally, people on the beach, fetching water or bathing, and always they stood for a moment and looked at us before they turned and walked back up out of the sun into the trees.

When we got back to the house there was no sign of the cats—at least not any that were alive. The yard was strewn with mangled carcasses darkened by ants and clouds of black flies. The cats that survived had fled, and they never returned. The pogrom had been a success, one from which none of us would ever recover.

I found our mother in her bedroom. She seemed to be in some kind of shock. She lay rigid on her back on the bed, her arms folded across her chest, her face frozen in a vaguely pained grimace, her eyes gazing blankly at the ceiling. I looked down and stared into that face, into those eyes that pretended not to see me. A sudden blink of an eyelid revealed that she was conscious.

I turned and started toward the door.

"I saw you two running away this morning," she said.

I stopped and turned back around without saying anything. She hadn't moved on the bed. Only her lips moved.

"You were both fully dressed and you were running away. You knew about this. You knew what he was going to do, and you were trying to get away in secret."

Now she sounded hurt, betrayed.

"We didn't want to see him kill the cats," I said, my throat swelling.

She sat up. Her tangled red hair fell across her face.

"You ran away with your sister—the two of you—and left your brother and me to face the music—like a pair of rats. He's the only one of you with any gratitude or guts. He's out there right now, cleaning up that mess, burying it so *I* don't have to see it."

She was full of rage now. I had the awful feeling that the massacre was about to set off a storm of retribution that punished without distinctions. I cringed and started to back slowly out the door.

"Has Dad come back to stay?" I asked, hardly able to speak.

"Get away from me," she said. "I don't want to look at you."

I turned, trembling with relief, and ran through the house looking for my sister.

THE DAY MY SISTER was to leave on the train, Sunday, our mother insisted that we all attend "one last Mass as a family."

"Heaven knows what people already think of us," she said. "Your sister's not leaving 'til late tonight. At least we can make a display."

Our father was on the veranda as usual. She came out already dressed and made-up and confronted him through the black face net of the hat she always wore to church. For a short time, while our father was away, these appearances in her dark Sunday dress delighted people with the rumor that she was secretly a widow by her own hand.

"Well, Murray, you better hurry up and get ready, or we'll be late."

He didn't move from his chair, but sat leaning forward with his elbows on his knees, and looked up at her with an expression of astonished disgust.

"You know I don't go to church."

Sometime ago, the last time this issue was raised, he claimed to have been given a special dispensation from the local bishop, who had appealed to Rome on his behalf. Being inside a church, being so directly in the presence of God the Creator, evinced a bodily reaction so intense that it took him days to recover from the trauma. The bishop had understood—the experience of such ecstasy can be extremely painful to the corporeal being, which must struggle to hold onto the spirit. The Vatican also understood. Our father, in spite of his intemperance, obviously had the proclivities of a saint easily possessed by the Holy Ghost—a physically volatile condition which distracted his fellow parishioners from their worship. Quietly, he reminded her of the bishop's so-called ruling.

"It's because you're possessed by the devil, not by God," said our mother. He didn't move, but said firmly: "I'm not going."

"I think you should make the effort just this once. Your daughter's leaving. Just this once let them all see us as a family."

"I'm not going, and that's final."

"Then let's see the bishop's letter, the document that pronounces you an unstable saint." She took a step forward, glaring down at him.

"It's with the bishop. In his files. Do you think I have to carry proof like a passport in a foreign country?"

"But he must've written you a letter."

"Let's not talk about it anymore. He told me personally."

"You went to his residence?"

"No."

"I wouldn't have thought so."

"He was with Phil O'Brien at the golf club. His Grace happened to be passing through."

"O'Brien! My God! What did the old bishop do? Did he just look at you drunkenly over a glass of whiskey and a stacked deck and say, 'Oh, by the way, Murray, old boy, the Pope's granted you that dispensation and declared you a candidate for saint-hood. Bottoms up!"

"The first Australian saint!" My sister squealed with delight through her bedroom window. "To think, all this time we've been within his holy glow and we never knew! We've missed out on grace! This must mean God has abandoned us! Oh fa-ther, father, Saint Murray, forgive us and make us worthy!"

"Leave me alone, will you!" Our father shook his head and raised his hands and eyes to heaven.

"Did they all get down on their knees at the golf club when they realized who had come amongst them?" called my sister, still unseen. "*Who it was* they were drinking with, had been drinking with for all these years!" Her green laughter pealed out of the house. "No wonder he always loses at cards! He's a saint! He's actually giving his money away. Brothers, mates, down on your knees!"

My mother burst out laughing, joining in with my sister.

"Shut up," he mumbled. "I don't always lose."

"No I won't shut up!" said my mother, taking a deep breath and regaining her serious composure. "Not until you take your family to church! Show the town that we have some unity, that we mean something together."

"I'm sure we already mean quite a lot," he said, laughing.

OUTFLANKED, he finally relinquished in the face of an unbeat-able barrage of ridicule. We drove to town in silence. The river road was not yet dusty in the morning light, striped with the shadows of gum trees from one side; on the other side orange groves covered the slopes of the red sand ridge. There were huts facing the road, interspersed between the rows of trees, made of large gray bricks and mortar with corrugated iron roofs where the Sicilian workers lived. It was Sunday and no one was to be seen picking fruit, knotted handkerchiefs covering their heads. We would see them in church dressed in tight-fitting dark suits, the married women and the daughters in black veils and colorful dresses.

We passed Aborigine encampments amidst the trees along the riverbank, dark glinting twisted corrugations, the smoke of a campfire, dogs running about—then the river and the forest were gone and we were out on the plain. The sky was a high bright blue dome above us, the horizon vast and empty beyond the bright yellow millet and wheat fields. Then there were tan Brahman cows with loose awkward humps on their necks and red beef cattle and black-and-white dairy cows and white and parchment-colored sheep dotting the plain. Then more orchards, green and geometrical, and then the forest and the river glittering through the trees. As we entered the town and approached the church our father clearly grew agitated, although he still said nothing.

The church, surrounded by tall date palms, was a bastard Gothic structure made of red bricks and cement with a high arched portal and an arresting steeple tower. It had been built with Christian nobility, with a bell that resounded throughout the town. And with great Catholic intent. It was a citadel of Celtic and Latin passion, mythology, and superstition, a thick-walled fortress against the heat, and the dryness of a Protestant invasion into an already dry land.

Our father made it as far as the church door, where he stopped and lit a cigarette.

"You go on. I'll be in in a minute."

Our mother didn't say anything. Dutifully, we followed her inside, the little red hen leading her children—late—a spectacle to behold. Our father, stooped and wild haired, smoked at the door.

The Mass was well in progress. Roof fans whirred slowly below the high rafters, but the air was hot and still. The crowd knelt with their heads bowed, listless and strained, lulled into a torpor by the incomprehensible monotone of the priest at the altar. As always, he appeared to be sleepwalking his way through the service. His dull voice rose occasionally in a strange trancelike singsong that quickly sank back into a deadening, almost drunken murmur.

Then the murmur stopped. The priest turned and faced the people, and the people rose with a sigh of relief. The altar boys sat down on the altar steps, the priest put a Bible under his arm and walked slowly toward the pulpit, and the people sat down and gradually began to fan themselves.

Father McInnery climbed the steps to the pulpit slowly. His somnambulant pale blue eyes gazed emptily through thick spectacles at some ineffable nothingness. His robes weighed heavily upon him, his knees were weak, and outside the mid-morning heat had now finally descended with its whitish glare and the loud incessant buzz of cicadas.

There was a long moment of silence broken by an occasional cough. He stood in the pulpit, his eyes half-closed, his hands on the balustrade, his heavily oiled black hair parted down the middle, and began to rock slowly back and forth. People shifted uneasily in their seats, waiting for him to begin.

"Today, my dear brethren," he intoned in the same slow monotone, his eyes now fixed on a turning roof fan indirectly above him. He seemed to stare at it for an incredibly long time before he spoke again.

"Today, my dear brethren, we are made aware." He looked up again at the fan.

"We are made aware that—"

He did not really get to finish his sentence, nor, for that matter, his sermon. There was a sudden, loud, rending, and even volcanic explosion of holy possession in the back of the church. Our father's stentorian fit of coughing, choking, retching, and spitting resounded throughout the building. It echoed in the high-arched vaults of the ceiling and drowned out the hapless priest, who, still gazing at the fan, continued to drone obliviously.

A few heads turned. The coughing harangue faded and seemed to stop, then erupted again in a more violent choking spitting barking attack that quickly took on the disturbing intensity of a drowning man.

Our mother sat rigid, her face taut, perspiring through her makeup, her eyes fixed on the altar, a poor widow publicly humiliated by the ludicrous and despicable and all too physical ghost of her husband. She suffered in stoic silence, inert, wooden, mannequin-like, believing that her own display of dignity gained her the sympathy of the congregation. Our father was like the heat, the dust, the place itself—something to endure and rage against all at the same time, something about which she had no choice.

The coughing gradually subsided. Then there was an eerie silence, beneath which the priest's solemn monologue continued its ceaseless and dull pace. Our mother took a deep breath and allowed herself to sit back. There was a deadly stillness in the crowd. Then, from the side of the building, standing outside beneath an open window next to the pulpit, our father launched another prolonged assault of even greater voracity. My sister and I were both in tears, our bellies aching, trying to smother our laughter as each mounting upheaval filled the church with the phlegmatic roar of God's emphysema.

I saw the boiling lava of shame fill our mother's face. Beneath the makeup she had turned a blazing red, her powdered skin glowing pink and white beneath the dark hat and veil. Tears were streaking her cheeks and she was grinding her teeth, making her jaw muscles twitch.

Unfortunately, this sight of her only added to my own hysteria. I stuffed my tie in my mouth, unable to contain myself, looking down at my shaking body, tears burning my face. I felt my sister shaking beside me as I gasped for breath, and tried to imagine what it was going to be like later on, when it was no longer funny but the reason for a bitter harangue. But it didn't help.

After the service she herded us out quickly. We all three waited in the car while our father lingered, having recovered enough from his attack to stand around and chat with some of his mates. We drove in silence out of the town, our father muttering behind the wheel, occasionally gesturing with his hand as his private conversation with himself grew more heated. At one point he said out loud, "Oh, gedday, Murray," and then muttered, "you bloody ratbag!" My sister and I both burst out laughing. "Surprised to run into yourself again, Dad?" asked my sister, and we were both beside ourselves, lying across the seat. He remained obliviously absorbed. Our mother kept her eyes on the road and said nothing. By the time we were home he was cursing loudly and his face was red and angry.

"Somebody say something you didn't like, Murray?" asked our mother. He didn't answer, appeared not to even hear her. He parked the car and got out and slammed the door and walked off, still muttering, pulling his tie off as he went. We watched him disappear into the orchard. A sudden warm breeze raised cobra-like threads of red dust between the rows of trees and flapped his wide cotton trousers against his legs.

As we got out of the car my sister said, "We're all mad, every one of us. We're a mad family." Immediately our mother swung around and hit the side of my sister's face with her handbag, knocking her back against the car. My sister put her arms up to protect herself and stood there, her head down, patiently enduring the blows that followed. Soon our mother was worn out. She stepped back, dazed and trembling, and then turned and started toward the house.

"That's the last time you'll get to do that," said my sister. "I hope you enjoyed it."

She knew that this was dangerous, would more than likely provoke a second attack, and she stood defiant and ready as our mother turned back around and faced her. But she did not come at her. She knew that this time it would be useless; the hopeless force that drove her blows would quickly be exhausted and its weakness openly exposed. It truly had been the last time and my sister had won and if she hadn't quite won was well on the road to victory. She was leaving.

"Yes, I did," said our mother, taking off her gloves.

"Come on," I said to my sister. "Let's go for a walk."

"Lunch will be ready soon," said our mother.

"We don't want any lunch," said my sister.

We walked down through the forest to the river and followed the bank for some time. Then we stopped and sat down. We looked out from the shadows at the white glare of the river and the dark current beneath it, swirling and rippling and moving steadily by before us. Her face was flushed and her cheekbone bruised with a growing blue blotch where she had been hit, but her expression was serene and distant. I watched her for a little while, fascinated because I had never really seen her like this before. I grew agitated and stood up.

"Sit down," she said. I did so and she looked at me and smiled and then turned back to the river.

"They don't matter, you know." She kept her eyes on the water. The light off it was hitting both of us full on, on either side of the face, filling us, blinding us, even as we sat half in the deep shade of the trees. I saw it enter her eyes, turning them to a translucent sea green. They were no longer eyes but brilliant sparkling sun-filled opals, the pupils mere specks, strangely liquid blemishes in the magically glowing green stones.

"Let's just stay here for a while," she said. "And listen to the river. It's going to be a long time before I hear it again."